Pine Bluff Jefferson County Library
200 East 8th Ave.
Pine Bluff, AR 71601

THE
MOSES
VIRUS

A NOVEL

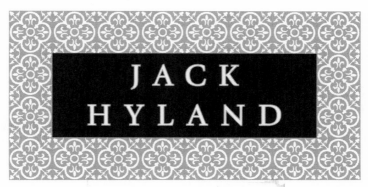

JACK HYLAND

Pine Bluff Jefferson County Library
200 East 8th Ave.
Pine Bluff AR 71601

TAYLOR TRADE PUBLISHING

LANHAM • NEW YORK • BOULDER • TORONTO • PLYMOUTH, UK

Published by Taylor Trade Publishing
An imprint of Rowman & Littlefield
4501 Forbes Boulevard, Suite 200, Lanham, Maryland 20706
www.rowman.com

10 Thornbury Road, Plymouth PL6 7PP, United Kingdom

Distributed by National Book Network

Copyright © 2014 by Taylor Trade Publishing

All rights reserved. No part of this book may be reproduced in any form or
by any electronic or mechanical means, including information storage and
retrieval systems, without written permission from the publisher, except by a
reviewer who may quote passages in a review.

British Library Cataloguing in Publication Information Available

Library of Congress Cataloging-in-Publication Data

Hyland, Jack, 1938–
    The Moses virus / Jack Hyland.
        pages cm
    ISBN 978-1-58979-908-0 (cloth : alk. paper) — ISBN 978-1-58979-
909-7 (electronic) 1. Archaeologists—Fiction. 2. Biological disasters—
Fiction. 3. Forensic archaeology—Fiction. 4. Power (Social sciences)—
Fiction. 5. Rome (Italy)—Fiction. I. Title.
    PS3608.Y53M67 2013
    813'.6—dc23

                                                    2013014803

♾™ The paper used in this publication meets the minimum requirements
of American National Standard for Information Sciences—Permanence of
Paper for Printed Library Materials, ANSI/NISO Z39.48-1992.

Printed in the United States of America

And it came to pass, that at midnight the Lord smote all the firstborn in the land of Egypt, from the firstborn of Pharaoh that sat on his throne unto the firstborn of the captive that was in the dungeon; and all the firstborn of cattle.

Exodus 12:29

Sunrise crept across the red tile rooftops, washing away the blues and grays that had hidden Rome during the night. From the terrace of his apartment on Via Gregoriana near the top of the Spanish Steps, Tom Stewart watched as the city started to come to life. Shops opening. Bread deliveries being made. People beginning their workday. He imagined that the rhythms of this eternal city remained unchanged for two thousand years. The bells chimed six in the tower of the Trinità dei Monti, the church at the head of the Spanish Steps, and the sounds were echoed by church bells across the city.

In the distance, Tom saw the majestic dome of St. Peter's. It dominated the skyline, casting a shadow over the remnants of the ancient empire. It had become the symbol of Rome to the world and the center of faith for tens of millions of believers. Tom's sense of awe in seeing the basilica remained as inspiring and humbling as it had the first time he saw it as a student more than twenty years ago.

Tom was a trustee of the American Academy in Rome, a scholarly organization, located on the Janiculum, the highest of Rome's hills. Each year, the twenty-five American archaeologists, artists, architects, writers, musicians, and scholars who had won its coveted Rome Prize spent time in its palatial residence, free to pursue their various fields of study. As a trustee, Tom spent every other summer there to attend administrative meetings. On this particular June trip, Tom was also busy editing the most recent draft of his new textbook on forensic archaeology.

Tom was well liked by his fellow trustees. Bright but not overly bookish, with an ironic sense of humor and an easygoing manner, he was a popular professor at New York University. A former competitive swimmer, he kept in shape by swimming nearly every day. He had dark brown hair, almost black, and a strong, classic face which some said made him look like the Roman emperors or statesmen pictured on busts carved by great Roman sculptors. He spoke Italian with a decidedly American accent, having taught himself the language over the years. Aside from New York, Rome was his favorite city, the perfect mix of ancient and modern.

This morning Tom was going to the Palatine Hill in the Roman Forum. Doc Brown, a professor of archaeology, a member of the Academy, and an old friend, invited him to observe the excavation of an underground passage discovered last year. If Doc's theory was correct, it could lead to the rooms of Emperor Nero's fabled imperial palace, called the *Domus Aurea*, or the Golden House. If he was right, it would be a find of historic proportions. Tom was excited for the opportunity that promised to be the crowning glory of his friend's career.

He took his apartment building's ornate elevator to the ground floor and passed through the genteelly run-down lobby. He had been lucky to find this apartment in such a desirable part of the city. Not only was it reasonable, but, despite its shabby appearance, it was run well. It even had Wi-Fi.

He headed into the Piazza Trinità dei Monti, in front of the Hassler Hotel, to hail a cab.

"Buongiorno," Tom said to the taxi driver as he pulled up abruptly. "Il foro Romano, per favore, vicino al Colosseo el'arco di Costantino."

"Sì, signore."

The taxi lurched forward and sped down the hill, along the Via del Corso, a street full of shops and eateries, into the Piazza Venezia.

Part of Rome's magic for Tom was that its many layers of past, present, and future were all jumbled together. Standing high on the hill overlooking the piazza was the monument to Victor Emmanuel II, ridiculed for years as resembling a white wedding cake, yet important for honoring the first king of a united Italy in 1861. Behind the monument lay the Roman Forum, once the center of the Roman Republic and later the Roman Empire. On the same square, in the Renaissance Palazzo Venezia, Mussolini had had his headquarters. In the ancient palazzo, a photographer was busy shooting an impossibly thin model for some chic fashion magazine.

The taxi stopped near the Arch of Constantine. Tom leaned forward, paid his fare, got out and checked his watch: 6:35 a.m. Right on time. He looked around at the deserted area on the edge of the Roman Forum. He spotted an iron fence with a gate, behind which he could see the familiar signs of an archaeological excavation. It took him back to his own experience of being on an excavation in Arizona.

The Academy's "dig" was located on the Palatine Hill, one of Rome's fabled seven hills. As Tom passed through the gate, he saw wheelbarrows, picks, shovels, and brushes of various sizes; wooden tables and plastic tubs filled with water for processing pottery; and a number of sifters, containers with bottoms made of wire screen to filter dirt removed from the dig. It felt good to be on a site again, he thought. It had been a while.

Dr. Robert Brown gave him a welcoming wave. Brown was the senior archaeologist at the American Academy and highly admired in his profession. Despite his imposing reputation, everyone called him by his nickname, "Doc," which gave him the informality he preferred. Doc was slight in stature, probably—Tom guessed—no more than five-feet, six inches, wiry, with an aesthetic face that reminded Tom of a portrait of a saint found in mosaics on some floor in a Romanesque monastery. Doc talked quickly and with passion. His students at Bryn Mawr College loved him. His specialty was late imperial Rome, and he was bristling with anticipation to get started.

"You made it," Doc said, shaking Tom's hand.

"Wouldn't miss it. Nice day for a dig."

"Great day. Let me show you around. We're almost ready to start."

At the trustees' meeting of the American Academy at its New York office last November, Doc had briefed everyone about his amazing discovery of the ancient underground passage during his excavation the year before. Upon hearing Doc's enthusiastic presentation, the trustees and patrons had agreed to provide most of the funding for this year's dig. With the green light from the trustees and most of the money raised, Doc's proposal went out to dozens of foundations. No one was willing, and Doc despaired that his project might not go forward. Then, in a surprise development, Belagri, a global agribusiness, took an interest and provided the balance of the funds needed.

Excavations in the Roman Forum were permitted to only a few qualified groups, the American Academy being one. Upon seeing Brown's report, the Ministry of Italian Cultural Properties and Activities had approved the excavation, anticipating a historic find, and was following the events closely.

The Forum was still empty because the Roman authorities kept the tourists out until after nine in the morning. Once in, the tourists swarmed over most of the Forum with their cameras and their picnic lunches. Fortunately for those doing excavations, the iron gates and fence kept the tourists out.

"Our plan today is to enter the underground passage at the end of the mosaic floor, once we've cleared away the surface debris. If you don't mind doing some crawling, you can join us," Doc said to Tom. "That's if you're up to it."

"Count me in," Tom replied enthusiastically. Twenty-two young men and women, dressed in T-shirts, coveralls, and work shoes were gathered around, already engaged in their tasks. Doc's crew included mostly American college students who paid for the privilege of participating in this archaeological dig as part of their coursework.

"Here, let me introduce you to my team. Actually, I think you know Eric Bowen," Doc said, as he gestured in the direction of the closest of the workers.

Eric looked up from one of the laser surveying instruments that he and another student were adjusting.

"Yes. How've you been, Eric?"

"Good to see you again, Dr. Stewart."

"Please call me Tom. How's your father?"

"Okay . . . Tom. He's fine. He's supposed to visit next month."

"Give him my regards. I'll see him in September at the trustees' meeting."

Tom looked at the instrument Eric was holding.

"Is that your total station?"

"Yes," said Eric, with an assurance that Tom found amusing. "Totally digital. We can download the data to model building equipment."

"They're getting more sophisticated every year."

"Can't work without high tech these days," Doc added. With that, he escorted Tom to a number of locations where he met individuals in charge of drawing the frescoes that had been discovered, others who were marble and stone experts, and the site historian, Bill Erickson, a doctoral candidate at Yale.

Doc stopped near the site. "The underground passageway—just fifteen feet away from here—may lead us to rooms of Nero's palace that have been lost for two thousand years. His palace was a gigantic complex. It covered three of Rome's seven hills, three hundred acres in all. Nero built furiously after the fire in 64 that devastated Rome, and he didn't stop building until his suicide four years later. But all his work was buried or built over by the emperors who followed.

"We believe that much of Nero's complex lies unexplored—just waiting for us at the end of the passageway."

"What did the superintendency do to protect the underground passageway from 'visitors' over the winter?" Tom asked Doc.

Doc replied, "They installed a security cover after we finished our campaign last year and removed it just prior to our starting up again."

Tom watched as the team worked diligently under Doc's direction. It took a good couple of hours to remove the remaining pile of rubble around a large, flat segment of the ancient mosaic floor. Then, they broke for coffee. Tom was surprised to see an attractive Italian woman working alongside the rest of Brown's team.

"Alexandra Cellini, a graduate student at the University of Rome," Doc said, noticing Tom's interest. "She signed on with the team to learn American archaeology techniques. She goes by Alex, and her English is flawless."

"What's her specialty?"

"Ancient European history, but archaeology is of special interest to her. She's bright and a whiz on the computer. Her mother's American and her father was an Italian diplomat of some kind. Pretty well connected. She's been a real asset to the team."

At this point, Doc spotted a man who had entered through the gate in the iron fence and was walking toward him. Doc's face reddened slightly, and he said to Tom, "I may be stooping to a new low."

"How's that?" Tom asked.

"Here comes the press. My main sponsor of the excavation suggested that I get some publicity. It may help with future funding. So, I invited a reporter I met from the *International Herald Tribune*—one of those modern reporters who also takes his own pictures. There's a chance we'll be making history today."

"I believe you'll be making history," Tom replied. "That's not what I call stooping to a new low."

Doc relaxed. "I know, I know. I'm uneasy about seeking publicity just to raise money."

"Don't worry," Tom replied. "Think of it as helping the Academy and your students."

"Right," Doc said.

The reporter joined them. Doc shook his hand, saying, "Jim. Jim Ruchet, I'd like you to meet a trustee of the American Academy, Tom Stewart. He's a famous forensic archaeologist from New York and is in Rome for the summer working on a book he's writing."

Ruchet, looking jaunty, was wearing a loose-fitting Hawaiian shirt and white khaki trousers. He had a small digital camera in his hand and sported a wide smile. Tom thought that Ruchet looked more like a photographer than a reporter. Ruchet shook Tom's hand. "Glad to meet you. Are you ready for history?"

Tom replied, "You bet."

Doc said to Tom, "Jim made a name for himself for being Marilyn Monroe's photographer."

"That chapter is long over," Ruchet said. "I became more interested in writing than pure picture taking."

For the next five minutes or so, Doc briefed Ruchet, giving him the names of the members of his team and their roles. Ruchet recorded Doc's conversation. After Ruchet had been filled in, Doc said, "Jim, we're ready. Before I drop down into the passageway," Doc nodded toward the opening of the passageway about fifteen feet away, "do you want to get a shot?"

"How long do you think you'll be in the passage?" Jim asked.

"I don't have a clue," replied Doc. "One, two, maybe three hours. Depends on what we find."

"Uh-oh," Ruchet said. "My editor thought I'd be here for a half hour, and I have to be at the American ambassador's residence in another forty-five minutes. The U.S. secretary of state is in Rome. If you don't mind, let's take several shots now. Admittedly they're 'before' rather than 'after,' but the text can cover your results even if the photograph doesn't."

Ruchet walked to the passageway entrance. "Doc, stand at the edge, explain something to Tom—that's your name, isn't it? Tom, go shake hands with Doc. Smile, both of you. Doc, make it look like you've just found hidden treasure."

"But I haven't," complained Doc. "Not yet, anyway."

"C'mon," replied Ruchet, "this is a publicity shot. For the newspapers. Stop thinking about it too much."

Doc and Tom stood near the passage entrance, smiled and shook hands. Jim took a number of quick shots, then made a discreet exit.

Doc placed his fingers in his mouth and whistled. "Listen up!" The entire team stopped talking and gathered around him. "We're ready to lift the entry stone and drop down into the passageway. Take your positions. I'll go first. Eric, you're behind me. Greg Bator will be at the entry, and he'll keep you all informed with everything he hears from us over our two-way radios."

The anticipation in the group was electric. Two of the strongest workers carefully levered the large flat stone with crowbars. Slowly, the stone, which was about four feet in diameter, yielded and was moved away from the edge of the hole it had covered. Everyone took turns looking down into the dark space.

Doc dropped into the passageway, and then Eric followed him. As a precaution, they had two-way radios and ropes tied around their waists that fed out as they moved into the tunnel. There was always the risk that the age and unknown state of the passageway could give them trouble. Both Doc and Eric also had oxygen sensors and were wearing helmets equipped with lights. Kneeling by the entrance, Greg began to pass along Doc's and Eric's comments as they called in. The rest of the crew watched eagerly, gathered in a circle around the entrance to the passageway.

After a few minutes, Eric radioed to Greg, who repeated for everyone else to hear that Eric and Doc had come upon some kind of wall that blocked their way. Fifteen minutes later, Greg reported that Eric and Doc had managed to dismantle enough of the crumbling stone so that they could slip around it and advance further into the passageway.

"They're in! The passageway seems clear," Greg called out to the group.

Then there was silence.

Greg waited a few minutes, then called Eric. No response.

He tried again. Nothing.

"Maybe they're busy with a major find," Tom said, knowing Doc could get so wrapped up in his work that he forgot everything else.

"But, they're not moving. The tie ropes went slack," Greg said.

"Give them a tug," Tom suggested.

Greg pulled on the ropes, got resistance which meant that the ropes were still tied to the two archaeologists, but they didn't pull back to signal everything was fine.

Something was wrong.

"How stable is the passageway?" Tom asked Greg.

"We've no way of knowing. Our instruments couldn't penetrate that far."

Tom called down into the tunnel several times. Silence.

"We've got to get someone down there. If there was a cave-in, they might be in trouble."

"I'll go," Greg said, hooking a lead line to his belt and grabbing a flashlight. "I'll let you know what's down there." He handed Tom the radio.

"Take a mask," Tom said. "The dust might be intense."

Greg nodded, put on the mask offered by another team member, and jumped down into the tunnel.

Every minute Greg was gone was agony for the crew. The tautness of his lead line was a good sign. Greg was still moving forward. Then, suddenly, it went slack. Everyone was paralyzed with fear.

"Greg, what's happening?" Tom radioed in.

Silence.

A few minutes later, they heard scrambling. Greg appeared at the opening. Tom gave him a hand to help him up.

Ripping off the mask, Greg gasped, "They're not moving. They're just lying there. I tried to . . ."

"Calm down. Tell us what you saw."

Greg was breathing hard. "It was dark and narrow. I called to them as I went through the tunnel. I saw a light. The tunnel got bigger. I kept calling. Then, I saw them. They were on the floor in a large room. I shouted. I shone the light on their faces. They were covered with some kind of . . . green moss. Their eyes were wide open like they had seen something horrible."

"And? What else?"

Greg stared up. "They're dead."

Tom had to think fast. "We need to get an ambulance."

"Dr. Stewart, I can call the Carabinieri," Alex Cellini offered, taking out her cell phone.

"Good," Tom responded immediately, glad that the Italian military police would be here soon. But a few thoughts began to gnaw at Tom. Why had this tragedy happened? Was there any physical danger to the Academy's team? He was now the senior person from the American Academy present—he had to call the director, deal with the police, protect the Academy's reputation. And what else? Would he have to deal with the press? From the pleasant pastime of watching an archaeological dig in the famous Roman Forum, he was suddenly at the center of some very unpleasant action.

Alex nodded and punched in the emergency number. She spoke to the operator, then turned to Tom. "Help's coming. I told them we need a doctor and ambulance."

"We have to go after them," Greg said, still visibly shaken by the horror of the scene he had come upon.

"No," Tom replied quickly and firmly. "It could be extremely dangerous to go down there. We can't help them. It's better to wait for medical help."

Within moments, they heard the wail of the Carabinieri siren. The flashing blue lights of a squad car appeared at the Arch of Constantine, followed by an ambulance two minutes later.

Two police officers stepped out of the squad car and asked their questions in Italian. Alex answered them and then translated for Tom. "They want to know who's in charge, and what happened. I told them that you're a trustee of the American Academy and the senior person here."

Tom gave the carabinieri the highlights of what had happened with some help from Alex. The EMT crew from the ambulance attended to Greg. His body was trembling as he relived the quick deaths and the mysterious green mold. The officers found nothing wrong with Greg, however, and asked him if the men might have died from a cave-in.

"Their bodies," he said, "were lying there, free of any debris."

The carabinieri put up a cordon around the area, making certain that the perimeter around the dig was sealed off.

"We have to retrieve the bodies," the senior officer said. "Since we don't know what caused their deaths, we've got to take precautions. I've requested our Squadra di Hazmat unit. They'll collect the two bodies and get them to our labs. This excavation will be sealed until further notice."

Tom realized that the situation was now in the carabinieri's hands. He took a moment and called Caroline Sibelius, director of the American Academy, and filled her in.

"Doc and Eric dead? I can't believe it. What happened?"

"It's unclear. The police are removing the bodies to do an autopsy."

Caroline was silent. "Well, it'll be all over the news tomorrow, then. I'll contact the families. Please ask our group to come back to the Academy as soon as they can. Call me the moment you know more."

"Will do."

"I'll stay to translate," Alex offered as the other students collected their things and headed back to the Academy. The ambulance also left while the two carabinieri remained with Tom and Alex.

"I can't tell you how helpful you've been to me," Tom said to Alex.

"I really haven't done much—just calling the police," she replied. "What happened to Doc and Eric is overwhelming me—I've got no answers for this."

Tom saw that she had tears in her eyes and put his hand on her shoulder. In a quiet voice he said, "I've no answers either, but we'll find them."

Alex looked at Tom, and he looked back at her. Neither said anything further.

About thirty minutes later, a dark blue Land Rover Defender with a white roof and Carabinieri red stripe along the side, followed by a Mercedes Unimog 3000-5000 mobile lab, pulled up to the gate where Tom and Alex were waiting. An official in full uniform stepped down from the Rover and walked over to them.

"Dr. Stewart?"

"Yes, I'm Dr. Tom Stewart."

"I'm Lieutenant Giovanni Gabrielli from the Italian Environmental Protection Command," he said in English, extending his hand. "My sympathies for the loss of your colleagues. We're here to assess the situation." Two men emerged from the Unimog, tethered to the vehicle with long lines feeding them oxygen. The lines unspooled as they walked. The men were garbed in full white hazmat suits and gloves. The police officers directed them to the passageway at the site. Gabrielli, Tom, and Alex followed close behind.

"These men are equipped with a video data line so that we'll be able to see exactly what's in the tunnel. We can observe it on this mobile monitor," Gabrielli said, pointing to a small flat screen set up on a cart near the opening.

They watched as the men descended into the passageway with their flashlights at the ready. As they walked through the tunnel, they reported back to Gabrielli over the data line that they unspooled as they walked. As the two men came to the end of the passage, Tom could see on the video screen an opening into a large space, which had shiny walls.

The bodies were contorted as if something had caused them incredible pain before they died. There was nothing natural about the position of their bodies. They look broken, like rag dolls tossed against a stone wall. Tom was puzzled by a bright green substance, like pollen, on Doc's and Eric's hands. But he was struck by what he could see of their faces—looks of agony. It was sickening to imagine that Doc and Eric had suffered excruciating deaths. In the background of the video, Tom saw the dim remnants of something else. At first he thought they were mounds of rags, but as the camera moved closer, he saw that they were human skeletons clothed in what appeared to be lab coats.

Gabrielli then spoke to his two men in the underground chamber, ordering them to carry each of the bodies back through the passageway. On the video monitor, Tom and Alex could watch as the two officers enclosed each of the bodies in a black plastic bag, which was zippered closed. Making two trips, the men brought the bodies of Doc and Eric to the Unimog.

"We'll conduct an autopsy on the bodies and will be in touch with the American Academy as soon as we have the results. I'd like to schedule a call with you and the director of the Academy for tomorrow morning, perhaps at 10 a.m. Now, please accompany me to our examining station. We'll need a full report about what happened. After that, we'll take you wherever you wish."

As they left the American Academy's excavation site, Tom noticed that a crowd of tourists and reporters had gathered outside the gate. Caroline was right about the news. Tom grimaced.

Gabrielli must have noticed Tom's expression. "Sensational stories are difficult to contain. Deaths in the Roman Forum will be big news—international news."

"Can't be helped, I suppose."

"We'll of course not give out any information until we know what happened. But you should be prepared to be contacted by the reporters."

"I'll leave that to the Academy director."

The interview at the station did not take long. There wasn't much to tell. It all had happened so quickly.

A police car drove them to Via Angelo Masina and the main building of the American Academy. The car stopped and idled. Tom got out and turned to Alex.

"Thanks for your help today."

"Not a problem. Please let me know if there's anything else I can do." She took out a business card from her purse and scribbled on it. "Here's my cell number. Call me anytime."

"Thanks. I'll do that. Get home safely."

She gave the driver instructions. "Ciao, Tom."

"Ciao."

Tom walked up to the front gate of the American Academy. Norm Robertson, the guard, stepped out of his gate station.

"Sorry about what happened, Dr. Stewart."

"Thanks, Norm. I'm here to meet with—"

"Go right in. The director's expecting you. She said for you to meet her in the courtyard."

Tom climbed the front steps, walked through the vestibule to the courtyard. Its walls were covered with flowering vines filling the evening air with the scent of jasmine. Tables lined the outer edge of the courtyard under the alcove of the building.

The Academy fellows and residents, including Doc's archaeological team, had already finished supper and left. Tom waved at Caroline and John Connor, Caroline's predecessor as director of the Academy, and joined them at their table under an arch. Caroline Sibelius was a highly regarded art historian, and was now on sabbatical from Duke University in order to serve as director here. She was an expert on gothic architecture in Italy. Connor was the world's expert on Francesco Borromini, a highly influential late-Renaissance architect. He was also on sabbatical in Rome from his professorship at Columbia University.

"Tom," Caroline said warmly, "how are you? You've been through so much. Please sit down. Would you like a coffee or cappuccino or something to eat?"

"I'm not particularly hungry, but I'd like a cappuccino."

Caroline called one of the waiters over and asked that Tom be brought food and drink. Then she said, "I still can't believe that Doc and Eric are dead."

Tom recounted his arrival at the excavation early in the morning, taking Caroline and John through all the incidents, including the mysterious underground chamber where Doc and Eric were found.

The waiter brought the cappuccino and a small plate of fruit, cheese, and bread.

"Grazie."

"I had no idea this excavation was so dangerous. Doc seemed to indicate that it was fairly routine," Caroline said.

Tom sipped his cappuccino. "Yes, it should have gone off without a hitch. But I'm concerned about some of the bizarre elements that came to light."

"You mentioned a large room with shiny walls and skeletons?"

"Yes. Not what you'd expect to find in an ancient Roman palace."

"Also, from what you've described," John added, "Doc and Eric seemed to have died quickly and horribly without any warning at all."

"I've never heard anything like it," Caroline said. "As for the Academy community, they know only the bare facts of what's happened. I'd like to keep it that way until we know more."

"Agreed. Although the media will probably be pestering you," Tom said.

Caroline nodded. "I've already gotten calls, and Lieutenant Gabrielli's office telephoned to arrange a phone meeting tomorrow morning. I'd like you to attend if you can."

"Sure thing."

"Well, something leaked out," Connor said, breaking off a small cluster of grapes. "I had an odd telephone conversation this afternoon with Tim O'Boyle."

"Who's that?" Tom asked.

"The former chief archivist of the Vatican libraries. He's a retired priest. We've become friends since we both spend time at the Vatican doing research.

"Father O'Boyle expressed his sympathy at what happened in the Forum—just how he knew about it so quickly, I have no idea. He discreetly began to ask questions about what actually had happened, and how much detail we have. And, he asked about you, your connection to the Academy, your profession. Very polite, but probing. Finally, he asked the oddest of questions."

"What did he say?" Tom asked, startled by a perfect stranger's interest in his life. What could this unwelcome intrusion mean?

"O'Boyle said, 'Is this Stewart person a wholly ethical person? Is he totally trustworthy?' Just like that. Ethical, trustworthy—in my opinion, very odd questions. Out of order, really."

"I agree," Tom said. "How did you answer—if I may be so bold?"

"I told him 'very ethical, very trustworthy.' O'Boyle definitely had something on his mind, though I certainly did not know what it was. 'One final question,' he said. 'Is Stewart a man of action?'"

"How in the world did you reply to that?" Tom asked.

"I said that you were courageous and had walked through the chaos, destruction, and danger of 9/11 helping to identify human remains to give families of lost ones some closure. Wouldn't that serve as a proxy for 'action'?"

"Thank you, John," Tom said. "I'm honored by your answers."

"Well, here's the unusual part. Just before dinner tonight, he called back, somewhat nervously, to ask that I consider our prior conversation 'off the record.' Just not 'off the record,' but *totally* off the record."

"That's off the wall," replied Tom. "What's O'Boyle like?"

"Quite a likable guy," John replied, "with a wry sense of Irish humor. A serious scholar. Often, you'll find him in the Mithraic Temple in the third level of San Clemente Church."

"Mithraic Temple?"

"O'Boyle's an expert on this clandestine group—mostly Roman soldiers who kept their secret rites to themselves. He loves to sit on the stone bench in the anteroom, imagining, he says, he can hear the soldiers praying."

"John," said Tom, "that was two thousand years ago."

"I know, I know." He laughed. "In Rome, we all have our pet fetishes. His is harmless, and his research is well regarded. I've never heard him so anxious to understand the essence of someone's character, nor back away from this line of questioning so abruptly. I'd even say he seemed uneasy or afraid of something. I still don't get what he meant by 'man of action.'"

Caroline had been half-listening since she was preoccupied with the Academy's new problems, stemming from the tragedy in the Roman Forum.

"Tragic news travels fast, especially over the Internet," Caroline said. "I've received a few calls and e-mails from Doc's colleagues in Rome. Apparently, it's been on TV as well."

"How did the families take the news?"

"As you'd expect. They were devastated. Eric's parents will be on the evening plane to Rome to take him home. Doc had no immediate family, except for a sister living in California. She asked me to arrange to have him sent to a funeral home in her area. Of course, the Academy will pay all the expenses."

"Are you planning to have a memorial service for Doc and Eric in Rome?" Tom asked.

"Yes, I've been thinking about that."

"What about their personal items?"

"Greg Bator is collecting Eric's. Doc's are still up in his room here."

"Doc was a good friend. I'd be happy to help with that," Tom said.

"Thanks. I expect there isn't too much."

"It's been long day." Tom stood. "I think I'll head back to my apartment."

"Just ask Norm to call you a taxi," Caroline said. "You're sure you're okay?"

"I'm fine. Just a little shaken. See you tomorrow."

The taxi pulled up to the front door of his apartment building on Via Gregoriana. As Tom let himself in the front door of the building, he was too tired to notice a man standing in the shadows across the street. When the outside door closed and Tom was inside, the man spoke quietly into his cell phone and then walked down the street, disappearing into the night.

After showering the next morning, Tom dressed, then let himself out onto the terrace, the best feature of his apartment. From the terrace, covered with planters filled with red geraniums blooming like crazy, he could see all of Rome stretch out before him. The thought struck him—the ghastly events of yesterday—they changed everything. The news would be in the papers, too. He walked down the nine flights and into the street. It was a three-minute walk to the Hotel de la Ville, where he knew he could buy the morning's *International Herald Tribune* and have breakfast.

The Hotel de la Ville was full of tourists, but he had no problem getting a table. After ordering, he glanced at the main headlines on the first page. Good, he thought, no mention of the incident. Then, below the fold, in the lower right-hand side of the front page, there was a photograph of him in the Roman Forum shaking hands with Doc. The headline read: MYSTERIOUS DEATHS AT THE ROMAN FORUM. The opening paragraph said:

Two archaeologists from the American Academy in Rome were killed yesterday while exploring an underground passageway on the Palatine Hill. The Roman Superintendent of Cultural Affairs stated that the roof of the passageway collapsed, and the cave-in resulted in the deaths of the two men. One of the archaeologists killed, Dr. Robert Brown of Bryn Mawr College in the city of Philadelphia in the United States of America, was heading the excavation sponsored by the American Academy in Rome. There had been hopes that the passageway might lead to new finds in the vast, mostly still buried, Golden House of Emperor Nero. The number two archaeologist, who also died, was Eric Bowen, a graduate student at Yale University in New Haven, Connecticut.

Professor Thomas Stewart, a trustee of the American Academy in Rome and a professor of forensic archaeology at New York University, was the senior Academy official present and was questioned by the Carabinieri. Dr. Stewart is pictured with Dr. Brown just before the latter dropped down into the passageway and perished. A spokesperson for the American Academy in Rome said there would be an official statement once the investigation was finished. The underground passageway and the American Academy's excavation itself have been officially closed until further notice.

The article went on but had no further information of consequence.

Cave-in? Tom thought. There was no evidence of a cave-in. Tom felt troubled. What could the reason be for covering up the truth of what had happened yesterday in the Forum?

More important, Tom was disturbed by the fact that the article had included his name and, even more, his photograph. He knew that if the Italian authorities were intent on hiding the truth of the cave-in, any reporter investigating the matter would be calling him to get more information simply because he had been identified in the article as having been there. He hoped that Caroline would handle the aftermath of this tragic event. After he'd finished breakfast, he hailed a cab in front of the Hassler Hotel and was back at the Academy in time for Gabrielli's phone call.

Lucia, Caroline's assistant, showed Tom into Caroline's office. "Thanks for coming, Tom," Caroline said. "Gabrielli's secretary telephoned to confirm that he'll call at 10 a.m. They asked for us to let them sort through Doc's belongings as part of the investigation. I told them I'd take the request under advisement."

Caroline continued. "Tom, have you given any more thought to what was going on yesterday with Doc's and Eric's deaths? Eric's parents and Doc's sister will surely be asking, and they probably won't buy the official explanation."

"I've been thinking that the arrival of an Italian Hazmat team points to some kind of chemical substance—likely a dangerous one—that caused their deaths, not a collapse of the roof of the passageway," Tom replied.

A look of concern flashed across her face.

The telephone buzzed. "Lieutenant Gabrielli," Lucia announced.

"I'll put it on the conference phone," Caroline said.

"Ciao, Lieutenant Gabrielli, I'm Caroline Sibelius, director of the American Academy, and I have Dr. Tom Stewart with me. We're at your disposal."

"Thank you. I'm sure you have seen the newspapers this morning?"

"Yes, but as I understand it, there was no collapse of the passageway," Caroline said.

"We had to adjust the story for the media because the deaths involve details we don't want widely known."

"Can you please be more specific?" Caroline asked.

"I'd like to, but I cannot."

Tom broke in. "Two of our friends and colleagues died yesterday. We need to know the reason why."

"I'm sorry, but the results of the autopsies must be kept confidential until the investigation is completed. Dr. Stefano Pulesi, senior director of the Laboratory for Communicable Substances, will be handling this stage of the investigation."

"What does this tragic event have to do with communicable substances? I thought this was a routine police investigation."

"Again, it's a matter of some . . . sensitivity. I'm sure Dr. Pulesi will be able to explain more."

"Does this mean that our Academy excavation will be suspended?" Caroline interjected.

"Yes, Signora. I'm afraid so. The passage will be sealed until further notice. We have posted guards there to prevent any curiosity seekers."

"Is there any danger to anyone who was there yesterday?" Tom asked.

"There's no danger. We'd like your help, however."

"How can we help?"

"We'd like to interview the members of the team present at the dig yesterday, including you, Dr. Stewart."

"I've already told the police what happened," Tom said.

"Yes, but perhaps there is some small fact you'll recall that will give us a lead. It's all part of the procedure."

"Understood. When can we pick up Doc's and Eric's remains?" Caroline asked. "Their families would like to make funeral arrangements."

Gabrielli was silent for a moment. "I'm afraid that we had to arrange for the cremation of the bodies due to the nature of the situation. The ashes will be available later today."

"Cremated? On whose authority?"

"By order of the Italian Security Agency."

"With all due respect, Lieutenant Gabrielli, this is entirely unacceptable. The families expect to take possession of the bodies and will be in Rome later today. I must contact the American Embassy."

"Your embassy has already been informed. I'm sorry, but there was no other way. Dr. Pulesi will be in touch concerning the interviews."

"Under the circumstances," Caroline said, "I'm afraid we need to contact our attorneys before we can cooperate further."

"That is unfortunate. It will only delay matters."

"Good day, sir." Caroline hung up.

Caroline and Tom looked at each other in astonishment. Tom offered, "First the cover story, now this. It doesn't add up."

"It's a mess any way you look at it. I'll need to tell the rest of the group not to speak with this Pulesi or any other official until they hear from me. The families will be furious about the cremations."

Tom stood. "I better get started on Doc's things."

"First door on your left, third floor—it's Room 272," she said, as she picked up the phone.

Doc's apartment was a one-bedroom apartment with a generous living room and a separate kitchen, which had windows looking over the central courtyard of the main building. When he opened the front door, Tom looked around. Sunlight streamed in the windows, and he could easily see the two giant cypress trees in the courtyard. The other two matching cypresses had become diseased and were replaced by attractive slim younger trees, whose size better suited the space.

What faced Tom was clutter. Clothes, papers, artifacts—all were a jumble on the desk at the window. Nothing out of the ordinary, Tom thought to himself. Doc was always a bit disorganized. Tom went over to the desk. There were several books on Nero's Golden House, including one with extensive diagrams of one author's speculation of how the palace rooms had been configured before they were destroyed or buried by the emperors who succeeded Nero. Doc had marked a few diagrams, putting question marks on Post-its. Doc seemed to be looking for something specific. Tom also saw some work papers concerning the dig in the Roman Forum, letters from Doc's sister, from colleagues at Bryn Mawr, a restaurant receipt.

Then, a single piece of paper caught Tom's attention. The paper was a work order dated September 17, 1943, from an Italian construction company for some work in the cryptoporticus at the American Academy in Rome. The name of the Swiss Institute was stamped on the paper, and countersigned by Lily Ross Taylor. There was an approval stamp with the initials "PF" next to that. Tom recognized Lily Ross Taylor's name and knew she had been one of the Academy's earliest female fellows, the first woman director of the American Academy and a classicist from Bryn Mawr College. Why would Doc have this old work order? Tom wondered.

Tom put the paper in his pocket and went about sorting everything into piles to be packed later and sent to Doc's sister. After about an hour, he returned to Caroline's office.

"Did you find anything interesting in Doc's room?" Caroline asked.

He showed the old work order to Caroline. "Strange. Doc and I were just talking about Lily Ross Taylor last week. She was quite a personality. We have a file on her in the library, and he must have found it there."

"I'd like to go through her file. That work order seems a little out of the ordinary even for Doc."

"Marina will help you find it. I'm waiting for callbacks from the American Embassy and the Academy attorney. Let's meet for lunch later."

"Works for me. You know—I never expected to be using the Academy library for finding out about World War II Swiss work orders. My editor will have a hard time believing this when I miss my deadline with my new book."

Caroline replied, "Join the crowd. My book schedule is five years overdue—my job as director is more like being a hotel keeper than a resident scholar: unexpected guests, broken water pipes, international crises."

"Okay, I get it. See you for lunch. Will you have Lucia tell me where and when?"

Caroline nodded and picked up her telephone.

The main reading room of the Academy library was a haven for scholars. It was something from another era. The vault in the main reading room, painted off-white, soared high overhead, and the tables and shelves were dark Italian walnut. With its open stacks and welcoming design, and the large bronze candelabra in the center of the room, it reminded Tom of the library from his college days at Columbia University.

Marina Calzona, the Academy's librarian, was a somewhat portly middle-aged woman who wore her glasses on a necklace. She smiled when she saw Tom. For his part, Tom couldn't help returning the smile.

"Dr. Stewart, how nice to see you. I'm so sorry about what happened to Professor Brown and Eric."

"Yes, it was a real tragedy. A great loss to us all."

"What can I do for you?"

"I'm looking for information about one of the former fellows, Dr. Lily Ross Taylor."

"Of course," she replied. "I have it right here. I hadn't filed it after Professor Brown returned it a few days ago. He said he might want to look at it again. Poor man." She crossed herself. "So young. May he rest in peace."

Marina retrieved the bulging file and put it on the counter. "There's an open desk there on the right. Just bring the file back when you are finished."

"Thanks for your help."

Tom took the file to the small desk and began to look through it. There was a list of Lily Ross Taylor's publications, her awards, and public references to her scholarship and historical role in the Academy. Standard stuff, Tom thought. There were a few photographs in the file. Ross had worn her hair in a crew cut and dressed in mannish clothes. He could picture her, a feisty and controversial figure at Bryn Mawr, a conservative women's college at the time. Then, he found a small brown envelope wrapped loosely with a string. Someone must have opened it and had done a poor job of retying it.

Tom found two letters inside, one dated August 1, 1943, and the other dated September 26, 1943. The first was a carbon copy from Lily to her sister in Bryn Mawr. Tom glanced quickly through it:

Rome is exceedingly interesting. Today, Sunday, August 1, there was a solar eclipse, with the moon covering the sun, darkening the Eternal City. The newspapers were trying to tie this event to everything else that has been happening. Speaking of events, two days ago, American bombers attacked Rome, aiming to destroy the rail yards of the main train station, the Termini. Some of the bombs went astray and five hundred Romans were killed and many more were wounded. The Church of San Lorenzo, where the Pope's predecessor is buried, was damaged. Pius XII hurried there where he prayed, offered money and sympathy. When he left, his long white coat was covered with blood. I don't know what to think. Of course, with the Allies landing in Sicily and

American bombers over Rome—that's all good news. But inno-cent people getting killed upsets me.

Then, last week, on July 24th, Mussolini was voted out of of-fice and a constitutional monarchy with a democratic parliament replaced him. This is wonderful news. But, now everyone expects the Germans to invade Italy.

Rome, as you can see, is in turmoil. I'm safe at the Swiss In-stitute—with the American Academy closed, I've got nothing official to do, so I spend my days in the Swiss library.

There is one unusual thing. Two days ago, on July 30, a cardinal and a priest from the Vatican—all at the official request of Pius XII—visited the Swiss Institute and the American Academy. They arrived and were greeted with as much fanfare as the dour Swiss know how to do—which isn't much. It seems they really wanted to visit the grounds of the American Academy, so I took them around. They were very secretive, so I have nothing to report, except the oddity of their visit.

If I were superstitious, I'd wonder about the moon blocking the sun and the coincidence of the cardinal's visit. But I'm not superstitious.

Love to you and your family,
Lily

What had the cardinal and his colleague wanted at the Academy? No higher-ups in the Church had ever visited the American Acad-emy to Tom's knowledge. Nor had top Italian politicos, except one famous visit by Mussolini, captured on a Pathé News clip, when the music fellows played "Turkey in the Straw" in his honor.

In the September 26 letter, Lily's sister's anxiety for Lily's safety was evident. She closes by pleading with Lily to get out while she could. "I know you feel great loyalty to the Academy, and I know how stubborn you are, but please do yourself and us all a favor and get out of that country, *now*. Our papers are filled with reports of the Nazi occupation of Rome two weeks ago and rumors of what they'll do. I hate to think."

Tom saw nothing in the correspondence that mentioned construction work or the PF, but why would she talk to her sister about this anyway? However, what was unusual was the date of her letter. About the time she signed the work order—it was very close to Germans taking control of Rome. Was there a connection?

Tom had to admit that, so far, he saw only a few dangling pieces of information, but nothing that gave him enough to tie a story together. It was, he thought, like most archaeological puzzles: a jumble of many bits of evidence. He'd have to lay them out on a table and wait until an inspiration happened. In this case, he sensed there were more pieces to discover before he could draw any conclusions.

After about an hour or so, Tom felt a tap on his shoulder and looked up to find Marina standing there. "Signora Sibelius asked that you join her at Lo Scarpone's for lunch. She'll meet you there in fifteen minutes. Do you know where it is?"

"Thanks, Marina. I do know where it is." He closed the file and handed it to her. "Thanks again for your help."

Caroline waived to Tom from her table on the terrace of Scarpone's, a small local restaurant a few blocks from the Academy. After he was seated and they had ordered, Tom asked, "Did you find out anything from the embassy?"

"The undersecretary was very polite, but all I could get was more political double talk. Eric's family will be landing in a few hours, so I couldn't leave word for them, and, frankly, I don't have much to tell them. I hope you were more successful checking out Doc's room."

"Not really. There were two letters; one, dated in August 1943 from Lily to her sister in Bryn Mawr and one from Lily's sister to her in September 1943."

"That was an increasingly dangerous time in Rome."

"How could she be at the Academy after Italy and Germany declared war on us?"

"When it looked like Italy would join Germany in declaring war on the United States, just after Pearl Harbor, the director of the Swiss Institute contacted the Academy to offer to take over the Academy property, to prevent the Italian Fascists from confiscating it. I believe Lily was instrumental in promoting this idea at the time."

"I assume the Academy's board jumped such a generous offer."

"On the contrary—the trustees in New York never made a decision. They suspected that the Swiss offer was just a power play to get our land and building. They never sanctioned the move. Once war was declared on the United States, the Swiss didn't wait for an official invitation—as the Americans moved out, the Swiss came in, uninvited, taking charge and protecting the Academy. Lily insisted on staying to watch over things. For the next couple of years, she was safe so long as Swiss neutrality was honored by the Germans and the Italians. In late 1943, Mussolini was deposed and Germany invaded Italy—then she knew she had to get out of Italy. She escaped by getting on a merchant freighter, which took her to England. From there she was put on a U.S. Air Force plane for the States. It's all in her official report in the records back in New York."

"It doesn't explain Doc's interest in her or what the work order for the American Academy's cryptoporticus with approvals by the Swiss Institute and 'PF' mean," Tom said.

Caroline shrugged. "Maybe it has something to do with his research for the dig in the Roman Forum. Lily was his mentor at Bryn Mawr, you know, and perhaps she mentioned it to him."

"Yes, I remember now. He took her position after she retired. It still seems a bit odd."

Caroline nodded. "The cryptoporticus of the Academy's Main Building contains the lower section of the library and, besides that, there was only a vast storage area. Until our recent renovations, people rarely went down there."

The waiter brought their meal, and they began to eat.

"By the way, Lucia said that a number of reporters have called to see if they can interview you."

"I expected that. I'd prefer not to be involved."

"Lucia will run interference for you, but all this attention isn't good for the Academy. We operate in Rome on the goodwill of the Italian government so we have to be careful. The embassy reminded me of that as well."

Caroline looked at her watch. "I expect Eric's parents have landed and are probably on their way to the Academy right now. I need to get back." She signaled the waiter for the check. "The memorial service for Doc is tomorrow at four in the afternoon at the Protestant Cemetery. You've been there before, haven't you?"

"Several times—a beautiful place. Of course I'll be there," Tom said.

As they walked back to the Academy, Tom asked, "Do you know the director of the Swiss Institute?"

"Reasonably well," she replied, "Georges Lundell. Quiet guy. Good scholar. Oddly enough, he loves to polka. Why do you ask?"

"Call me crazy, but this work order has me intrigued, and I'd like to read their records of the time."

"I'd be happy to call him to set up a meeting for you when I get back to my office. Lucia will let you know."

"Thanks. Good luck today, with Eric's family."

It was late afternoon. Tom was back in his apartment, working on his book, when his cell phone rang.

"Dr. Stewart, it's Lucia. Dr. Sibelius asked me to tell you that you have a meeting with Dr. Lundell at 10 a.m. tomorrow at the Swiss Institute."

"Thanks, Lucia. I'll be there."

Taking a break, he checked his NYU e-mail. There was a message from Alex asking him if there was any news and, if there were, to call her. He took out her card and called.

"Pronto."

"Alex, it's Tom Stewart. Just got your e-mail."

"Thanks for calling. I was wondering if there were any new developments."

Tom told her that he'd spoken with Gabrielli and that Stefano Pulesi of the Laboratory of Communicable Substances would be taking over the investigation.

"That's unusual."

"Yes. It seems it's all superconfidential. He would not give us any information."

"Not surprising. That agency is very secretive. Did they mention anything about precautions about the remains, like cremation?"

Tom was surprised at Alex's remark. "In fact they did. How did you know?"

"Standard procedure for containment, but it seems strange in this situation."

"That's what I thought when I heard it." Tom had to admit to himself that he didn't have anything else to say about the Roman Forum incident, but the idea of seeing Alex again appealed to him, so he plunged ahead. "Are you by any chance free for dinner tonight? Maybe at eight?"

"Yes, if we can make it a bit later. I've got a paper to finish."

"Perfect. Say around nine?"

"That's fine. Why don't you come to my place for a drink, and then we'll go to a little place around the corner."

"Via del Pellegrino, right? Near the Campo dè Fiori?" he said, looking at the card.

"Yes, that's right. See you then. Ciao."

He returned to working on his book, and became so engrossed that he lost track of the time. It was 8 p.m. when he finally looked at his watch. Tom quickly showered and changed. He got a taxi to take him to Alex's address.

When the cab let him off on Via del Pellegrino, he walked through a stone archway into a courtyard. Diagonally across from the arch, Tom saw Alex's house, a three-story stone building painted a Roman burnt red color. He rang the buzzer, and Alex appeared at the little balcony one floor up. She waved and then buzzed him in. Entering on the ground floor, Tom passed through the kitchen where he saw an Italian woman bent over a stove. She looked up when he passed through, giving him a smile and a wave. There was a beautiful, ancient wooden table in the middle of the kitchen/dining room.

Tom walked up a narrow spiral stairway. Alex stood at the landing in the living room, waiting for him to arrive. Off the living room was the small balcony containing planters filled with geraniums and ivy. The plants spilled over the edge of the balcony and swayed with the slightest breeze. Alex described the floor above as a bedroom, bathroom, small study, and a second terrace over the first, also filled with planters. "I guess you passed Ana, my cleaning lady, in the kitchen. She doubles as a cook when she has the time, and I've asked her to make soup for tomorrow. It's always better when it rests overnight."

There was a pitcher of flowers on a sideboard in the living room as well as two glasses and a carafe of red wine and a bottle of white wine. "Would you like some white or red wine, or, perhaps, something else?" she asked Tom.

"Some white wine would be fine," he replied. Tom watched her as she moved to the sideboard to fill their glasses. She was dressed informally in a loose red blouse and jeans that fit her well.

"I was sorry to see your name in the paper this morning," she said, handing him his wine. They sat down on the sofa. "Now the reporters will never leave you alone."

"Yes, but forewarned is forearmed. Caroline is handling the press. So far I've been able to avoid them."

"Are there any more developments?"

"Lieutenant Gabrielli called the Academy this morning to say the authorities are putting a lid on further publicity. They sealed the passageway and stopped excavation. Then they handed the case over to Pulesi. At the moment, we know nothing else."

"There's got to be more to it," Alex said. "Sealing the passageway and stopping excavation—very unusual. And assigning someone from the Communicable Substances Lab? It may be that what killed Doc and Eric was not only very lethal but highly contagious. Remember the green moss that Greg mentioned? Maybe it's involved somehow."

"Killer green moss? It all sounds more like a sci-fi movie," Tom said. "Doc was an archaeologist, not a terrorist."

"If Gabrielli or Pulesi is worried about contagion, there may be some real danger."

"Still, it doesn't fit," Tom said. "Traces of a deadly virus in a Roman emperor's palace buried for two thousand years? How could that be?"

"Epidemics are frightening and hard to control. Viruses or plagues—periodically, they appear and do cause horrendous destruction."

"You seem to be quite interested in this."

"I've made human plagues a specialty," Alex replied, "particularly ones that had devastating impacts on society. Some plagues, like the black death, wiped out huge numbers of people. There was widespread panic. Even powerful institutions like the Catholic Church were affected. Think about it. If death kills most of your family and most of your neighbors, just how mighty would you think God is? Or, His Church? I could talk about this for hours, but I don't want to bore you."

"This isn't boring to me," Tom said. "When was the first plague?"

"You'll find the earliest recorded plague in the Book of Exodus. Ten plagues fell on the Egyptian people sometime around 2000 BC during the reign of Pharaoh Ramesses II. The plagues nearly destroyed Egypt, though we don't know the numbers of people killed.

"You could say Moses was the first leader to use plagues as weapons against his enemy. Essentially biological warfare." Alex paused, embarrassed because she was doing all the talking. "I told you I could go on for hours. You must be hungry. Let's go to dinner."

"Yes, let's go," said Tom, laughing. "We can finish this discussion later."

Passing through the stone archway, Alex turned left onto Via del Pellegrino heading away from the Campo dè Fiori. Almost immediately, she turned left again.

Tom hesitated for a moment, though he wasn't sure why. They were in a passage so narrow Tom guessed traffic couldn't get through.

Alex, sensing Tom's hesitation, laughed. "This is an alleyway called Arco di Santa Margherita—it's a shortcut to the restaurant. It's perfect for me."

The alleyway ended at the front door of La Taverna di Lucifero, on a quiet side street that also ran into Campo dè Fiori.

Alex explained that the restaurant was built around a column from Pompey's gladiatorial arena.

The restaurant itself was busy, but the owner knew Alex and showed them to a quiet table in the back. After they ordered, Tom asked, "So, how'd you get into archaeology? You don't seem like most of the graduate students I've known."

"It's a long story."

"We've got time."

"My father was an Italian diplomat and my mother's an art historian, born in the United States."

"No wonder your English is so perfect." Almost without realizing it, Tom was leaning forward, just slightly, over the table to catch every word Alex spoke. He was having a great time. She, too, seemed totally engaged in their conversation. At one point, Tom caught himself, wondering if he had been served yet, then looked down and saw his plate empty of food, waiting to be picked up by their waiter. Alex saw Tom gaze downward, realized what he was thinking, laughed, and said, "Yes, we've eaten and are waiting for coffee."

She laughed. "Thanks for your compliment about my English. I appreciate that. My mother and my father eventually divorced when my mother found out that my father was not only a very good diplomat, but that he turned out to be devastatingly attractive to younger Italian women, too. My mother left him and returned to live in New York. She never remarried. I am an only child, and, when they divorced I bounced between New York and Rome. I know living in New York and Rome sounds glamorous, but I never wanted to live that way.

"I went to college in the States—Smith College, where I majored in European history. Afterward? I moved to New York City. I loved the city, but living with my mother turned out to be too claustrophobic for me. She's wonderful, but she never got over my father.

"So, I moved back to Rome. Every street goes back two—or three—thousand years. That's when I really discovered history because I was living in the middle of it. For me, there's so much to learn. I quickly decided to get my master's degree in ancient European history at the University of Rome and that led to my working on my PhD."

Tom asked, "Is your father still alive?"

"My father died five years ago. Despite his philandering, I loved him and enjoyed the meals we had together in his favorite restaurants. He left me some money, and I bought my house."

"You never married?" Tom asked, and immediately blushed. "I'm sorry—that's pretty forward of me."

"I'm not going to take that as an intrusive question, which of course it is," Alex said. "I've had plenty of opportunities," she said, looking straight at Tom. "But, I've never found the right person at the right time." Then she added, "I'm thirty-one, and my birthday's March 1. I thought I'd save you the trouble of asking."

"Thanks," replied Tom, blushing again. "I can congratulate myself for my discretion. But, I'll persist, how did you become interested in archaeology?"

"A man I met at the university is an archaeologist and last summer joined the team at the American Academy's excavation in the Roman Forum. I was intrigued. This spring I signed on as a volunteer."

Tom asked, "Is this friend of yours on the dig as well?" He tried to sound casual.

"I'm not seeing him, if that's what you're getting at. He's in Greece at an excavation with the American School in Athens. Now I've told you my story, what's yours?"

"I'm forty-five, by the way, with a birthday on January 29," Tom began.

"Aquarius," Alex said. "But why are you telling me your birthday?"

"Turnabout is fair play. Anyway, I grew up in Saginaw, Michigan, with a mother and father who married very late. My father was sixty before he married for the first time. I was born five years later. My mother, thirty years younger, was an adjunct instructor at the University of Michigan where my father was an English professor. They fell madly in love with each other and, when I was born, spoiled me rotten.

"Still, I never had a father to play baseball with or toss a football to. He was more like my grandfather, but there were compensations. I often wondered what it would have been like to have parents who were much younger.

"I couldn't wait to get away from Saginaw to go to college. I went to Columbia where I studied archaeology as an undergraduate and then stayed on for my PhD."

"Why archaeology? It seems like an unusual major for an undergraduate."

"I wrote a paper senior year in high school on Howard Carter's discovery of Tutankhamen's tomb in Egypt. I read everything I could find on the topic. I got an A+. I guess that I never lost my enthusiasm for archaeology."

"Was your specialty Egypt?"

He smiled. "At first, of course. I wanted to follow in Carter's footsteps. But my advisors said Egyptology was too crowded a field. I became a generalist, eventually specializing in forensic archaeology."

"And are you married?" Alex asked politely, but directly.

This time it was Tom's turn to smile. "Never found the right person. Several long affairs, some for the right reasons, one for the wrong, but none that worked out."

Alex said nothing.

After dinner, as Tom followed Alex to the restaurant's front door, he caught the scent of her perfume. It smelled of jasmine. He liked walking behind this striking woman, with olive gray eyes and brownish black hair.

"Why not treat ourselves to a gelato at the most famous café of them all, Giolitti's?" Alex suggested. "It's only two blocks from here, near the Pantheon."

"Beautiful night for a stroll. Lead the way," Tom replied.

Alex walked with Tom through the Campo dè Fiori, where crowds of people were still wandering around, though the shops were closing down for the night. As they passed by the center of the piazza, Tom and Alex paused at the tall, hooded, brooding statue of the philosopher Giordano Bruno. Tom said, "Burned at the stake by the Catholic Church because he chose not to believe that the earth was the center of the universe."

"Slight correction," added Alex. "Bruno was burned because he wouldn't shut up about the matter."

"Noted. Do you think things have changed that much?"

"That's rhetorical, right?" said Alex, as they continued toward their destination.

They enjoyed the walk, watching the crowds filling the old narrow side streets even this late in the evening. Cars and motor scooters threaded through the streets, picking their way carefully to avoid the pedestrians. Somehow, they all coexisted peacefully.

At the Pantheon, Tom and Alex stopped in front of the massive entrance. The façade was lit up.

"This building is a miracle," Alex said.

"What I admire," Tom replied, "is that it has survived emperors and popes, pillages and wars. It has stood proudly through two millennia. I imagine it will be here in another thousand years."

"The Eternal City?"

"Yes. I guess that's why I love it."

As Tom and Alex moved on, they failed to see a man standing in the shadows watching them. He followed them at a discreet distance. A few minutes later, Tom and Alex were inside Giolitti's, the glittering Belle Epoque café, crowded with tourists anxious to sample from the café's wide range of desserts, ice creams, and coffees.

"I'm interested in learning about your work in forensic archaeology," Alex asked. "It sounds fascinating."

"Basically, I'm a theoretical archaeologist, which means I'm rarely at work at an archaeological dig. But I spend my time with the results of such digs, analyzing the finds, particularly human remains, but also other objects, all of which create a picture of the society and lives of the group being studied. I teach the methodology of forensic archaeology at the graduate level."

"Sounds very analytical."

"Not really. I've had my best results when I've played my hunches—like a gambler in Vegas. I deal with fragments—often there's no complete picture. Imagine a jigsaw puzzle with half the pieces missing. It's very practical. Also, the police academy in New York City has me lecture their detectives. I create a scenario and show them how to analyze the physical clues at the scene of the crime. "

"Sherlock Stewart?" Alex joked.

Tom laughed. "Hardly, but it's fun. I like working with the police. Right after the events of 9/11, I spent several weeks with the police in the rubble of the World Trade Towers helping to find and identify human remains. There was often so little left that all we had to go on were teeth and body fragments that yielded their DNA."

"What a depressing experience that must have been," Alex said.

"Identifying someone, however, gave that person's family some sense of closure. That was satisfying. Oh, here's something less gruesome. I'm also called by WNBC, Channel 4 News—when there's some crime being reported on, either local or national. Chuck Scarborough, the veteran news anchor, interviews me for my opinion about the facts of the case. This makes me a minor, a very minor, television personality. It's been interesting, however, and taken me into situations in which I wouldn't have otherwise been involved."

"You know," Alex confessed, "I've never been able to help myself. When I saw actors and film equipment in the process of making a movie in New York City, I was one of the crowd who loved watching. And once or twice I went to NBC television broadcasts at their studios in Rockefeller Center." She smiled. "I'm hooked. I'm intrigued by your 'celebrity.'"

Tom laughed, but was very pleased by Alex's interest in his 'minor' celebrity status.

They left Giolitti's close to midnight and walked back to Alex's house where they said good night.

"I had a wonderful evening," Alex said. "I'm glad you suggested it."

"We'll do this again soon. I'll be here for the rest of the summer."

"I'd like that. Buona notte."

Tom found a taxi near the Campo dè Fiori and told the driver to drop him at the piazza in front of the Hassler. It was a pleasant summer evening, and he was in a particularly good mood.

In the midst of his short ride to the top of the Spanish Steps, Tom checked his cell phone. There were many messages from reporters wanting to speak to him. He erased them all.

5

Sometime after midnight, three men dressed entirely in black approached the locked gate outside the archaeological precinct on the Palatine Hill in the Roman Forum. With one movement of powerful steel cutters, the lock was removed. They opened the gate quietly and slipped in. Two carabinieri posted to guard the site, about twenty feet away, were smoking cigarettes and talking.

The intruders advanced quietly toward the guards. The intruders were prepared: two shots, fired silently from a sleek black pistol, struck the guards. The carabinieri looked surprised as they crumpled to the ground, unconscious as the fast-acting agent did its work. The intruder with the pistol said, "They'll be out for at least two hours. Let's get going."

One of the three intruders stood guard over the fallen carabinieri while his two accomplices pushed aside the rock that covered the underground passage. They put on gas masks, dropped down into the tunnel, and began moving forward in the passageway. They had headlamps and moved without a word, reaching the large underground tiled room within minutes. The two men were searching for something in the now spotlessly clean—and empty—abandoned laboratory.

Despite their thorough efforts, they found nothing. Disappointed and anxious not to delay things too long, they turned and began to walk back to the beginning of the underground passage-way and climbed up to the surface, empty handed.

"The boss won't be happy," the third intruder said. "What about them?" He pointed to the bodies of the two policemen.

"Just leave them there. Let's go."

At 6 a.m., two carabinieri walked up to relieve the night guards. The first thing they noticed was the open gate and the snapped lock.

Rushing up the hill to the American Academy site, they found the two guards, conscious now, sitting in the dirt, holding their heads.

"What happened?"

"We were attacked in the middle of the night." The two cara-binieri stood, brushed themselves off, and walked to the entrance of the passageway.

"Over here," the other officer said. "Somebody moved the stone."

Shining a flashlight into the passage below, they saw nothing out of order. One of the newly arrived carabinieri said, "We've been told to alert headquarters if we find anything suspicious." With that he grabbed his cell phone and immediately called his supervisor.

Tom woke up early, exhausted. He hadn't slept well.

A fragment of a dream he had had during the night flashed into his mind. It was an image of Doc's and Eric's contorted bodies. He had woken up in a sweat. Now, at 6:30 a.m., he forced himself to get up, shave, and go out for breakfast at the Hotel de la Ville. At the newsstand in the hotel, he picked up a copy of the *International Herald Tribune*. As he skimmed through the paper while he ate, he looked for any articles about the deaths in the Roman Forum. There was a short article with no new information, but a reference was made to speculation that there was more to the story than the Italian officials were admitting.

After all, the reporter had written, the Italian authorities had ordered a Hazmat team to the site, and Hazmat means hazardous materials.

Pleased, however, to be finding nothing new about himself in the article, Tom immersed himself in the depressing articles about the economic conditions in Europe.

"Un altro caffè, signore?" The waiter asked.

Tom looked at his watch. He'd better get moving to make his appointment at the Swiss Institute. He declined a second caffè, paid the check, and left to get a taxi.

At the front gate of the Swiss Institute, Tom gave his name and was immediately shown to the director's office. Georges Lundell rose from his desk and walked toward Tom, extending his hand. He was tall, thin, with dark hair thinning on top. He wore brown horn-rimmed glasses with lenses that made his eyes look considerably larger than they were.

"I'm sorry for the death of your colleagues. It's a sad affair for all of us." He spoke English with a decidedly German accent.

"Thank you. It certainly was a shock."

"So, how can I be of assistance? Caroline mentioned something about a research question."

"I'm interested in the period when the Swiss Institute acted as custodian for the American Academy during the war. It would be helpful if I could see your annual reports for 1942 and 1943."

Lundell seemed surprised. "May I ask the reason for your request? It is rather specific."

"I'm doing some research into Academy history for the other trustees, especially the period during the war and shortly thereafter."

"Yes, that was certainly a chaotic time. I'll arrange for the reports to be brought to our research room on the second floor where you can read them without interruption. I'll have my assistant escort you there. Please let me know if I can be of any other assistance."

Lundell called his assistant—a sturdy brown-haired woman with an attractive face. He introduced Monica to Tom. Monica smiled, through lips covered with bright red lipstick. Her eyes were deep blue. She was cheerful, but Tom guessed she also had firm German training and would heroically do all her tasks.

"I appreciate your help," Tom replied to Lundell as he and Monica left the director's office.

After about twenty minutes waiting in the research room, Monica brought Tom the two official reports from 1942 and 1943 he had asked for. They were very detailed and confirmed that Lily

Ross Taylor was in residence at the Swiss Institute, and that two representatives of the Vatican had visited the Institute in July 1943. Further, there were a few documents relating to the visit.

The first document was an official announcement from the director of the Swiss Institute that Cardinal Visconti would be there on July 30, 1943, at 3 p.m., a guest of Lily Ross Taylor, director pro tem of the American Academy in Rome.

The second document was a bit more cryptic. It read:

Memorandum for the File—Confidential:

On July 30, 1943, Cardinal Visconti, accompanied by a young priest, visited the Swiss Institute. They said that Pope Pius XII had sent them to visit the Institute but also the American Academy, which is under the protection of the Swiss. No reason other than Vatican business was offered. The director of the Swiss Institute and Miss Lily Ross Taylor of the American Academy, a guest of the Institute, accompanied Cardinal Visconti to the American Academy on the Janiculum Hill where Miss Taylor showed them through the buildings. They requested information about the large rooms in the basement of the main building. When they had completed their tour of the American Academy, the cardinal asked the director and his associates to keep his visit confidential.

Signed: Frederick Schumann, secretary

Odd, Tom thought. Why would a senior official of the Vatican be interested in the Academy's cryptoporticus? Had the work order he had found in Doc's papers been connected to this visit? There was also a signed photograph of the cardinal, Lily Ross Taylor, the director of the Swiss Institute, and a young, unidentified priest, all standing in the main receiving room of the Institute. The cardinal's arms were inside his robe; he was standing erect, with no smile on his face. Visconti looked stern, totally businesslike. There was no humor in his face. On the other hand, the young priest, the Swiss director, and Lily Ross Taylor—the others in the picture—were captured by the camera laughing with each other, appearing to be having a good time talking.

Tom read through the rest of the records for that year and found nothing of import. Monica had been waiting for him to finish, sitting at a nearby table reading the day's German newspaper. Tom signaled to her, and Monica came over. "Do you need any more documents?" she asked very politely.

"I'm finished," Tom replied. "Dankeschön."

"You speak German?" she asked.

"Ein bisschen." Tom laughed.

Again, very politely, very efficiently, and with no trace of humor, Monica led the way back to Lundell's office.

"Did you find what you were looking for?" Lundell asked.

Tom replied that the reports had been helpful. "I learned that a Cardinal Visconti had visited your Institute and asked for a tour of the cryptoporticus of the main building of the American Academy. Do you know anything about this man Visconti?"

"I do. Intriguing man, even frightening. Very austere. I've studied Vatican history, particularly the modern period. Cardinal Paolo Visconti was one of the most powerful cardinals—some say the most powerful man in the Vatican next to the Pope himself. He was called the 'Red Pope,' being a cardinal, and head of the PF."

"PF?" Tom asked.

"He was the director of the Sacred Congregation for the Propagation of the Faith or the *Sacra Congregatio de Propaganda Fide.* Hence the nickname PF."

"I'm not familiar with that organization."

"It was founded in the seventeenth century, and it still exists today as the Congregation for the Evangelization of Peoples or *Congregatio pro Gentium Evangelizatione,* although it does most of its work out of the public eye. It is the agency in the Roman Curia originally meant to enforce Church practices around the world. Think of it as the Pope's police force though its role has softened over the years. In 1901, the Pope commissioned the Pontifical Biblical Commission as one of its sub-agencies, responsible for investigating scholarship and archaeological discoveries that could in some way impact Church doctrine."

"Why would the Pope send Visconti to visit the American Academy? The Academy has always been nondenominational."

"It does seem out of the ordinary. I don't know."

Tom stood up, graciously thanked Lundell, who offered to make himself available any time Tom might want. In parting, Lundell said, "I've invited Caroline and the rest of the Academy to the Institute Saturday night. We thought it might help the Academy lighten up after the horror of recent events. We're having a polka evening with a genuine polka band."

Tom couldn't suppress a grin at the thought of German-Swiss scholars dancing polkas.

Lundell seemed to take Tom's grin as encouragement. "The band is quite good, and we'll have plenty of beer and wine. Please accept my invitation for you to join us."

Tom thanked Lundell for the invitation and shook hands with the director and left to return to his apartment.

His cell phone rang. "Signore Stewart, it is Lucia. Signora Sibelius asked me to remind you of Dr. Brown's memorial service today at 4 p.m. There's an Academy van leaving at 3 p.m., and there's room on it if you're planning to go."

"Thank her for me, but I'll make my way to the service on my own."

"Also, a Father O'Boyle telephoned and asked me to give you his cell number. He'd like you to call him."

Tom took down the number. "Thanks for the message."

Tom dialed, and O'Boyle picked up after the second ring. Tom introduced himself and said, "What can I do for you?"

"Thank you for calling me back," the man said in a soft Irish brogue. "I won't take much of your time. It's about the unfortunate incident in the Roman Forum. I've information, which may be extremely important to you. Could we meet? I'd rather not discuss it over the phone."

Tom was puzzled at the urgency in O'Boyle's voice. He didn't sound like the good-natured librarian John Connor described.

"I'm rather busy today, Father O'Boyle. Perhaps later in the week."

"Dr. Stewart, the sooner the better—as it's a matter of some urgency. Would it be possible for us to meet sometime this evening? Perhaps around eight?"

"Yes, I can meet you then. Would this be at the Vatican?"

"No, not there," he said quickly, then caught himself. "I'd prefer you meet me at the Jubilee Church."

"I don't know where it is," said Tom.

"Jubilee is a new church, commissioned by Pope John Paul II for the Millennium Celebration. I'll be in a pew halfway to the front of the church."

"Give me the address, and I'll get a taxi. How long a drive is—"

"No taxis. It's too . . . expensive. Please let me give you the instructions by public transportation." O'Boyle went on to tell Tom how to get there. It was complicated. "And, please come alone."

O'Boyle hung up.

Tom had to admit he was very curious. Perhaps O'Boyle would shed some light on what had happened to Doc and Eric.

The Protestant Cemetery was located in southeastern Rome, at the Porta San Paolo alongside the pyramid built in 30 BC by a private citizen, Gaius Cestius, praetor and tribune of the people of Rome, as his tomb. It was a small-scale Egyptian-style marble-covered pyramid, the most unique mausoleum in Rome.

Tom had been to the Protestant Cemetery previously and found the grounds as beautiful as he remembered them, with its trimmed boxwood hedges under the shade of pines and the tall cypress trees mixed with green, well-watered lawns. A number of illustrious people were buried there, including English poets John Keats and Percy Bysshe Shelley. Tom was among a group of about a hundred friends and acquaintances of Doc's, there to honor him. They gathered around a small hole in the ground, which had been dug to hold the bronze container carrying Doc's ashes, and that would be covered by a marble plaque in his honor.

Several of Doc's colleagues in archaeology from the American Academy presented short remarks on the life and achievements of their friend. Michael Lowell, a classical scholar at the American

Academy and head of the Department of Classics at Brown University, read some poetry in Latin, which moved a number of those present to tears. Tom found his own rusty Latin was adequate to give him the gist of what Lowell had said, but not the nuances. He made a note to himself to practice reading some Latin poetry.

As Tom glanced around, looking at the crowd, he suddenly noticed two men in the shadows of a large cypress staring back at him. Tom turned away, but when he looked again, they were gone. Knowing that he was being watched was very disturbing to him—he didn't like it at all. What could they want?

At the conclusion of the ceremony, Tom saw Caroline talking with an impeccably dressed, stunning blond woman. Beside her was a man who looked like a staid businessman in a sharp gray suit. Caroline motioned for Tom to join them.

"Let me present Crystal Close and Robert Parker, both from an international genetic seed company called Belagri. They provided money for Doc's excavation in the Roman Forum. They are very kindly paying their respects to Doc and Eric." Turning to Crystal and Parker, Caroline said, "Dr. Tom Stewart is one of the Academy's trustees, a distinguished forensic archaeologist and professor at New York University."

Tom shook hands with them.

"We're very sorry for your loss," Crystal said. "Dr. Brown was quite passionate about his work."

"Yes, he was."

"Our chairman, Hermann Bailitz, is fascinated with archaeology. When he heard about Dr. Brown's plan to uncover some of the lost rooms of Nero's Golden House, he directed our foundation to donate funds to the effort. Brown's research showed great promise. Dr. Bailitz was very dismayed at the unfortunate turn of events."

"As were we all," Caroline added.

"It must have been difficult for you, Dr. Stewart, to be present at the death of your colleagues," Robert Parker said. "I gather that the Italian authorities sealed the site and shut down the excavation. Do you think it will be reopened after the investigation is complete?"

"We don't know," replied Tom.

"A pity," Crystal said. "Dr. Bailitz asked us to convey to you that our foundation remains committed to the work started by Dr. Brown. Should the dig be reopened, we hope the Academy will use the unexpended money from our grant."

"That's quite generous of you," Caroline said. "We're eager to continue the excavation provided it's safe, and we can find a new senior archaeologist for the dig."

"Good. The foundation will be ready to work out the details."

"Are you in Rome for long?" Caroline said. "We'd like to give you a tour of the Academy facilities."

"Thank you," Crystal said. "Actually, our executive team is in Rome for a couple of days on a corporate retreat. When we heard about this service, we took time to pay our respects. We have a facility on our property next to Hadrian's Villa, forty minutes by car from here. We need to be getting back now."

"Perhaps you could join us for lunch tomorrow?" Parker said.

"Thank you, but I'm afraid I'll have to pass," Caroline said. "But, Tom, maybe you'd like to go?"

"I'm . . . well, I'll make time. Yes, I'd like to join you. Just tell me where and when."

Crystal smiled. "Excellent. Let's say lunch around 1 p.m. Give me your e-mail address, and I'll have someone send you the directions and our telephone numbers."

Tom handed her his business card.

With this, Crystal shook hands with Caroline and Tom, as did Parker, and they walked to an awaiting limousine.

"What do you think of all this?" Caroline said to Tom. "I was surprised to see them here."

"It was a strange coincidence, but they seem committed to the project."

"Frankly, their offer seems a bit too good to be true. Let's see how receptive the foundation is. Thanks for going tomorrow."

"Anything to keep the funding alive. Doc would appreciate it."

"You'll need a car to get there. Why don't you take mine? Come by the Academy tomorrow morning, and I'll give you my keys."

As he was leaving, Tom saw Alex talking with the other members of Doc's archaeological team. She waved at Tom. He hoped that she might be joining them for dinner. He had a meeting with Father O'Boyle, so he smiled and waved back.

About 6:30 p.m., Tom followed Father O'Boyle's instructions and headed to Rome's major train station, the Termini, in the southeastern part of the Eternal City. People of all nationalities moved in and out of the giant train terminal. O'Boyle had told Tom to look for a trolley station near the main entrance. Tom found it and boarded a car just about to leave for Rome's southern suburbs. Tom kept alert to see if anyone might be following him. There didn't seem to be anyone, but Tom did notice that an old man with a decided limp remained on the trolley for the entire ride, and looked at him occasionally.

After about an hour, the trolley came to its final stop. Tom headed for a bus stop about a hundred yards away, as O'Boyle had instructed him. A few minutes later, a bus pulled up and Tom boarded. A teenager and the old man with the limp lined up behind Tom to get on the bus. The ride to the Jubilee Church took another twenty minutes and was the next to last stop. The bus left Tom directly across the street from the Jubilee Church.

The church itself was a modern, concrete structure. It looked to Tom like a white boat with three billowy sails. Odd, thought Tom, until he realized that the sails represented the folds on a nun's cap. The white church was surrounded by a stone plaza broken up by a few grassy areas. There was a bell tower to the front of the entrance.

Tom entered the main door. The soft light from the ebbing sun streamed in the narrow window at the altar and through the high-curved windows of the nun's cap. Inside there was a peaceful silence. Beneath the whiteness of the interior walls, there were pews of brown oak. One person sat midway toward the front of the church, his head bowed in prayer. Otherwise, the church was empty. Tom walked slowly toward this person. "Father O'Boyle?"

The man crossed himself, then turned toward Tom. "Doctor Stewart?"

"Please call me Tom," he replied.

O'Boyle stood up, with some difficulty, and held out his hand. Tom realized that O'Boyle shook hands firmly, but his hand trembled a bit. He had a full head of white hair. He was dressed in his priest's black cassock.

"Thank you for coming," O'Boyle said and gestured for Tom to sit beside him in the pew.

"Stunning church," Tom said.

"Think it's a bit odd that an old codger summons an American TV personality to a new church in the middle of nowhere?"

Tom paused, not sure what O'Boyle would say next.

"Tragic," O'Boyle continued, looking at their surroundings. "This church was built for the millennium celebrations, but when they were over, it was forgotten. No one in Rome wants to come out this far to worship. The local people prefer their own churches. Even the priest here is part time."

"Seems like a waste," Tom replied evenly.

"That's only the half of it," the old priest said. Then he seemed lost in thought for a minute or two.

"Father O'Boyle, about the tragedy in the Roman Forum . . ."

O'Boyle was abrupt. "That photograph of you and Doc Brown at the opening to the underground passage has gone around the world."

"What do you mean by that?"

"You are tied by that newspaper to the story, like it or not."

"I understand. Should I be worried?"

"Readers of that story will assume you have information they want. Information they want badly. You will have to take action to defend yourself."

"But I know nothing," Tom said impatiently. "What does this all have to do with the dig? With Doc and Eric? With me?"

"Doesn't matter," O'Boyle said. "You need to know more to defend yourself."

"If this is true," Tom said, "are you prepared to help me? In fact," Tom continued with some irritation, "if I'm supposed to defend myself, what am I supposed to be concerned about? The odd green moss? The crazy, inexplicable deaths of two American Academy colleagues? Someone coming after me, thinking I know something—which I don't?"

O'Boyle sighed. "I don't know. What you might learn might make you more vulnerable."

Tom said, "It's up to you. If I'm in trouble, I should know enough to defend myself."

O'Boyle said nothing. He fixed his eyes on Tom. He leaned slightly forward. "I checked up on you. The Vatican has you in their files."

"What?" Tom said, unable to hide his surprise.

"The record shows that ten years ago a guard in the Sistine Chapel apprehended you for trying to make off with something belonging to the Church."

Tom repeated, "Ten years ago . . . Okay." He laughed, recalling the memory. "I'm guilty."

O'Boyle looked puzzled. "Why are you laughing?"

Tom replied, "I had been visiting the work area in the Sistine just under the ceiling where Michelangelo's great fresco was being restored. An official photographer was taking Polaroid pictures—before and after—of the restoration. He gave me a discarded one."

"What happened?"

"I rode down from the scaffolding in the elevator with the photograph in my hand—in complete innocence. I left the elevator. A guard, seeing me holding the photograph, came right over to me and confiscated the Polaroid."

"That's it?" O'Boyle asked. "The Great Vatican Theft? Well, we've always been accused of caring too much when a lone sparrow falls."

"So, I'm a sparrow?"

"We all are," O'Boyle retorted. "Thank God for the Vatican security system."

O'Boyle was amused by this exchange, but fell quiet once again.

Tom broke in, "Father O'Boyle—about the Roman Forum . . ."

"Ah, the deaths in the Roman Forum and the reasons for them. Well, to understand, you have to go back a number of years. Ever hear of Imhotep the Younger? Or the archaeologist Charles Babcock?"

"I haven't heard of them, though Imhotep's name rings a bell," said Tom.

"You might want to learn a lot more about them. The Vatican paid close attention. That's where it started."

"What started?" asked Tom, lost by O'Boyle's elliptical comments.

Father O'Boyle said nothing for a moment as Tom waited patiently. Then O'Boyle continued. "This was before my time. The Propaganda Fidei had their proof, and the matter was closed—forgotten about."

Tom thought about what O'Boyle had said. It sounded like gibberish. He decided to wait the old man out.

"In 1933 Hitler came to power. Increasingly he became a threat to Europe and the Vatican. Then, in 1939, a new pope was named: Pius XII." O'Boyle seemed to be looking at the past, and he did so with pride.

"Pius had previously been Vatican ambassador to Germany and had dealt with Hitler. He not only didn't trust Hitler, he feared Germany would inevitably invade Italy, destroy the Catholic Church, and seize its property. As world events progressed, and Germany's aggressions were more evident, the Pope became obsessed with the risk the Vatican faced."

"How do you know all this?" asked Tom.

"My superior was the head of Propaganda Fidei—the Red Pope, as he was called. He was a member of the inner circle, close to the pope himself."

"Why was he called the Red Pope?" asked Tom, believing he already knew but wanting confirmation.

"The Propaganda Fidei is a secret organization, with strong financial resources, answerable only to the pope. Its head, a cardinal, is extremely powerful."

"You were part of this organization?" Tom said.

"I was a young priest from Ireland, assigned to the Cardinal—Cardinal Paolo Visconti."

Tom did a double take. "Visconti?"

"Do you know of him?" O'Boyle asked, surprised.

"I believe so," Tom replied. "Please go on."

O'Boyle continued, "Visconti was an ambitious man who had risen quickly. When he was made head of Propaganda Fidei, he was in fact the second most powerful man in the Church.

"Everyone knew of the pope's concern about protecting the Church from Hitler. But no one had a solution. Then, in early 1942, Hitler provided us the answer to our problem."

"How is that?" asked Tom.

"A few German scientists, fearing for their lives at the hands of the Gestapo, escaped from Berlin and came to Rome. Each had a relative or ancestor who was Jewish. They knew that eventually they would be rounded up and shipped off to the concentration camps.

"Cardinal Visconti liked to say that Divine Providence had intervened— and he, Visconti, as God's agent, had then pulled strings that provided sanctuary for the scientists. These men had worked on top secret biological weapons projects in Berlin."

"Wait a minute," Tom exclaimed, with some fear mixed with anger. "You said biological weapons. Poisons. Is this what Doc's and Eric's deaths were all about? Killed by some biological weapon?"

"Let me finish," O'Boyle said. "Visconti gave the German scientists access to the Propaganda Fidei laboratory located four stories underground in Vatican City. The Germans soon found the earlier project of the PF, which I told you about."

He didn't like what he was hearing at all, but he had to let O'Boyle finish.

O'Boyle continued. "In searching through PF projects of the past, the German scientists discovered one from ancient Egypt. They saw a great challenge, and Visconti found his solution to protecting the Vatican from a German invasion."

"And what was this?" Tom asked.

"There were three canopic jars from ancient Egypt in the PF's inventory, one containing remains of grain, another the bones of a cow, and the third—human tissue fragments. PF research had verified that a powerful virus had killed the cow and the humans. The scientists proposed to reconstruct the virus, and if they succeeded the virus could be used to defend against the Germans.

"Visconti presented his project to His Holiness, who had reservations but allowed the project to proceed so long as it was done in total secrecy and not in the PF's lab in Vatican City."

Tom had begun to see where this story was headed. "By any chance, was this experimentation performed in the Roman Forum in a secret lab?" Tom asked.

O'Boyle smiled. "Very good. You catch on fast. As Visconti's personal assistant, I came up with the location, under the Forum, part of Nero's gigantic Golden House near the Trajan Baths. There were vast underground rooms, some known and explored, others just speculated about, waiting to be discovered. Perfect hiding place. I supervised. We built an up-to-date laboratory in a month, working around the clock as each day Germany's power increased.

"Finding traces of the virus in tissue samples from the canopic jars, the scientists performed trial after trial. Most ended in failure. But these scientists were brilliant, motivated, and persistent. Finally, we had a breakthrough. First, minute traces, then a small supply. The virus had shocking properties."

Tom noticed the gleam of pride in O'Boyle's face and excitement in his voice.

O'Boyle suddenly interrupted himself—he seemed to be shying away from his telling. Tom needed to keep O'Boyle on track. The old priest was vacillating. Suddenly, he said, "What was it like being so close to Michelangelo's work on the Sistine Chapel ceiling?"

Tom was floored by the digression, but decided to play along.

"Where the work was already restored, the colors were shockingly bright pastels rather than the dull colors I had studied in art history in college. The wax and smoke from the oil torches burning for the last five hundred years lay thick on the surface of the painting."

O'Boyle's curiosity about the Sistine ceiling was not yet satisfied. "What part of the painting were you able to inspect?"

Tom said, "I was standing within a foot of the most dramatic moment in the entire ceiling."

"Which was?"

"The inception of the human race. Adam lying on a cloud with his left arm stretched toward the right hand of God, whose finger was about to touch Adam's, causing life to surge from God to man."

O'Boyle said, "And, did you?"

"Touch God's finger and Adam's finger as well? Absolutely."

"Of course. Well, what was it like?"

"Sublime." He had touched the finger of God, the finger of man and the painting surface left by one of the greatest artists who ever lived and at the peak of his artistry.

Tom paused, then said, "Father O'Boyle, we are diverting from your story of what happened in the Roman Forum. Please go on. Once the virus had been reconstituted, what was next?"

O'Boyle obviously wanted to tell his story but found parts of what happened difficult to relate. He continued, "What I'm telling you, I've told no one else."

"Really?" asked Tom. "You are revealing this to me, but no one else?"

"It's a hard secret to keep," O'Boyle acknowledged with a sigh. "In your case, I believe you must learn what happened if only to save yourself." There was a brief pause, then O'Boyle continued. "Visconti insisted on a human trial to test the potency of the virus. I begged him not to do this. Even the scientists said it was not necessary. But he was adamant."

"Where in the world did you get human guinea pigs?" asked Tom.

O'Boyle looked pained when asked this question. He said, "From San Giovanni, a huge hospital near the Roman Forum. We selected a small number of patients with terminal diseases."

"Who allowed you to do this?"

"Those who ran the hospital. They knew the power of the Vatican and looked the other way. They never asked any questions after they gave us the permission.

"We took over a remote ward in a small building, on hospital grounds but separate from the main facility. It was originally used to treat lepers. Our scientists sealed doors and windows. A small container of the virus was set off in the ward. We watched in horror as the patients inhaled the virus and immediately began to have difficulty breathing. Some got out of their beds and thrashed around, their faces and bodies contorted in pain. In less than an hour they were all dead. We had never seen a more lethal virus."

"But if the virus is as lethal as you say, wouldn't it spread rapidly to ordinary citizens of Rome if used in an attack? And, what happened at the Academy dig? Sounds like it escaped somehow—but what kept the virus from spreading after Doc and Eric were killed?"

"This was our dilemma," O'Boyle said. "We had no way of stopping it. We were told by weather experts that Vatican City and parts of downtown Rome would be blanketed in the lethal virus in no more than three hours under normal prevailing breezes."

"A doomsday weapon."

"Precisely," O'Boyle said soberly. "We never intended to release the virus, just to use it to demonstrate its power to kill German soldiers. I argued with Visconti that it was unconscionable for us to possess a weapon so inhumane. To no avail. He believed that God had created it for Moses to use against the Egyptians and had resurrected it to protect His Church against the Germans."

Tom stopped, frozen with horror. "Moses? Against the Egyptians?"

O'Boyle's reply was short. "That's where the virus came from. Visconti began referring to our weapon as the 'Moses Virus' or by its Latin equivalent, *Pestilentia Moseia.*"

Tom asked, "You've explained the Moses Virus. Now come back to the present. How did it kill Doc Brown and Eric Bowen?"

O'Boyle replied, "I'm coming to that. One day a lab technician didn't follow protocols. The virus escaped and wiped out the entire PF staff except one scientist who had been home sick. All hell broke loose in the Vatican. The pope was both furious and horrified. I don't think he had believed the virus could be reconstituted. He saw how wrong he had been. Pius immediately ordered Visconti to abandon the lab, destroy the virus and all the related documentation."

"But," said Tom, "Visconti didn't, right?"

"Visconti ordered the supply of the Moses Virus removed from the lab—but not destroyed. The lab, however, was sealed shut—the fully clothed, contorted bodies of the PF lab technicians left inside. To my knowledge the lab remained undisturbed for about seventy years, until your colleagues stumbled into it. They must have come in contact with traces of the virus."

"Did the pope know what Visconti did?"

"The pope never found out—he thought Visconti had shut down the lab and destroyed the virus. Visconti covered his tracks completely. He swore me to secrecy. It was as if the whole lab never existed."

"Weren't there loose ends?" asked Tom.

"You mean the supply of the Moses Virus? Visconti had me hide it in a top secret location, which I did."

Tom persisted. "And you kept the secret?"

O'Boyle stirred, uneasy. "Well, I did say that it was a hard secret to keep. The Holy Father's personal secretary once commented to me about the matter, though I held my silence. But it did seem like he knew something."

"If a very few people knew, what would any of them do to keep the Church uninvolved?"

O'Boyle answered immediately, "Your incident in the Sistine Chapel shows how long the Church's memory is. Nothing will stop a two-thousand-year-old institution from defending itself against outsiders."

Tom asked, "What about another loose end? The German scientist who had been sick the day of the accident?"

"He knew what had happened—his colleagues were dead, and the lab was treated as if it had vanished. There was only one option for him, and he took it."

Tom said, "He vanished, too, right?"

"Out of sight. Out of the country—Switzerland, we heard. Then, after the war was over, we discovered he had turned up in Israel."

Tom now summed things up. "Ghastly story of a killer virus in a Vatican lab with a worldwide disaster narrowly averted. What's more, as you've yourself said, there are some loose ends—the scientist gone to Israel, Visconti, or the pope's secretary. You, too, are a loose end. So what, Father O'Boyle, does this have to do with me?"

O'Boyle's voice lowered to little more than a whisper. "A worldwide disaster, as you put it, may still be possible. And you, Tom, are in grave danger."

"Explain why," Tom replied.

"I hid the Moses Virus twice—first, right after the lab accident and, second, just before the Germans invaded Italy. I did my work well, and though the virus was never found, from time to time I'd awake in a cold sweat from a nightmare. A recurring dream. The world destroyed by some evil force that had found my hiding place, which stole the supply of the virus and set it loose in the world."

"But that never happened," Tom said.

"Not yet," O'Boyle replied.

"Pope Pius XII died in 1958 and took his part of this story to his grave—unless he left a secret diary of his time as pope. I don't know if he had such a diary or not. Some popes have and some haven't.

"Three years later Visconti, an old man by then and retired, summoned me to his house. I had then been reassigned to the Vatican Libraries. I found him ill. He asked that I hear his confession, which I did. He was consumed with guilt about the Moses Virus. He asked me twice about the location of the supply of the virus and, twice, I told him. Did he tell anyone where it was? I don't know.

"At the end of my visit, he pressed a small envelope into my hand. It was sealed and inscribed in Latin, "Do Not Open Until My Death, Paolo Visconti." He reminded me of my priestly oath of secrecy. Then, too weak to continue, he fell asleep before I could ask what it contained. Several days later, I read in the newspaper that he had died."

Tom realized that O'Boyle was under a great internal need to unburden himself of the secret that Visconti had shifted to O'Boyle's shoulders. But it still wasn't easy for him to tell this part of his story.

O'Boyle continued, "That night, I opened the envelope. There was a bank check made out to me for several thousand dollars and a short note with a letter. The note said that the letter was addressed to a Swiss banker whom Pope Pius XII knew. I was asked by Visconti to contact this banker and say that Cardinal Visconti had been entrusted by Pope Pius XII before he died to ask a last request on the pope's behalf. The request was for the banker to provide a secure resting place for 'a Vatican treasure of immeasurable value.' The note ended with further instructions regarding this 'treasure.'"

"The cache of the Moses Virus."

"Precisely," O'Boyle said.

"What did you do?"

"I followed my instructions to the letter. The Swiss banker was only too happy to help as his bank had been given tens of millions of dollars of Vatican assets to manage. From then until now, I considered the matter closed. That is, until your colleagues met their horrible fates. The publicity and suspicion that the Italian government is covering up the escape of a powerful virus is being watched by a number of foreign governments.

"How is this information about the supply of virus getting out?" Tom asked.

O'Boyle scoffed. "The Italian government leaks its secrets like a sieve. Money changes hands, and news that the authorities are trying to downplay the event in the Roman Forum gets around. The word 'dangerous virus' is enough to alert groups in a number of countries. The stakes are huge—some will want to gain control for themselves, others will insist on possessing it to keep others from using it."

O'Boyle continued, "Perhaps the German scientist is still alive somewhere in Israel. Some group, somewhere, will assume there is a supply of the virus. This may explain the break-in of the underground lab the other night. Every group will connect you with Dr. Brown and will come after you to find out where the virus is."

O'Boyle took a deep breath. "You must for your own protection find and destroy the Moses Virus. The hunt is on then. You are the only public face connected to it."

Slowly Tom realized he was being given a mission by this old Irish priest. He suddenly felt the full force of his predicament. If he succeeded, he might live. He was suddenly afraid. "Tell me how to find this supply," he said to O'Boyle. "I'd go to the Italian authorities, but—listening to you about how information gets out—I don't know whom to trust. What's more, I'm not sure what I'd tell the American authorities if I even knew whom to contact. Right now, I've learned what you've told me, but who would believe me? It all sounds preposterous."

At this moment, Tom heard some scuffling coming from the back of the church. He turned to see who made the noise. So did O'Boyle. In the back row, Tom spotted a lone figure sitting. This figure, a man, was looking at the ceiling, but that didn't mean he wasn't straining to hear everything being said. Tom recognized that he had seen this man before. It was the man with the limp, the man who had been on the trolley from the train station and then on the bus with him.

O'Boyle stiffened. "I've already told you too much," he said between clenched teeth. "I must be sure the information will be safe with you."

In exasperation, Tom said, "My friends and colleagues died from the Moses Virus. Others could be in jeopardy. You . . ."

"I must pray on it further. God forgive me." And with this Father O'Boyle rose and shook Tom's hand. As he faced the altar, he bowed slightly, crossing himself. Then he walked somewhat unsteadily to the front of the Jubilee Church and out through a side door on the right-hand side.

Tom remained behind for a few minutes, dumbfounded by what O'Boyle had told him. It explained a great deal. But what could he do now? Then Tom rose, walked to the back of the Jubilee Church. The man with the limp was gone. Strange, thought Tom, could he have followed me all the way from the Termini? Tom left the church through the door he had entered. Out on the stone plaza, he looked back at the Jubilee Church, rising in majesty, impressive in its grandeur.

What irony, Tom thought, the Catholic Church is the source of hope and salvation for more than a billion people, yet it created a supply of the world's most deadly virus, capable of killing millions. How could this be possible? Why wouldn't O'Boyle help him find the virus?

Tom retraced his steps, finding the trolley station with a car ready to begin its return trip to the main train station. He arrived in central Rome at the Termini and found a taxi at the stand, which took him back to his apartment. It was late, and yet he was too wired to sleep. He checked his e-mail. More reporters. There was also a message from Belagri, from Crystal Close's assistant, with driving instructions to their facility at Hadrian's Villa.

Belagri, Tom puzzled, what brought them into the picture? He knew something about the company's reputation—not good, but perhaps times had changed things. He Googled "Belagri." The first two searches made clear to him that dealing with Belagri would not be straightforward.

One article was entitled "Terminator Seeds." It reported that Belagri's technology produced plants that had sterile seeds so that they would not flower or grow fruit after the initial planting, requiring customers to purchase new seed from Belagri for every planting. The article pointed out that opposition from environmental organizations arose from farmers' dependency on Belagri seed, especially farmers in the third world who had few resources.

The second article concerned Belagri's "predatory" lawsuits. These accused Belagri of suing farmers to intimidate them and to defend its patents, particularly in the area of biotechnology, essentially to monopolize the market for its seeds around the world.

So much for helping mankind, Tom thought. To him it was clear that Belagri had something else in mind, and it was not likely to be anything good for the world's farmers.

Before he turned off his computer, Tom quickly deleted the messages left by reporters, all asking for information, then sifted through his office e-mails. Most were routine until he found one from Brad Phelps, his department chair at New York University: "The news about Doc Brown and the excavation horrified us all. Please let me know what's happening as soon as you can. Can we do anything to help you?"

Tom typed a simple reply: "I'm still shocked by Doc Brown's and Eric's deaths. The police continue to investigate but say nothing. I'll keep you posted on any further developments."

7

Tom awoke early. It was a beautiful day, destined to be very hot, he thought. His terrace, however, was still cool, and he feasted on the luxury of looking out over the city. The red geraniums on the terrace loved the sun. "I guess they don't get skin cancer," he muttered, half out loud and fully in jest.

His cell phone rang. "Pronto," he said.

"Dr. Stewart?" inquired a distinctly Italian voice with a strong accent. It reminded Tom of a Columbia classmate who had grown up in Naples. Very musical cadence.

"This is Tom Stewart. Who is this? I don't see any identifier on my telephone."

"Our calls are masked. Sorry. My name is Pulesi, Dr. Stefano Pulesi. I'm the chief investigator . . ."

"Aren't you the senior director in charge of viruses and other communicable diseases?" Tom asked.

"That's what I'd like to speak to you about. Could we meet? Perhaps in my office?"

"I can do that," Tom replied. "Where do I go?"

"We're located in the Quirinal Palace."

"Isn't that the official residence of the president?"

"It is, but there are certain government offices here as well. If you walk from your apartment or from the Hotel de la Ville, along Via

Sistina, down to Piazza Barberini, then up to the Quattro Fontane, turn right onto Via del Quirinale, the main entrance is midblock, opposite the refurbished stables. A ten minute walk—certainly no more than fifteen minutes. Or, you can take a taxi."

Tom asked, "How do you know where I'm living?"

Pulesi laughed. "We make a point of knowing as much as we can."

"Like where I live and where I eat my breakfast?"

"That, too, although I am surprised you don't go to the Hassler Hotel for breakfast—it's closer," Pulesi replied, pausing.

Tom was shocked by how much Pulesi seemed to know.

"Well," Tom replied, "I prefer the Hotel de la Ville—it's less formal."

Tom mulled over his next comment. Then he said, "Okay, I'll come to your office."

"Fine," Pulesi replied, "shall we say 9:30 a.m.?"

"See you then." Tom looked at his watch. It was 7:45 a.m. Time for breakfast at the Hotel de la Ville.

Tom left his apartment building, walking up Via Gregoriana toward the Hassler. He looked to the left and right, but spotted no one suspicious. At breakfast he also looked around the room but saw no one observing him. Tom realized the irony—he was relieved because he couldn't spot anyone obviously watching him. Yet, if he was in physical danger, perhaps being watched by the Italian government might be of some help to him. He concluded, I'll never see them—they're clever enough not to let me catch them tracking me.

The *International Herald Tribune* had a follow-up article on Doc's and Eric's deaths. Eric's parents had spoken angrily about the Italian government's unauthorized cremation of their son's body. The reporter conveyed his belief that the government was lying and covering up what happened. The fact that a group from the laboratories for communicable substances had shown up at the Roman Forum was enough evidence that a biological contaminant of some kind had been present. As was the cremation of the bodies. The article hinted at all of these factors, but at least it didn't name Tom again.

After breakfast, Tom set off down Via Sistina. Ten minutes later, about 9 a.m., Tom found himself standing in Quattro Fontane, at the crossroads of Via Sistina and Via del Quirinale. He immediately spotted the famous Borromini church, San Carlo. He was half an hour early. He found the front door locked and no one around. Typical, he thought, it's supposed to be open and it's closed to the public. Only in Italy.

Tom proceeded down Via del Quirinale. Just before he came to the main entrance of the palace, he saw Bernini's church, Sant' Andrea al Quirinale. Since he was still early for his meeting with Pulesi, he walked in through the open front door of the church. He liked the interior but preferred Borromini's San Carlo with its complex geometric forms. In the pews, as he passed by, were four musicians with string instruments preparing to rehearse.

Tom had visited this church on a number of occasions. He remembered the fascinating black stone sculpture of Saint Stanislaus Kostka. Saint Kostka was shown either dead or dying. Tom felt an urge to visit the sculpture. He found it in a room upstairs. Tom imagined that the saint was sick with a fatal flu or virus—dressed in a black robe lying on a black marble bed. He studied the saint's face. But no enlightenment came. Nothing telling him about the fates of Doc and Eric, either.

Glancing at his watch, Tom knew he had to get to Pulesi's office. As he returned to the main body of the church, Tom could see and hear the four musicians who were deep into rehearsal of a Bach piece. The music reverberated in the large space as sunlight streamed in from windows high above the altar. The beams from the sun caught the specks of dust in the air and gave the appearance of tangible shafts of light landing on the musicians and on the empty pews. Tom was struck by the peacefulness of the moment, especially when contrasted with the disruption of his own life.

Tom emerged from the Bernini church at 9:25 a.m. He stood at the top of the steps looking some yards away, across the street, to the front entrance of the Quirinal Palace. He was about to descend the church steps when he was stopped by the startling image of a stunning blonde leaving the Quirinal Palace entrance in a bright, lemon-colored dress. He looked more closely, almost transfixed. He wasn't sure, but the woman seemed a lot like the Belagri officer Caroline had introduced him to at the Protestant Cemetery. If it was she—Crystal Close—could she be visiting Pulesi, and, if so, why?

Tom stood still. He watched the woman in the lemon-colored dress. He felt like an eavesdropper or stalker. She was waiting, looking first to her left and then to her right. She's impatient, Tom thought. Abruptly, almost in front of him, a dark blue Fiat limousine pulled out from the curb and drove toward her. Tom remained transfixed. He didn't think she had seen him. The woman—surely it was Crystal—got into the car, and it merged into the traffic.

Tom had seen the whole pageant and now started down the steps of the church. But there was more to come. A sleek black Fiat with darkened windows emerged out of nowhere and quickly followed the blue limousine. Tom was mystified by what he had seen, but had no explanation. He crossed the street and headed toward his meeting.

At precisely 9:30 a.m., Tom entered the address that Pulesi had given him. It was in the midst of the vast sweep of offices in the Quirinal complex. He was immediately shown into Pulesi's office.

Dr. Stefano Pulesi rose from his desk as Tom entered. He was a tall, slim man with dark hair, an aquiline nose, and a warm smile. He had dimples on both cheeks when he smiled, which Tom found disarming. Pulesi wore a business suit.

"Welcome, Dr. Stewart. I'm glad to meet you," Pulesi said and thrust his hand forward, giving Tom a firm handshake. For all of Caroline's talk of Italian bureaucrats, Pulesi seemed very different to Tom.

Pulesi continued. "Let me get down to business. Lieutenant Gabrielli has told me about his conversation with you and Director Sibelius."

Tom said, "We were surprised to hear that your agency is involved."

Pulesi paused. "As you know, the official story is that your colleagues were killed by a cave-in. In fact, we believe that they were killed by a highly toxic virus. So toxic, the only parallel we know is the Spanish flu of 1918 to 1919. That virus caused a pandemic that spread around the world, killing as many as 50 million people—3 percent of the world's population. This virus could be worse, and it seems it may have been manufactured in quantity in the underground lab where the bodies were found."

Tom was shocked into silence. *Fifty million* repeated itself like a drumbeat in his brain. Father O'Boyle's concerns mingled with the idea of vast numbers of victims. The image of the dead in lab coats in the underground room presented itself. As these images collided, Tom began to get hold of them.

"What's happened to the skeletal remains that were also in the lab?"

"We've removed them," replied Pulesi.

"Why do you think the dead bodies were there?"

Pulesi said, "Maybe an experiment gone disastrously wrong."

"But why would anyone put a lab underground in an ancient building in the Roman Forum?" Tom asked, trying to see how much Pulesi knew.

"Secrecy, for one thing—nobody would ever suspect an underground lab in the Roman Forum. And also, deniability. A lab in the Roman Forum would be difficult to trace . . . to the Vatican, or to anyone else."

"Then," Tom stated, "are you telling me that this is the work of the Church?"

"It's the only group I know that cares this much about secrecy and could get away with something like this," said Pulesi.

"When was this lab in operation?"

"We think the lab was built decades ago, perhaps during the Second World War. I was hoping that you might shed some light on the situation."

"I'm afraid I can't help you there. It's the first I'm hearing of it."

"Do you think Dr. Brown knew it was there?"

"As far as I know, his work involved hunting for the underground rooms of Nero's palace. It sounds as if he stumbled on the laboratory, as you call it, and died as a result."

"I see," Pulesi replied. "A tragic accident."

Tom asked, "You mentioned a highly toxic virus. But in an abandoned laboratory, empty for decades, wouldn't a virus die?"

Pulesi said, "We know now that traces of the virus were absorbed by a green moss whose primitive structure incubated the virus, keeping it alive. The odds of this happening are infinitesimal, but it did happen."

"Wouldn't that moss be excessively dangerous?"

"We've had crews scouring that area around the clock. That laboratory is spotless. We have retained a few minute samples of the virus residing in the moss, which are being analyzed under extremely rigorous conditions."

"When will you have any more information?"

"We are working closely with our European and American counterparts to unravel this mystery."

"What group in the United States do you work with?" asked Tom.

Pulesi replied, "The Centers for Disease Control, in Atlanta. Do you know anyone there?"

"No," said Tom, "I'm just curious."

O'Boyle was right, Tom thought. The information about the virus is being circulated, and news of it will leak out.

"I'm sure you understand this matter is highly confidential. Anyone gaining possession of a virus as toxic and contagious as this could be extremely dangerous."

Tom asked, "Just how dangerous is this virus?"

Pulesi was quiet for a few seconds, perhaps debating with himself how much to reveal. Then he continued. "The virus works faster and, like the Spanish flu virus, it is particularly lethal for younger, healthier people."

Tom interrupted. "But why are younger people singled out?"

"The research the CDC has done on the Spanish flu shows that deaths were most likely caused by cytokine storms."

"What in the world is that?" Tom asked.

"When your immune system fights pathogens, cytokines signal your immune cells to travel to the site of the infection. Normally your body keeps this process under control, but, when the immune system encounters a new and highly dangerous invader, there is an exaggerated response called a cytokine storm.

"If the 'storm' occurs in the lungs, then fluids and immune cells accumulate, blocking off the airways, resulting in death. Ironically, a healthy immune system—as found in younger people—becomes a liability since the cytokine storm is more powerful and therefore more lethal. The Spanish flu killed far more young people than anyone expected. This virus is similar to the Spanish flu in this way. There's more, however."

"What do you mean, 'There's more'?" asked Tom.

Pulesi said, "Every person who gets the virus spreads it to everyone he or she meets. The number affected grows geometrically. In the case of the Spanish flu, the public estimate of 50 million dead may in fact have been as high as 90 million—we just don't know. Think about that today—with airplane travel and with a more lethal disease as well."

"I get it," Tom said slowly. "I understand."

"Let me give you my cell phone number," Pulesi offered. "To the extent you can, please keep me informed about any developments, and I will do the same." As he said this, Tom admitted to himself that he had no intention of committing to tell Pulesi what he might find out.

"One more thing," Pulesi said. "We've heard rumors—very recently—that there is a considerable supply of the virus, somewhere."

"Can you tell me where these rumors are coming from?" asked Tom.

"I'm sorry," Pulesi replied, "I've said enough."

Tom asked, "If your group has scoured the underground lab, and destroyed what you found, wouldn't that mean there'd be no supply of the virus left?"

"Apart from what we are testing, we've destroyed all other minute traces that survived. The rumors have to do with a substantial supply which exists and is hidden somewhere. Certainly there is equipment in the lab designed to create large amounts. While the virus supply may have been manufactured and once stored in the lab, I can assure you that there is no virus in the underground lab. Whoever is eager to find it must look elsewhere."

Pulesi let this statement sink in, then continued, "You may be contacted or followed or even threatened. I hope not, but if you should be, please let me know at once. We are here to help."

"Threatened?" Tom asked.

"Threatened," Pulesi answered. "I can think of a half dozen groups of different nationalities that would do anything to possess a supply of deadly virus. Unfortunately, the newspapers present you as the only person who was present at the disaster and who, therefore, may know something."

Tom froze. O'Boyle had hinted that Tom was in jeopardy, and Pulesi had just come out and declared Tom's vulnerability. Tom felt like he was standing on a precipice looking down at a dangerous fall in front of him, alone, with no one to help him. And then, oddly, he was being offered assistance from an Italian bureaucrat with some compassion in his voice. "Dr. Pulesi—thank you for your offer. I'll keep in touch with what happens." With this they ended their conversation.

Pulesi walked Tom to the front entry of the building. They shook hands, and Tom left. Outside, in bright sunshine, he spotted an empty taxi, hailed it and within twenty minutes, a little after 10:30 a.m., he was walking up the front steps of the American Academy to Caroline's office.

Caroline greeted Tom and handed him the keys to her Lancia, telling him it was parked in front of her house next door. "The newspaper reports have turned ugly," Caroline said to Tom. "Reporters are now speculating that the Italian government has something to hide."

Tom replied, "That's the way I read it this morning. I've gotten dozens of e-mail requests for information. They're grasping at straws."

"At least we were able to calm down the Bowens. We agreed to set up a scholarship in Eric's name at Brown. This afternoon, they'll be flying back to New York with his ashes and personal effects."

"The scholarship's a great solution."

"By the way, how'd your visit go at the Swiss Institute?"

"It was interesting, but didn't reveal much. I confirmed that in 1943 Lily Ross Taylor was staying at the Institute after the Academy closed, and that a powerful cardinal, Paolo Visconti, asked to visit the Swiss Institute and the American Academy as well."

"The American Academy?" Caroline asked, surprised. "Now I've heard everything."

"This is your morning for surprises, then. Visconti insisted on seeing the Academy, but specifically the cryptoporticus, which he and his colleague spent time visiting alone."

"Cryptoporticus? I wonder why." Caroline thought for a moment. "It's a huge space, part of it being the lower floors of the library. The rest—in 1943, anyway—was filled with trunks, bicycles, books, archaeological artifacts from some of the Academy's excavations, the photographic collection—in short, anything that anyone wanted to store until their next visit."

"Is it self-contained?"

"Almost entirely. Wait a minute. Maybe the cryptoporticus was not the cardinal's objective. Maybe it was Trajan's aqueduct. There would have been an old iron grate on the floor of the cryptoporticus leading to the aqueduct."

Trajan's aqueduct, or the *Aqua Traiana*, was finished around AD 112. It was the last great aqueduct to be built in Imperial Rome. It entered Rome at the Janiculum Hill, ran under what was now the Academy's Main Building, then down the hill, across the Tiber—on a special bridge—and underground again to the Baths of Trajan. It was rediscovered when the building was being constructed in 1913–1914.

Tom paused, trying to picture the Roman Forum. Then he remembered—Trajan had had his public baths built over the only remaining section of Nero's Golden House. Precisely, he thought, where Doc's underground passageway in the Roman Forum led.

Caroline, oblivious to Tom's silence, said, "About a year ago, the Rome gas company was digging in the street outside the Academy and broke into the aqueduct. This brought the gas company's work to a complete halt while our archaeologists, including Doc, documented the aqueduct. I remember that he was excited and became especially involved in all of this."

"I'd like to take a look if that's possible."

"That's easy to arrange. I'll have Fabio, the head of our work crew, show you around. He knows all the nooks and crannies."

"Thanks," Tom said, "but I'd rather explore it myself."

"Okay. Here," she said reaching into her desk for a flashlight, "You'll need this—it's dark down there. I'll have him open the grate. There's an iron ladder beneath the grate that leads down to the floor of the aqueduct." Then, as an afterthought, Caroline smiled and said, "Oh, by the way, watch out for the killer mosquitoes."

"Mosquitoes?" Tom asked.

"A few years ago, before the recent renovation, an open grate covered the entrance to the aqueduct. The Academy that summer was overrun by hordes of vicious mosquitoes. No one could find out where they were coming from until Fabio saw them flying up through the grate leading to the aqueduct. It turned out they were breeding in a small pool of stagnant water trapped by debris from construction at the Norwegian Academy farther down the hill."

"Should I be worried?" Tom asked.

"Not at all! I was just joking with you—they've been gone for years, and the grate's been replaced by a solid cover. I'll call Fabio." Caroline picked up the phone, then paused. "You know," she added to Tom, "if you want to go exploring down in the aqueduct and then drive to Tivoli for your lunch with Belagri, I recommend you wear a pair of our workers' overalls. That way you won't get your street clothes messed up."

Tom was about to say that he'd skip the overalls, then guessed that Caroline might be making a good point. He nodded his agreement, and Caroline called Fabio.

Fabio was waiting at the grate on the floor of the cryptoporticus when Tom arrived. He was wearing the blue bibbed overalls everyone on the Academy's main workforce used as a uniform. He carried a crowbar, flashlight, and had an extra pair of blue overalls for Tom.

Fabio pried the grate open with the crowbar, its rusted hinges squealing. Tom could see the iron ladder going down a further twenty feet.

"I will wait for you."

"No need," Tom said. "I may be awhile. May I have the crowbar?"

Fabio was a bit surprised, but handed it over. Tom thanked him again, telling him he'd return it when he was finished. Fabio waited until Tom climbed down the ladder, then left.

At the bottom, Tom turned on his flashlight. He was on a stone floor under a vaulted ceiling in the aqueduct that had once carried one of Rome's largest supplies of water.

The aqueduct was large enough for Tom to stand upright, and the tunnel itself could accommodate just barely two men walking abreast. He was struck by the silence in the tunnel. As he began to walk, even his footsteps seemed to be muffled. The air was close and humid. After twenty yards or so, the floor of the aqueduct began to tip downward to follow the slope of the Janiculum Hill to the Tiber.

Tom heard scuffling sounds. He stopped. His flashlight picked up nothing unusual. He started to walk again. He heard more scuffling. This time, his light shone on a half dozen pairs of eyes staring at him. Rats. Tom lunged toward them, and they scattered off down the aqueduct.

Tom wondered what he should be looking for. If Cardinal Visconti had been interested in hiding something, he certainly wouldn't leave it on the floor of the aqueduct. The sides were smooth, as was the ceiling.

The floor of the aqueduct continued to pitch downward. Tom walked carefully on the sloped pitch. Nothing seemed out of place. Was this a fool's errand? he asked himself. He stopped. Visconti needed a place to hide something valuable. Then it came to Tom—there must be a room whose entrance would be disguised.

Tom moved to the edge of the aqueduct and shone the light along the wall. He stared in the direction of the beam. There was no aberration in the surface. He crossed to the other side of the aqueduct and shone the light on that wall's surface. Nothing.

Tom walked forward twenty feet and repeated the same procedure. On the third try, he saw a slight bulge in the wall. He walked to that spot. He spotted what looked like crumbling plaster on the wall to his right. When he shone his light at the area, it became clear that a patch on the wall was not made of the same material as the rest. He put the flashlight on the floor of the aqueduct far enough away to light the patch on the wall. Then he lifted his crowbar and chipped at the wall. Little by little, he pried the plaster away until a hole the size of a basketball revealed a wood surface beyond.

Tom began attacking the surface plaster in earnest. Chunks began to fall on the floor of the aqueduct as the outlines of a door emerged. Within twenty minutes of tough work, he uncovered a wooden door. Tom pushed the door, which was not locked, and it swung inward with a loud creak, revealing a small room.

When Tom examined the door, he found that it was much heavier than normal. While it appeared to be made of wood, it was a steel door covered with a wood veneer. And when the door closed, the steel fitted tightly in the door jamb.

The room, about seven feet high and ten feet deep and wide, had been hollowed out of the earth, and then lined with steel and covered with wood. The workmanship was simple but impressive. On the side of the room farthest from the aqueduct there was a small, marble-topped table covered in dust. Just above the table, on the wall, there was what appeared to be a compartment covered by a sliding wood panel. The compartment, carved into the wall, was about as big as a large safe-deposit box. The panel was warped, and Tom had some difficulty opening it. When he had it half open, he shown the flashlight inside. Empty.

This must have been where Visconti hid the virus, Tom thought. When O'Boyle retrieved it, he must have had the wall plastered over. It all makes sense.

Tom closed the door to the secret room. Then he turned and began to walk back toward the ladder. Retracing his steps uphill was hard work. He found the ladder and climbed back up into the cryptoporticus. Fabio was waiting for him, and he replaced the cover over the opening to the aqueduct.

It was getting late and Tom needed to be on his way to the Belagri lunch. He left a message with Lucia for Caroline, removed his plaster dust–covered overalls, washed his hands, and was pleased that his street clothes looked to be in reasonable shape. He went to the main entrance of the Academy and walked to the white Lancia parked in front of Caroline's house. He got into it, started the engine, and drove off.

Once on the autostrada, Tom went over what he knew about the tragedy in the Roman Forum. He kept coming back to Doc, who certainly knew about the Trajan aqueduct nearly a year before his ill-fated excavation. His dig was near Trajan's Baths. Could Doc have made the connection between the two? Maybe, maybe not.

Tom also knew that Doc and Lily Ross Taylor had spent many years on the Bryn Mawr campus. Surely their common ties to the American Academy had made them friends. Might Lily have told Doc about meeting Visconti? Did Lily even know about Visconti's interest in the Trajan aqueduct? Far too much was still unknown to make valid connections.

The traffic out of Rome was light, so he had no trouble navigating his way to the small town of Tivoli, which was located slightly to the north of Rome and twenty miles to the east. For two thousand years, Tivoli has been a favorite place for wealthy Romans to escape the heat of the Roman summer.

Tivoli's attractions were its clean air and beautiful location on the slopes of the Tiburtini Hills. In addition, there are sulfur springs and the waterfalls of the Aniene River—which Emperor Augustus said had cured him of insomnia. Hadrian's Villa is four miles southwest of Tivoli. It was built between AD 118 and 134 by Emperor Hadrian. The grounds consisted of 300 acres, filled with full-scale reproductions of the emperor's favorite buildings from Greece and Egypt—now mostly ruins.

Tom arrived at Hadrian's Villa shortly before 1 p.m., the time Crystal had specified for lunch at the Hotel Adriano restaurant. He parked in the area reserved for visitors to Hadrian's Villa and was surprised that there was only one tourist bus and a handful of cars. Tom thought it odd that one of the most famous Roman sites was so little visited. On the other hand, he guessed, there was little left that is not in ruins.

As he walked from the parking area along a line of huge cypress trees, Tom guessed they might be more than fifty feet high. The Hotel Adriano was located on the way into the grounds of Hadrian's Villa. He could see under the trees that surrounded the hotel and restaurant that there were a number of tables spaced around with enough room so that conversations at one table need not be overheard by those at nearby tables.

On the far side of the garden, at the farthest point from the hotel itself, three people were already sitting at a large table—two men and a strikingly attractive blond woman whom Tom recognized as Crystal Close. And, Tom noted, Crystal was wearing a bright, lemon-colored dress. She *was* the woman in yellow.

As Tom approached, all three stood up. Crystal smiled and extended her hand. "Good afternoon, Tom," she said, fastening her gaze directly on Tom's eyes. "You remember Robert Parker. He's not only the head of Belagri's foundation, he's the senior executive in charge of our marketing and promotions. And this is our head of research, Dr. Ralph Winch."

Tom shook hands with Parker and Winch, and then everyone sat down. Crystal asked Tom if he'd like something to drink. A young waiter named Pietro came over and presented everyone with menus and took their drink orders. "You'll love the food here," said Crystal with a big smile. "This place has been owned by the same family for a couple of generations. Our chef, Maria, is Pietro's grandmother. The Belagri facility is located next to the grounds of Hadrian's Villa, and our people eat here frequently."

"It certainly is a lovely place," Tom said.

Pietro returned to take their luncheon orders, then he withdrew into the kitchen. Crystal said, "Thanks for coming this far to meet with us. We are fortunate that we happen to be the only guests at the restaurant this afternoon. Do you know much about our company?"

"Only by reputation."

"We're the leading factor, worldwide, in biogenetic research in agriculture. Dr. Hermann Bailitz, our chairman and president, has a mission—to rid the world of hunger, but of course to do so at a profit. We develop modified seeds and related products that dramatically improve crop yields. After lunch, if you'd like, we can show you through our facility. We own facilities in each of the countries where we do business. Growing conditions vary enough that we need to test our products in each of these markets."

"I've heard that Belagri is somewhat controversial."

"Anyone on the cutting edge of science is," Crystal replied smoothly. "Some people think we upset the natural balance by introducing genetically modified seeds. I assure you, our products are tested, retested, and tested again, and only made available when fully approved by all relevant official bodies."

Pietro brought the first courses, after which the conversation turned to general topics including Tom's study of forensic archaeology.

Pietro cleared the dishes, then brought cappuccinos or espressos for everyone, and a plate of complimentary amaretti cookies.

"I'm still a bit surprised by your company's interest in archaeological excavation," Tom said.

"As I mentioned," Crystal said, "our chairman has a particular fascination with the ancient world. We support explorations all over the world. He is an amateur historian and firmly believes that the past informs the present . . . and the future."

"An unusual position for the chairman of a global company to take."

"Yes, he is quite an interesting man."

"Still, Nero's Golden House seems a bit outside your core business concerns. How could it inform your agricultural research?"

"There is much we can learn from the ancient world, so long as we remain open to the lessons of history," Parker said.

"No disputing that," Tom said.

Winch took over. He had steel gray eyes that stared coldly, directly, at Tom as he spoke. The tone of his voice was self-satisfied, as if he thoroughly enjoyed showing whomever he was talking to that he was the brightest person in the room. "The culture of the ancient Mayans produced a city on the top of a mountain—Machu Picchu, but the Mayans disappeared. Were they wiped out by disease, a virus? We don't know. In our Old Testament, at the time of Moses, there was a virus or viruses that killed crops, animals, and humans."

Tom felt himself tightening up inside at the mention of a killer virus. He also realized that Winch was watching him very carefully while he talked. Tom wondered if Winch had seen Tom react to the mention of viruses. Maybe, Tom thought, I'm overreacting.

Winch pedantically continued. "What kills crops and animals is as important to us as what heals or improves them. It would be a major advancement for Belagri and for the world to find out what happened at Machu Picchu or determine the nature of the biblical plagues to prevent them from ever happening again. I wonder, for example, what happened at your excavation in the Roman Forum. It's hard to believe that the fuss is about a collapsed roof over the underground passage."

Tom noticed that Winch was still observing him with piercing interest. Tom said nothing.

Before Winch could finish his rambling thoughts Crystal interjected, "Ralph has just given you a hypothetical example that illustrates our chairman's interest in archaeology. Ralph's division is responsible for following up on all leads that can help Belagri protect the global agricultural community and our interests."

"I understand," Tom said, agreeably. Then, ignoring Crystal's efforts to change the subject, Tom decided he ought to smoke out what Winch was hinting at. "I'm interested, though, Dr. Winch, in your question regarding the Roman Forum. What did you have in mind?"

Winch replied, "Hazmat teams were dispatched to the site immediately. We read that the bodies were cremated—that's an unusual precaution. The cause for the incident is said to be a collapsed tunnel, but press reports question the truth of that statement. What, Professor Stewart, is going on? It sounds to me like a cover-up for an escaped deadly virus. In the Roman Forum? Does that make any sense?"

Tom decided that he didn't like Ralph Winch. The man had a staccato method of asking tough questions in a way that seemed meant to intimidate.

"Dr. Winch," Tom said, "I'm totally in the dark about what happened to Doc Brown and his colleague. I'm sorry I can't tell you any more—I'd like to know myself."

Winch sat back, staring at Tom. He had a look of smug satisfaction on his face, which Tom concluded meant that Winch hadn't believed anything he had said. Tom stared back.

Parker broke in to ease the tension, changing the subject.

"We admire your work in forensic archaeology, Dr. Stewart," Parker said. "Am I correct that you are writing a new textbook?"

"Yes, but this tragedy at the Forum seems to be taking up a great deal of my time."

"Regrettably. However, we would like to support your work at NYU. Your skills in forensics would be particularly useful in our attempts to derive knowledge from the past. If we could call upon you from time to time as a consultant, our foundation is prepared to make a sizable grant to your department at NYU."

"That is quite generous," Tom offered, "but I'm busy with my coursework and other consulting commitments. I'm not sure I could . . ."

"It would not be very time consuming. Perhaps an occasional peer review of our research reports," Winch said. "And, any insight you can give us on special projects would be helpful. We had a similar arrangement with Professor Brown."

"Approved by his department at Bryn Mawr, of course," Crystal was quick to point out.

"It seems interesting. Of course I'll need to check with my dean, Dr. Brad Phelps, first."

"We understand. If you or your dean has any questions, we'd be glad to answer them," Crystal said. "We have in mind a grant of $500,000 payable to NYU, spread over some mutually agreed period, such as five years."

Tom was shocked—this was a huge sum of money. He reacted quickly. "I appreciate your most generous proposal. Let me think about it and speak with Brad. I'll do this right away. Whom should I contact regarding my decision?"

"Please call me," Crystal said. "Once we hear, we'll forward the paperwork to Dr. Phelps." She stood. The other men followed suit. "Now, would you like to visit our laboratory? You might find it interesting."

"I'd like to."

The hot summer sun filtered through the trees as they walked the short distance from the restaurant to a low stone building.

"Belagri has owned this building for some time," Parker said. "We also have several farms in this valley, which Belagri keeps under continuous cultivation. We grow crops from the latest Belagri seed collections, and we test new fertilizers. Our objective is to evaluate all of our products being sold into a given market, so that we know what each farmer's expected results are likely to be."

Parker and Winch excused themselves to return to company meetings being held in a conference room in Hotel Adriano. Crystal said she'd join them after she showed Tom around.

Crystal proceeded to the Belagri facility, walking through the glass doors that led into the building, and Tom followed. Tom was immediately impressed with the facility. Contrary to what anyone might have expected from the nondescript exterior, the inside was starkly modern, well lit, and hygienically clean. Technicians wore white lab coats. To one side, there was a bank of refrigerated units.

"Many of the seeds must be stratified—have a period of cold prior to placing them in the ground to sprout. We can also keep seeds in cold storage for long periods of time."

As they continued the tour, Tom noticed that everything about the Belagri lab space was hyperprofessional, almost manically so. The five white-gowned Belagri employees were each introduced to him, by name, and each responded in a friendly way and explained their functions. They all spoke English.

"I'm impressed," Tom said to Crystal. "While I don't know much about this field, it certainly seems as if your work is first rate."

Crystal smiled a warm smile and said, "Yes. We run a tight ship. This is one of our smaller facilities. But I did want you to see it. We do great work, despite what you might read in the press about us."

Tom didn't respond. He was thinking—what were you doing earlier this morning in Rome then . . . were you meeting with Dr. Pulesi?—but he held his tongue.

"Well, that's about it," she said, as they returned to the front entrance. "Unless you have any questions, I'll let you return to Rome. I've got to get back to business."

"Thanks for lunch and the tour. I'll consider your offer and be back to you very soon."

"Fine. You have my number. Have a safe drive back to the city."

They shook hands, and Crystal walked back to the Hotel Adriano to join her colleagues, Parker and Winch. Tom watched her, a beautiful woman in a lemon-colored dress. A dangerous woman? He dropped that thought—he really had nothing to go on. Pulling out of the parking lot, Tom considered the meeting. "These people are slick, tough, corporate types, especially Winch. How much are they to be trusted?" He wondered now how Doc had dealt with them.

Then he returned to their offer. Tom was sure Brad Phelps would jump at the chance for the Belagri money. But was Belagri really sincere about being interested in his research in forensic archaeology, or was this a cover for their clear interest in what Doc Brown might have been killed by—a formidable virus? Pulesi had suggested certain groups might come after him. Was it possible that they were just trying to find out what he, Tom, knew?

THE MOSES VIRUS

Tom's route back into Rome took him through the town of Tivoli and onto the autostrada. There was little traffic at this time of the afternoon. Once on the highway, no more than ten minutes passed, however, before he became aware that he was being followed by a black Fiat sedan with darkened windows. Each time he looked in his rearview mirror, he saw the Fiat several car lengths behind. As he focused on the car, he guessed it was identical to the Fiat that had followed Crystal as she had driven off after meeting with Pulesi. He corrected himself—after meeting with Pulesi or someone in his office.

Tom picked up speed and passed several cars. He watched as the Fiat did likewise. He tried this again, and the same pattern repeated itself. As he got closer to Rome, the traffic began to build. Tom started to weave in and out, but the black Fiat kept a close tail on him.

Tom took the next exit. The Fiat was right behind him.

"Damn." Tom was in a part of Rome he didn't know. He was now on local roads, heavy with traffic, without much room to maneuver. "What do they want?" Tom said aloud in irritation and frustration.

Almost as if to answer that question, the Fiat pulled up directly behind Tom, and then began bumping into the rear of the Lancia.

Tom took a sharp right. The Fiat followed. They were in an old, industrial district. Wide streets. Narrow alleys. No traffic. Some abandoned buildings. Frantically, he looked for a way out. The Fiat accelerated and bumped him hard. He nearly lost control, but recovered. Out of the corner of his eye he spied an alley immediately to his left. He yanked the steering wheel to the left, and the Lancia's tires screeched, and, barely avoiding concrete walls, he sped through the narrow road.

Tom checked his rearview mirror. No Fiat. They'd double back. He had to find a way out.

The alley dead-ended at railroad tracks. An unpaved road barely wide enough for a car to pass, ran along the tracks. He took it. The Lancia squeezed along the narrow path until he was past the next building, then he turned right into another alley, which, with one more right turn, led back to the main street. He turned and headed onto the autostrada, but the Fiat was waiting for him.

Tom saw a sign for central Rome and followed it. Soon, the street opened up to four lanes. Business and apartment buildings lined the street on both sides. He was back on major roads, which would take him into the center of Rome. Tom looked for a police car hoping he'd be pulled over, and thus spook his pursuer.

Tom began to weave back and forth across the four lanes, cutting ahead of car after car, darting in and out of the bus lanes as well.

The Fiat stuck with him.

Suddenly, he heard a siren. A police motorcycle was flashing its lights behind him on his left. "Thank God," he said and moved over into the right shoulder of the road. As the traffic cop pulled over, Tom saw the Fiat speed by and disappear into the traffic.

He was never happier to get a ticket in his life.

Tom made his way back to the Academy, arriving at 6 p.m. Norm at the front gate recognized Caroline's white Lancia and waved as Tom drove by and pulled into Caroline's space.

Tom stopped at Caroline's office. She was there and invited him in. "I'd like you to meet Ambassador George Wilson. You probably remember that the State Department leases one of our buildings—the Villa Richardson—for the U.S. Ambassador to the Holy See, and George has been our neighbor since his appointment."

Tom extended his hand, and Wilson grabbed it. Tom was surprised how large the ambassador's hands were, almost like those of a full-time farmer. Wilson exclaimed, "I'm so sorry about what happened at the Roman Forum. We all are."

"Thanks," replied Tom. "The newspapers won't let go."

"I know," said Wilson. "Reporters are like that—eventually they'll tire. Well, I must be off. Can't keep God's Vicar on Earth waiting. Tom, if you need any help, just call on me."

With that, Wilson gave Caroline a kiss on both cheeks and walked out of her office. When Wilson had gone Tom said, "Here are the keys, but there's bad news. A car bumped into me on the way back into Rome. I don't think there's much damage, but I want to look at it with you."

"Forget it. That old Lancia has plenty of bruises from other skirmishes on Italian roads and streets. If you want me to look at it with you, let's do that tomorrow because I've got a dinner I'll be late to if I don't run now."

Caroline rushed off. Tom didn't feel like going back to his apartment quite yet. His adrenaline was still in high gear. He wandered through the Academy's *salone*, where several of the fellows were gathered around the pool table watching two fully engaged players. Others were sitting in chairs or on the sofas reading the daily newspapers. A couple of fellows were working at their computers. Tom went into the bar where he decided to have a cappuccino.

Michael Lowell, a classical scholar and fellow trustee, who had spoken at Doc Brown's memorial service, walked up to Tom. "How's it going?" he asked solicitously.

"If you mean, am I enjoying being hounded by the press, no, I'm tired of it."

"Well, as the Persian poet Attar of Nishapur wrote, 'This too shall pass,'" Michael said.

"I hope so," Tom replied. "Speaking of poetry, I was impressed that you moved everyone to tears at Doc's service when you read Latin poetry. I'm sorry to say that most of what you said was over my head."

"That's Latin poetry for you," Michael smiled. "Read it, and everyone will cry until you stop."

Tom laughed, as did Michael, pleased with his joke. Then Tom asked Michael, "You're a friend of Father O'Boyle, right? What's his story?"

"No one knows, really," Michael volunteered. "There are rumors he was on the fast track at the Vatican. But something went wrong—years ago—and he was sidelined to running the Vatican Libraries. No slouch of a job, either, but he was not part of the inner circle. He ran the Vatican Libraries exceedingly well. We all admire him. Why do you ask?"

Tom said, evasively, "No particular reason. We had a conversation, and I enjoyed meeting him—that's all. It's getting late. Guess I'll head back to my apartment. Good night, Michael."

Norm was still on duty at the Academy's front gate and called a taxi for Tom. By 7:30 p.m., he was in a taxi on his way to his apartment, and he admitted to himself that he was exhausted.

Just before retiring, Tom sat at his desk, sipping a glass of wine and eating some grapes from the refrigerator. He e-mailed Brad Phelps in New York to get NYU's reaction to his working with Belagri.

Brad,

At their request, I met with representatives of Belagri, an international genetic seed manufacturer. They supported Doc Brown's dig and periodically consulted with him. They've offered $500,000 in funding over a five-year period to NYU if I give them advice from time to time on forensic archaeology. They're known as a tough, litigious company, and a very successful one as well. The offer is generous—maybe too generous. I'm really not sure what their agenda is. I'm assuming NYU would like me to accept this, correct?

I'm also being hounded by reporters wanting information on the incident. And the attitude of the Italians is odd—the man in charge of the investigation as much as confirmed to me this morning that there's a highly dangerous virus involved and that European and American government groups—and others as well—are nosing around trying to get their hands on a supply of this virus. Where this trail leads, I've no idea. I'm hoping the ruckus around the incident all dies down so I can focus on editing my book. Please give me your reaction to the Belagri grant proposal. Tom.

Tom wanted to pursue two names Father O'Boyle had mentioned—Imhotep the Younger and Charles Babcock, archaeologist. A quick search on the Internet revealed that Imhotep was chief architect for Ramesses II, one of the most powerful of all pharaohs, who ruled for the exceedingly long time of thirty-five years. Imhotep built cities, temples, and monuments, all for Ramesses II, and died at ninety years of age in 1213 BC. Imhotep was descended from Imhotep the Senior, the world's first architect, who designed the step pyramid at Saqqara a thousand years earlier.

For his work, Imhotep the Younger was treated like royalty, and when he died he was buried in a tomb befitting the most powerful priests.

Tom discovered that there were unexplained mysterious aspects to Imhotep the Younger's death. Remains of other human bodies were found in the tomb, all of which were discovered to be in contorted positions—as was Imhotep. His tomb lay undiscovered for 3,135 years, until Charles Babcock, an American archaeologist, came upon it by accident in 1922.

There was an odd postscript. In the months after its discovery, Babcock was busy going through the artifacts in Imhotep's tomb, making a record of his finds. Suddenly, without any warning, Babcock contracted an unknown disease and died within hours. His death was treated as a most sensitive matter by Egyptian authorities. At that time, there was a rumor going around of a pharaoh's curse, which claimed the lives of a number of people associated with Tutankhamen's tomb. Tom figured that the Egyptian authorities were trying to quell the pharaoh's curse rumors.

Tom paused in his research. Babcock, the American archaeologist, and Imhotep the architect, were connected by Babcock's excavation in Luxor in 1922. So what O'Boyle may have been hinting at was for Tom to find out more about Imhotep's tomb.

Tom learned very little more about Babcock or Imhotep that seemed relevant. He was about to give up when he discovered a current reference to something found in Imhotep's tomb.

On February 20, 2011, Professor Darby Smith, American archaeologist teaching at the American School in Cairo, announced the restoration of a wall painting discovered in the tomb of ancient Egyptian architect, Imhotep the Younger. The restored wall painting, more than three thousand years old, displays Egypt reeling from the onslaught of the ten plagues visited on the country by Moses prior to Pharaoh Ramesses II agreeing to permit Moses to lead the Hebrews out of Egypt. Smith gave credit to the restoration to a team headed by his wife. The team worked for seven years to restore and interpret the wall painting.

Tom checked his contact list on his iPhone. He still had Darby Smith's e-mail address. Why not contact him?

Tom immediately wrote the following e-mail:

For Darby Smith—you may recall we met at the archaeological conference at the New York Hilton two years ago. I've read recently about your restoration of the wall painting from Imhotep's tomb. Congratulations, by the way. For reasons I'll explain, it's important for me to understand something about what you and your team discovered. Could we talk by telephone? I'm in and around the American Academy in Rome, working on editing my new book. Kind regards, Tom Stewart, Professor of Forensic Archaeology, New York University.

Tom sent this message off to Smith. Tom was playing a hunch, that Father O'Boyle's suggestion that he should learn about Imhotep might provide insight into the origins and nature of the virus. Tom took a final sip from the wine, then, dressed only in his shorts and a T-shirt, he went out of his apartment onto his terrace. Rome spread out before him as if he was at the rim of a huge valley of twinkling lights. He filled the watering can and enjoyed walking around from one geranium box to another under the starry sky as he fed the plants. When this was done, having saved the best thing for the last, he called Alex.

"Hi—it's Tom."

Alex laughed. "I know. How are things going?"

Suddenly, Tom's fatigue vanished. "Are you interested in a nightcap?"

"Maybe," Alex replied. "Where?"

Tom took no time to reply. "The roof restaurant of the Hassler. The views are spectacular—it's a beautiful evening. We can have some snacks and wine. And, I'll tell you about my encounter with Crystal . . ."

Alex immediately responded, "Crystal—she's that blonde who was standing with you at Doc's memorial service?"

Tom, surprised, replied, "You remember her?"

"Tom. Of course. I didn't know who she was, but how could I fail to notice her? That black dress she was wearing was the most provocative mourning outfit I've ever seen! She's hardly what I'd call innocent or naïve."

"Appropriate then for a senior officer of Belagri—and, they offered me a grant."

"A grant? Okay," Alex said, "that's enough. I want to learn more. I'll meet you in twenty minutes."

It was earlier in the evening at the Basilica of San Clemente near the Colosseum. There were a few tourists still in the upper church, and a bell had just rung to announce that it was time to leave. The night watchman began making his final rounds. He was alone, as was customary at this time of the evening. He enjoyed his job and felt that he intimately knew all three levels of the church's famous history and would often tell his story to anyone who was willing to listen. He particularly liked his version of the story of St. Clement, the fourth pope, who ruled from AD 90 to 99, and was exiled to the Crimea and martyred after he was tied to an anchor and drowned.

The watchman looked around again, seeing two tourists earnestly studying the mosaics. He sighed. There was no obvious person to tell his story to.

"Nothing amiss," he muttered to himself as he completed his survey of the ground floor of the twelfth-century church. He paused at his favorite fresco in the church depicting the legend of a boy found alive in St. Clement's tomb beneath the Black Sea.

Candles flickered in the stairway to the first lower level, which was once a fourth-century church. He'd blow these candles out for the night after he checked the still lower levels. For now, they lit his way.

But as he made his way down, he noticed something different. "Strange," he said, "there's no reason for it, but the deeper I go, the less strength the candles seem to have."

The final flight of steps would take him to the catacombs level containing sixteen wall tombs, as well as the Temple of Mithras slaying the bull. The watchman was superstitious about this lowermost part of the church, this place where men used to meet in secret prior to Nero's fire of AD 64, which had destroyed the area. Men had met in secret to practice Christianity or its rival religion, Mithras. There was a gap in one of the walls through which he could see the ancient Roman street.

While the watchman was making his rounds, Father O'Boyle was sitting peacefully in one of his favorite places—on a stone bench in the anteroom of the Temple of Mithras. He knew that it was time to leave and was preparing to get up. He was surprised as a man in a dark business suit entered the temple, walked over, and sat beside him. Father O'Boyle did not recognize the man at all.

The man in the black suit spoke. "Father O'Boyle?"

"That's correct. What can I do for you?"

"It's about your conversation at the Jubilee Church with Professor Stewart."

"Oh?" replied O'Boyle, suddenly concerned his talk with Tom Stewart had been overheard and reported.

"I've been sent to ask you some questions."

"It's late, and I must be leaving. Perhaps another time," O'Boyle said, hoping to end this exchange.

The man rose, apparently willing to accede to O'Boyle's request to be left alone, but as he did, the man touched Father O'Boyle on the shoulder. Father O'Boyle looked at the man and recoiled. The stranger held in his hand a gun and pointed it directly at O'Boyle. "Get up," the man growled, his voice low. "We're leaving. Say nothing to anyone or I'll shoot them and you."

The watchman stopped in his tracks as he reached the lowest level, surprised to see two figures walking toward the stairs when normally everyone would have already departed. One of the men was clearly a priest, dressed in a cassock, walking slowly just in front of a man in a black suit. The man in the black suit walked with a slight limp.

As the watchman moved toward them, he recognized the priest. It's Father O'Boyle, he thought to himself. He's always down here.

The man in black guided Father O'Boyle up the stairs, and as they neared, the watchman saw the priest's startled, wide-open eyes. Father O'Boyle sought to make eye contact with the watchman, but as the priest passed, he did so without saying a word. The watchman was puzzled—he expected O'Boyle at least to say good night to him. Instead, it was the man in black who bade him a good evening. He spoke with a strong accent, but one the watchman could not place. There was no friendly banter with Father O'Boyle as the watchman was accustomed to. He watched as the two men slowly made their way up the stairs.

Then, because he still had his job to do, the watchman moved on.

Tom switched into khakis and headed up the street to the Hassler. He had plenty of time to order a glass of wine, some olives, crackers, and peanuts. As he looked around, he saw that the roof restaurant was almost empty.

In a darkened corner, there was a couple talking earnestly. The man looked American, middle-aged, wearing a suit. The woman who was talking very quietly to him was attractive, wearing a slightly too tight dress. What Tom could hear was a heavy Italian accent when the woman spoke. Tom imagined that she might be negotiating the price for spending some time with him.

True to her word, Alex was there in exactly twenty minutes. Tom saw Alex leave the elevator. She walked toward him. He quietly admired this sharp-looking woman as she approached.

He rose to greet her, offering her a seat with a panoramic view of the Eternal City. "I'm glad to see you," Tom said, and Alex gave him a warm smile in return. "I've ordered you a a glass of white wine. Okay?"

"Thanks. Now, if you don't mind, I'd like an accounting of your meeting with this company Belagri. And, of course, I'd like to hear more about Crystal. Do you know the company?"

"Oddly enough, yes. When my grandfather died, my grandmother continued to run his farm in Illinois. It was 4,000 acres of corn alternating with soybeans on the flattest land you've ever seen. Flat all the way to the horizon in every direction."

"Where in Illinois?"

"On the outskirts of a small town in the middle of nowhere, called Teutopolis."

"What did this have to do with Belagri?"

"It was Belagri seed that the farmers in the area used. The surrounding farms were vast compared to my grandmother's property—hundreds of thousands of acres. Big businesses, really. The Belagri seeds were like a drug. Using them led to bigger, better crops. But each year the farmers had to reorder new seeds whose prices, set by Belagri, kept rising.

"I remember my grandmother, who didn't use Belagri seeds, telling me of small farmers caught in the ruthless cycle of dependence in good times and bad. These farmers were gradually squeezed out of business by the economics that made the largest farmers wealthy and kept Belagri rich."

Alex looked intently at Tom. "And you want to get into bed with this company?" she asked. Alex suddenly blushed, probably thinking that if she had paid more attention to her brain, she would have used a different image than "getting into bed." She looked at Tom again. He had not reacted right away. Then he responded.

"Not particularly, but I'm sure that my dean will push me to accept their offer. Grant money is not easy to come by, and they've offered an amount that will be difficult to turn down."

"How much?" Alex asked.

"Five hundred thousand dollars."

Alex whistled softly in surprise. "I agree. No one would turn that down."

Tom then told her about the black Fiat with the darkened windows that tried to run him off the road on the way back into Rome.

"You should report this incident," she said, aghast.

"I didn't get the numbers on the license plate, nor do I have any idea who it might have been. And I'm not sure whom to trust."

"This horrifies me. Why not tell Caroline?"

"I've already put the Academy in the spotlight with the newspapers mentioning my name and printing my picture."

"You had nothing to do with this. You and I just happened to be on the scene, and you were the senior person."

"Still," Tom went on, "Caroline is concerned about negative press. The Academy doesn't need it."

"You've got to be the judge. Your life is involved. You don't know that someone may come after you again," Alex said.

After they finished their drinks and conversation, Alex suggested that it was time for her to be getting home. Tom paid the bill. As they walked toward the elevator, Tom noticed that the table, where the American and the Italian woman in the too-tight dress had been whispering to each other, was empty. Two glasses drained of their contents remained.

Alex commented, "They're gone—I'll bet they're in his room."

Surprised that she had noticed, Tom replied, "Think so? Will money change hands?"

"You can be sure of it," Alex said and laughed.

Tom was amused that they had both observed the scene, though nothing had been said until now.

They walked out of the hotel to the taxi stand. Tom put Alex in a cab and asked if she might like to have dinner the next night. "I'd like that very much. I'm free. Just tell me the time and place. Please watch out for Fiat sedans with darkened windows."

Tom said, "I will, and I'll call you tomorrow." Then he walked slowly back to his apartment. He was savoring the peacefulness of the evening, especially the warmth of his conversation with Alex. Her concern for his safety was reassuring and offset to some extent his own anxiety at what had been happening to him.

As Tom approached his building, he saw two men standing on the sidewalk smoking cigarettes to the right of the front entrance. Not thinking anything of it, he took out his key and approached the door.

"Dr. Stewart?" one of the men said, moving closer to block Tom's way.

Doing a double take, Tom was suddenly apprehensive. "Yes?" he replied warily.

"We want what you've found."

"Found?" Tom said, "I don't have a clue what you're talking about."

One man pushed Tom against the apartment building wall. "The Roman Forum. There's a supply of the stuff, and we've been sent to warn you that we want it, and that we'll be back to get it."

"Look," Tom said. "What's this got to do with—"

"Shut up," the man said and backed off. "Have it your way. We'll be back. And next time, we won't ask so politely."

The two men walked away quickly and disappeared into the darkness. Shaken, Tom entered his apartment building. He took the elevator up to his apartment, quickly checked to make certain no one was inside, then locked and double-locked his front door; he also double-locked the door to his terrace.

The shock of this encounter made Tom restive. As Alex had warned, another threat happened—this time with two men and no Fiat with darkened windows. How could they know about the virus? Or that there was a supply of it? And who were they? Could these two men have been sent by a group O'Boyle had speculated about? Why was he being pursued? Gradually, he calmed down and went to bed. He began to go over the turbulent events of the day and became overwhelmed with them. Eventually, sleep came and Tom recalled nothing further until he awoke the next morning.

9

When Tom checked his e-mails, there was a message from Darby Smith.

Glad you've contacted me. I'd be delighted to show you what we've found in Imhotep's tomb. I'd rather show you this in person, but, failing that, why don't we talk tomorrow at 11 a.m.? I'll assemble some photographs and an old video, which you can see on the Internet while I describe them. Have somebody at the Academy arrange for my call. By the way, I've been reading about you in the *International Herald Tribune*—publicity you probably don't want. Sorry about that incident in the Forum—very puzzling.

Puzzling, yes, Tom said to himself.

Tom decided to have breakfast at the Hassler Hotel rather than the Hotel de la Ville. He told himself he wanted a change and admitted he wanted to see if Pulesi's spies would figure it out. Also, he was curious.

The stuffy nature of the staff in the Hassler lobby confirmed his preference for the Hotel de la Ville. But once in the dining room, he looked around at his fellow diners—they looked about the same as those at the Hotel de la Ville. Then, across the room, he spotted the American businessman, eating alone, engrossed in his copy of the *International Herald Tribune*. So, Tom said to himself, I guess his tryst is over. He began to look through his own copy of the paper. Fortunately, there were no references to the Roman Forum tragedy or to himself. After breakfast, Tom headed to the American Academy.

As he ate, and afterward, as he left, Tom surveyed his surroundings, trying to identify who was spying on him. But no one stuck out. He was amused—the spies, who were certainly there, covered their presence completely. But his humor was dampened when he realized that this wasn't a game—a sobering thought as he left through the revolving door at the front of the Hassler.

When Tom dropped in on Caroline in her office, she asked, "By the way, I forgot to ask you last evening, how did your lunch with the Belagri people go?"

"Well, they certainly seem to have money to spend. They offered to make a substantial grant if I agree to act as their consultant on certain historical research projects."

"Seems a bit far afield for a global agribusiness."

"I'll bet Brad Phelps will say the same thing, but he'll also conclude that he's all for it." Tom paused before he continued. "The grant seems straightforward enough, although it's hard to know what they're really after."

Caroline nodded. "I'm sure they're up to no good."

Tom added, "By the way, I'd like to ask Lucia to set up a computer call for me. I'm doing some archaeological research."

"Certainly," Caroline said.

"Any news from the authorities about the investigation?" Tom asked.

"No. Pulesi is being very vague. But the number of calls from the media dried up yesterday. They seem to have lost interest, thank goodness. We can all get back to our lives."

Except that I'm being stalked, Tom thought to himself. He wanted to check into some of the things O'Boyle had mentioned. As Tom left her office, he said to Caroline, "I think I'll visit the library to do some homework."

"Happy hunting."

With Marina's help, he gathered a few books about the Trajan aqueduct and water systems of ancient Rome. After his discovery in the aqueduct the day before, he had to find out more. One of the books he selected was an historical study on the sources for Rome's water. There was a short summary of the Trajanic period in which it was stated that Trajan's aqueduct was built during the first century and early part of the second century, from AD 98 to 117, channeling water from Lake Bracciano, twenty-five miles northwest of Rome. When the water reached the top of the Janiculum Hill, it fed watermills for grinding grain. The mills were later destroyed by the Ostrogoths when they severed the aqueduct in AD 537 during the first sacking of Rome.

More than a thousand years later, Camillo Borghese, on becoming Pope Paul V in 1605, proceeded to have the aqueduct rebuilt but altered its path slightly, so that water would be diverted to meet the Vatican's needs, as well as to serve the suburbs west of the Tiber, which were suffering from a chronic shortage of water. The pope had a large fountain built near the top of the Janiculum Hill, just a short way down from the present position of the American Academy, to mark the success of the aqueduct's restoration and to glorify himself. This fountain became known as the Acqua Paola. The diverted water served the Vatican, while the former main tunnel running down the Janiculum was abandoned. In Roman times this main aqueduct crossed the Tiber on a bridge and proceeded to the Trajan Baths near the Colosseum.

Tom focused on the Trajan Baths—could Visconti have wanted to use the abandoned aqueduct for more than a place to hide something? In order to build the secret lab near the Trajan Baths and the hidden chamber near the Academy, there would need to have been an unobtrusive way to move things between both places. The old aqueduct would be perfect. It would permit someone to transport material to and from the secret laboratory. But where was the entry point? Wasn't the Academy too high profile to use for this purpose?

Looking at a map, it appeared that the likeliest place for the aqueduct to cross the Tiber River was the present Ponte Sisto, a footbridge, near Piazza Trilussa in Trastevere. There was a fountain

in the piazza, and Tom learned that there were water pipes crossing over the Ponte Sisto. Where did that water come from? As he
thought about it, Tom guessed that the abandoned aqueduct below
the Acqua Paola probably contained a water pipe or pipes feeding
the fountain in the Piazza Trilussa as well as feeding the flow of
water to another fountain across the Ponte Sisto. He concluded that
the downhill section of the abandoned aqueduct ended somewhere
near the piazza and the last section of the Trajan aqueduct that began just across the Tiber.

Lucia texted Tom while he was in the library: "Darby Smith at
the American University in Cairo will be ready to speak with you
tomorrow morning at 10 a.m. Attached is the password you'll need.
There's a computer in the office next to Caroline's. Ciao."

Tom texted his thanks. His time in the library had taken up the
entire morning, and then some. He adjourned for lunch, sitting at
one of the long tables in the courtyard. The sun lit up the cortile, bak-
ing everything in sight, but the tables were set in such a way as to be
pleasantly in the shade. Tom happened to sit next to two landscape
fellows who were planning to visit community gardens south of the
city near the terminus of the ancient aqueducts carrying water into
Rome. He took the opportunity to ask them about the construction
of aqueducts, not mentioning his interest in Trajan's. He was surprised
to find that they were only vaguely aware there was an actual aqueduct
forty feet directly under the tables where they were having lunch.

After a cappuccino at the Academy's bar, Tom decided to take a
field trip to test his theory about the path of Trajan's aqueduct and
where it crossed the Tiber. As he left the Academy to see where the
aqueduct led, he called Alex to set the time and place for dinner.
They agreed to meet at 8 p.m. at Otello's in the alleyway off Via della
Croce, not far from his apartment.

Leaving the Main Building of the Academy, Tom made a right
turn onto Via Angelo Masina and walked to the end of the street,
turned left and turned left again onto Via Garibaldi, passing the
huge Acqua Paolo with its churning water spilling out of three great
fountains, lit by lights, even though it was midafternoon. The de-
scent toward the Tiber was steep as Tom walked the next hundred

yards, turning right into Via di Porta San Pancrazio, which rejoined Via Garibaldi after another hundred yards. Tom realized his path roughly followed the path the aqueduct must have taken.

Via Garibaldi became Via di Santa Dorotea, which passed through Piazza di San Giovanni Della Malva and, after a left turn, into Piazza Trilussa. So far, so good, he thought.

Tom saw the modest fountain in the Piazza Trilussa and approached it. Standing with his back to the Tiber, Tom looked up at the Janiculum Hill. The end of the water pipe feeding the fountain had to be below one of the old streets leading off this side of the piazza. He spotted a small alley between two small buildings. An apartment house, about four stories high, painted a faded burnt Siena red, stood apart slightly from the next building, perhaps someone's private home, which was made of stone and covered with ivy. Tom walked toward the alley, which went back the depth of the two buildings. At the alley's end was a small stone structure no more than fifteen feet high, with a door marked with the insignia of Rome's waterworks.

Bingo, Tom thought. He tried the door. In true Italian fashion, the door was not locked.

Seeing no one watching him, Tom opened the door and walked in. At the back of the modest building, there was a door of normal height, which Tom pulled open, revealing the end of a tunnel. The height of the tunnel was about the size of the aqueduct he had been in at the Academy. At ground level, two pipes emerged from the tunnel, each about eighteen inches in diameter, which then plunged into the floor and disappeared. Tom guessed that one of these went to the fountain nearby and the other fed the pipes crossing over the Ponte Sisto.

Tom smiled to himself. Trajan's aqueduct ran under the Academy building, down the Janiculum, and crossed the Tiber. If he found the aqueduct on the other side of the river, he'd be able to follow it to the Trajan Baths, close to the underground lab.

Walking through the Piazza Trilussa, Tom crossed the Tiber on the Ponte Sisto, which was not as easy as it looked. As a walking bridge, it was devoid of car traffic, but it was filled with people sitting and talking. On the other side, at the end of the bridge, he noticed another small stone building marked with the same insignia. This time, however, there was a sign on the door. Tom translated the sign:

FOR OFFICIAL USE ONLY. KEEP OUT BY ORDER OF THE MINISTRY OF ITALIAN CULTURAL PROPERTIES AND ACTIVITIES.

This must lead to the final section of the ancient aqueduct, Tom thought. Visconti and his team of workers could have used this obscure entry to come and go from the lab without being noticed. That explained the mystery of how he kept it secret. The pieces were all falling into place.

Lost in thought, he made his way back to his hotel. He checked his e-mail before getting ready to meet Alex. There was a message from Brad.

In the e-mail, Brad confessed to some reservations about Belagri's reputation. He said, "They certainly have deep pockets. The proposal involves $500,000 in grant money. We can't look a gift horse in the mouth, Tom. You know how tight the budgets are. In this economy, grant money is exceedingly hard to find." Brad urged him to consider their offer very seriously.

Tom wasn't entirely satisfied by Brad's response, which seemed totally ready to take Belagri's money. Worse, he thought, Brad is leaving me with making the decision.

Otello's restaurant was busy when Tom arrived to meet Alex.

She was already there, waiting at a table in the garden. He waved and made his way over. Alex's table was under a maze of grapevines that grew prolifically on a yellowing old Plexiglas roof, there to protect outdoor diners from the lunchtime sun and the occasional Roman rain.

"It's good to see you," she said as he sat down.

"Likewise. Otello's nice, if a bit crowded."

They ordered a bottle of wine and the special of the day.

"How has everything been going?" Alex asked.

Tom replied, "I've done some research today. But last evening after I put you in the taxi—something happened that made me very uneasy."

Alex leaned forward, concerned. "Not again? Please tell me."

"I was at the front door to my building, and two men closed in on me and demanded that I hand over something they claimed I have access to from the Roman Forum."

Alex looked shocked. "First, someone almost runs you down in a car and then comes after you in the street. What's going on?" She paused, then continued. "You told me Pulesi is now in charge of the investigation. I inquired about him—Dr. Stefano Pulesi, isn't it? He's the head investigator of the agency the government set up after 9/11 to prevent bioterrorism. That suggests that something very serious must have been discovered with Doc's and Eric's autopsies."

Tom was startled by Alex's statement. She had obviously been doing some investigation herself—which pleased him, even if what Alex had found out bothered him. He said, "I spoke with Pulesi yesterday. His investigation confirmed that Doc and Eric died from a powerful virus. They breathed it in from spores in the moss that was growing in the abandoned underground lab."

"I see. So the green moss did play a role." She looked worried and perplexed. "In any of my research, there hasn't been a virus that acted that quickly in bringing about a person's death since—"

Tom immediately finished her sentence: "The Spanish flu. That's what Pulesi said and why he's involved. Apparently, this virus is similar and could be even more potent. He's alerted the Centers for Disease Control in the United States and its European counterparts. He's certain some other groups know about the virus and want to get their hands on it."

"Is this why Belagri approached you?" Alex asked.

"Probably."

"What will you do?"

"NYU wants me to accept Belagri's grant."

"Where there's grant money involved, there're always strings attached."

"I know," Tom continued. "Alex," he added, looking directly into her eyes, "I'm afraid there's more to all of this than Belagri. With the car chase, and my being stalked—neither was likely Belagri."

"Why not?"

"They barely knew me before lunch at Tivoli yesterday, and that was just moments before the car chase. Also, why offer me grant money and then harass me?"

"Good point. Then, who was it?"

Tom said, "I don't know."

Alex sat back in her chair, astonished. "If I'm going to help, I need to know everything."

Tom replied, "I don't want you dragged into this."

"I'm already in it," she said. "Talk."

After Tom had finished giving Alex a full accounting of O'Boyle's conversation with him—including the background of the Moses Virus, she said, "If you're right and other groups are after the virus, shouldn't you contact the Carabinieri?"

"No. I want to know more before I involve them. As for Belagri, I'm not sure whether Doc was involved with them beyond a straightforward consulting agreement—I don't think he was, but I don't know for sure."

"Why would Belagri be so interested in the virus, anyway? It has nothing to do with their agribusiness."

"That's the mystery. Maybe it's about creating superseeds resistant to such a powerful virus."

"Or something worse," Alex said, quietly.

"What do you mean?"

"Bioterrorism. Corporate warfare."

"You think it could be used as a weapon?"

"Anything's possible, I guess," Alex said without inflection. "With powerful weapons, there always seems to be someone who wants to control them."

The waiter showed up with their dinner.

Afterward, they walked through the quiet streets. Nearby, the Spanish Steps were crowded with hundreds of tourists, spilling out onto the piazza below. They passed the Spanish Steps. The moon shone brightly, giving the serpentine cobblestone streets a strangely beautiful look. As they walked and talked, they grew closer. Tom took her hand. She didn't resist. Eventually, they returned to the Spanish Steps, climbed all of its 138 steps, threading their way through the hundreds of students, tourists, and musicians gathered to talk, sing, or watch. At the top, they turned toward Via Gregoriana, and soon found themselves in front of his building.

"Here we are. Interested in a nightcap? I've got some bottles of pinot grigio in the fridge."

"I'd like that, thanks," Alex said and smiled.

Tom opened the apartment building's front door, made of steel and heavy glass, and they proceeded to the elevator.

"It's a little rickety, but it's reliable." The door squeaked as he slid it open for her.

Stopping on the ninth floor, Tom and Alex walked down the corridor to his apartment. The door was slightly ajar.

"Strange," Tom said. "I'm sure I locked it." He pushed it open.

"Hello," he said tentatively. He signaled to Alex to stay back.

Silence. Tom entered the apartment. "What the hell . . ."

The whole place had been trashed. Though the drawers of his desk were closed, Tom quickly determined that the contents had all been rearranged. Books in the shelves were in a different order than he had left them. Most importantly, his laptop was gone.

Alex joined Tom in the apartment.

"Oh, Tom. This is terrible."

Tom walked into his bedroom, then returned. "Nothing is missing except my laptop."

"I'm sorry. What about your book?"

"I backed it up on a flash drive, which I happen to have carried with me." He pulled it from his pocket to confirm that he still had it. "Luckily, there was nothing on my computer except a few stray notes."

"But why would only your laptop have been taken? What recent e-mails did you send? Or receive?" Alex asked.

Tom thought for a moment and replied, "I have a duplicate set on my iPhone. Let me see."

Tom scrolled through his incoming and outgoing e-mails. Suddenly he frowned.

"What's the matter?" Alex asked.

"I e-mailed my dean at NYU that I had spoken with a senior Italian government official investigating the Roman Forum incident.

I told him this official confirmed that a highly toxic virus was involved and that European and American groups were now on the alert."

"Anything else?" asked Alex.

"No, nothing else."

"This is serious. Tom. To break into your apartment, steal your computer. You absolutely have to call the Carabinieri and file a report."

"If I do call them, it'll be all over the news tomorrow."

"Well, it's not safe here. You can stay at my place until you sort things all out."

"Thanks, but I couldn't."

"No arguments," Alex said firmly. "I've got a sofa bed that my friends use when they visit. Let's pack your things and get out of here. Whoever broke in might be back."

An hour later, Tom and Alex were in a cab to her house.

After he was settled, Tom joined Alex in the living room. She had set out two glasses and a bottle of chilled white wine.

"Let's have that nightcap," Alex said, pouring the wine.

"I really appreciate your help, Alex."

"Niente. I have a friend who owns a small hotel not far from the Termini. I'll call her tomorrow and see if she'll let you stay at her apartment. It's on the top floor, which she normally uses, but this summer she's in New York decorating a boutique hotel she's opening near Irving Place—her latest project. I'm sure she'll let you stay. We'll give you a false name, right?"

"Thanks. I hate to think this is necessary."

"But it is," Alex said. "Do you know what I think?"

"No, what?"

"I'd guess that this break-in is more likely Belagri than anyone else."

"Why do you say this?"

She replied, "Belagri suspects you know a lot more than you told them. And they are extremely anxious to find out about this virus."

Tom was silent.

Alex said, "Tom, you're in a hell of a situation. Where is the virus?"

"I don't know. I can't find it without O'Boyle, and he as much as said he wouldn't tell me."

"And Pulesi or the Centers for Disease Control? They should be able to help, and they're certainly motivated to get hold of the virus. Or, what about the Catholic Church? O'Boyle's deeply involved with the Church. Are they involved?"

"O'Boyle told me all the records relating to the virus were destroyed years ago, so that no one currently in the Vatican knows anything about the virus. On the other hand, he warned me about the Church—the rumors that get passed around. I just don't know."

Tom went on. "The Italian authorities are another problem. They're notorious for leaking information and absolutely can't be trusted. The only Italian I'd be willing to say anything to would be Pulesi. I have to admit that Pulesi was very helpful when I spoke with him, though how do I know that people around him wouldn't talk? And," Tom added, "speaking of Pulesi, I saw Crystal Close leave his building just before I arrived."

"Crystal Close?" Alex's expression hardened, and she raised an eyebrow. "That woman gets around—inviting you to lunch, offering you a grant, and having a secret meeting with Pulesi."

"Wait a minute," said Tom, somewhat defensively. "I don't know if she met with Pulesi. It's a very large government building."

"Okay," replied Alex, "maybe she didn't meet with Pulesi. Maybe it was one of his people. How much does Caroline know?"

"Not much. Only that Doc was a colleague of Lily Ross Taylor's at Bryn Mawr. And, Caroline told me about the aqueduct."

"Might Doc have been looking for the underground lab?"

"Possibly, but I doubt it. Lily may have told Doc about Visconti's visit to the cryptoporticus, but I don't think there's any reason why Lily would have known about Visconti's interest in the aqueduct."

"Shouldn't you tell Caroline what's really going on?"

"I've been reluctant to. She's in a very tricky situation. She'd feel obligated to inform the authorities right away, go through channels, protect the interests of the Academy. It would all become a huge mess. And possibly wind up with the virus in the wrong hands. It's something I need to follow up myself at this point."

Alex, with some reluctance, agreed.

"I'm worried for you," she said. "What can I do?"

Tom shook his head. "It's too dangerous. If they continue to follow me, they'll follow you as well. I can't take that chance."

Tom put down his wine glass. "I need to convince O'Boyle to give me the name of the Swiss banker. Once I locate the virus, I'll turn it over to the authorities and let them take it from there."

"Which authorities?" Alex asked.

"What do you mean?" Tom said.

"Well, if you get hold of the virus, which group do you hand it over to? The Italians?"

"No, I don't trust them."

"The CDC?" Alex asked.

"Probably. But I don't know anyone there."

"So," said Alex, "we'll have to figure out how to get it to the right people there."

"We've got work to do," Tom concluded.

"Just be careful." Alex stood. "It's late and a lot has happened tonight. I think you ought to go to bed and get some sleep. I'm going to my bedroom upstairs. This couch pulls out into a bed and has clean sheets on it. Let me show you the bathroom. Will this all be okay?"

"I'll be fine," Tom replied. "Thanks."

"Right," said Alex. "If you're at all hungry, by all means go down to the kitchen. Anything you find is fair game."

Alex looked at Tom. "I'm glad you're here. I feel safer. I'll leave a note for Ana to add another place for breakfast tomorrow. Buona notte."

"I'm sure I'll wake up early enough, but please get me up if I oversleep. I've got a call scheduled at the Academy at 10 a.m."

"Okay. See you in the morning."

Alex gave Tom a light kiss. He hugged her.

Then she left Tom to go to her bedroom.

At precisely 10 a.m., Tom called Darby Smith. Tom was sitting in front of a computer screen that Lucia had set up for him.

Darby began by saying, "Good morning, Tom. I've read about the tragic event in the Roman Forum. It was played up big in the *International Herald Tribune*. Even a photograph of you. My condolences."

"Thanks," replied Tom. "It's been a brutal experience that shows no signs of terminating. The Italian authorities cremated the bodies and are treating the incident as if there were a deadly virus involved."

"Was there?" Darby asked.

"There might have been. If there were, it was a virus that lay dormant for many years. Most unusual. Anyway, I've got an idea that your restored wall painting might give me a clue."

"Really?"

"Yes. If you don't mind showing me your findings."

"Okay," Darby said. "Watch your screen. I'm starting with a tape I made a few years ago in the Valley of the Kings. My plan is to show you my own excavation—Tomb KV5, built as a mausoleum for Ramesses II's fifty sons, and then move to Imhotep's tomb, which is what you want to see. But there may be a connection. All right? Stop anytime for questions."

At that moment Tom saw on his computer screen a vehicle driving across a flat plain with mountains in the background. The vehicle was kicking up a trail of dust. Darby said, "The temperature here, today, like it was in the video, is 107 degrees, and it's dusty as hell, dry and very hot."

The vehicle crossed a bridge spanning the Nile. The sky was cloudless, the air clear. The vehicle traveled on a dusty road, with the rising walls of the Valley of the Kings off to the left, and ruins of mortuary temples to the right. The road ended at a visitors' center and parking area filled with an enormous number of air-conditioned buses.

"Here we are at the Valley of the Kings. There are sixty-three tombs, but I've always believed somewhere in this mass of stone there are more tombs to be found." Darby stopped his narration. "Is the picture coming through okay?"

"Yes," said Tom. "I feel like I'm actually experiencing it. In fact, memories of my first trip to Luxor are flooding back. It looks the same as I remember it."

"And it'll probably look just like this a hundred or a thousand years from now. It's timeless."

The camera moved to a shot of an unadorned stone stairway with steps leading below ground. Then the video continued down a half dozen steps into an anteroom lit by an electric floor lamp. Tom concentrated on everything he saw. The rough texture of the limestone walls seemed to have been carved flat. A student, off to the right, was photographing the fragments of a wall painting. An open pit was over to the left.

"We found some parts of a skeleton in that pit," Smith said, and Tom saw it as a flashlight shone on the contents of the narrow trench.

Darby continued. "Those bones may be the remains of one of Ramesses's sons, dragged here from his sarcophagus by robbers. His mummy probably contained precious jewelry that the robbers were looking for. If so, they unwrapped the mummy looking for the jewels, which they took, dumping the remains in the pit.

"Take a careful look at the skeleton. It looks normal, right? I want you to notice this skeleton since, when I show you the ones we found in the Imhotep tomb, they are considerably different—they are strangely contorted. Okay, enough of my dig. We'll move on to Imhotep."

Tom listened but said nothing.

Darby continued. "In the next valley, the noblemen are buried." The video showed small villages where Egyptian families had lived for the past two thousand years. Spotted in the midst of a village were entrances to tombs of high priests, rich merchants. The camera focused on a stairway of stone steps. "This tomb belongs to the master architect, Imhotep, who worked for the great Pharaoh Ramesses II. It was discovered in 1922 by Charles Babcock, an American archaeologist. Babcock was a very competent professional who made a remarkable find, which only a handful of people ever knew about because it was totally overshadowed by Howard Carter's discovery of King Tutankhamen's tomb just a few days earlier.

"As you already know, Tut's three cradled gold coffins were undisturbed for nearly three thousand years. The tomb contained the richest trove of artifacts ever found, from one of the most refined cultural periods of mankind: that's breathtaking stuff. Babcock didn't have a chance. Yet, in my judgment, what was found in his excavation may outshine the importance of Carter's discovery."

"I'm fascinated. Please go on," Tom said.

"Take a look at this," Darby said, his voice showing high excitement. The camera panned the interior of the Imhotep tomb. "This is a large square room hewn out of a rock cliff. The inner space is supported by columns, many of which were badly damaged or missing when Babcock first entered. Now we have restored or replaced them. On one section of the wall is a large painting three feet high and five feet long, which my wife and some other members of our team have been able to restore over the past seven years.

"When first found, this key wall painting was in terrible shape. There were certain discernible aspects, but as a whole it was indecipherable. With a great deal of work its story now makes sense. Only recently have we been able to read its hieroglyphs.

"What you're now looking at are enlarged details of the wall painting. Are you okay with hieroglyphics?"

Tom answered, "Not really."

Darby continued. "The wall painting depicts the ten plagues that devastated Egypt while Ramesses II was at the peak of his power. You can see dead cattle, rivers that have turned red with blood, soldiers dying or dead. This time of the plagues coincides with the story in the book of Exodus in the Old Testament. Moses pleads with Ramesses to let his people—the Hebrews—follow Moses to the Promised Land. Ramesses refuses. We guess that he refuses because his priests don't want to lose the manpower that the Hebrew slaves represented."

As Darby continued with the description of the mural, Tom's eyes surveyed as much as he could take in, allowing him to examine the painting for evidence of a reference to the virus. The more he saw, the more he realized that this magnificent painting was less involved in telling of the heroic exploits and accomplishments of Imhotep than it was in describing an incredibly devastating plague that threatened to lay waste to Egypt. There were depictions of the canopic jars, but he was more struck by the depiction of men dying, their bodies twisted in death by, Tom could only presume, the virus. Obviously, the artist or artists had a powerful story to tell—perhaps a warning for future generations.

Darby was saying, "Here are close-ups: the first plague was blood, where the fish of the Nile died. The second plague was a multitude of frogs that overran Egypt. The third plague was gnats, lice, or fleas—the word is translated differently. The fourth plague was flies, which only attacked the Egyptians, harming both people and livestock. The fifth plague was an epidemic disease, a virus, which wiped out Egyptian livestock: horses, donkeys, camels, cattle, sheep, and goats. And so forth."

"Amazing," said Tom. "The power and beauty of these hieroglyphics. Your wife should be congratulated."

"And her team," Darby added. "The tenth and final plague was the death of all Egyptian firstborn males—no one escaped, from the lowest servant to the pharaoh's own son. The firstborn of the Egyptians and of their livestock were killed—Egyptian culture was virtually obliterated. They are shown in the painting, but they are in horrible, twisted shapes, as if they died in excruciating pain."

Tom shuddered as he made the connection with the deaths of Doc and Eric and the skeletons found in the underground lab, but chose not to say anything to Darby about this.

"Tom, here's something I can't answer, but I'll point it out to you. How many plagues were there?"

"Ten," replied Tom.

"That's right. Count them, however, on the mural."

Tom, surprised, began to count them. "Eleven, not ten. That's what I count. But how is this possible? The Bible says ten."

"Okay," Darby replied. "Look at each of them, and compare them to the Bible's account."

Slowly, Tom went through the hieroglyphs. The pictures related to the Bible's text, except for the next to last one. This part of the Egyptian mural showed fire enveloping a group of Egyptians, a group of men, women, and children. This figure did not correspond to any of the ten plagues.

Tom was quiet. Darby said, "I don't have any explanation at all. Besides this panel not being a plague mentioned in the Bible, look at the drawing. There's one more aspect: this is the only drawing that shows three canopic jars."

"Four would be expected," Tom said. "Correct?"

"In a normal burial," Darby said, "there would be four, one each for the stomach, the intestines, the lungs, and the liver."

"What about the heart?" asked Tom.

"The heart was thought to be the 'seat of the soul' and had to remain with the body," Darby said. "Our mural shows three canopic jars, which seem identical to the actual canopic jars we found in Imhotep's tomb. I have to believe that the priests were sending a message by having only three instead of four jars. Furthermore, they were highly out of the ordinary since the contents were not Imhotep's internal organs, but samples of grains, cow bones, and human tissue."

"I would guess," Tom said, "the chief priests decided to preserve these items—certainly not for humans yet to be born, since the

Egyptians were focused on themselves and their next world. They might have been making offerings to the sun god, Ra, for his help in ridding Egypt of the plagues . . . or, perhaps the offerings were to ward off future plagues in Imhotep's afterlife?"

"Good guesses," Darby replied. "We'll probably never know for certain. But I suspect the contents of the canopic jars were to protect Imhotep from plagues in the next world. One other finding I should mention is that there were human skeletons in the tomb, which would not normally be there. I think that one explanation is that these bones were those of high priests struck down by the last and final plague, which may have killed Imhotep himself."

"So the virus struck more than the firstborn of the Egyptians?" Tom asked.

"The wall painting is clear about this, as were the skeletons we found in Imhotep's tomb. Obviously, these skeletons were not all first sons in their families," Darby said. "I think that the virus was horrendously powerful as well as pervasive. One of the canopic jars, examined and written up by Babcock in his papers, contained remnants of the victims of the plagues. And the skeletons found in Imhotep's tomb—most were in contorted positions—suggest that they were victims of the virus as well."

Darby produced pictures of the dead priests as they had been found in the tomb. "Here's what's left of them. After nearly three thousand years, many of these bones are held together by their thin, leathery skin, which keeps them in their contorted positions. To me, they died in extreme discomfort."

"I'm struck by how different these bones are from those found in your excavation," Tom said. He then added, "What you've found in this Egyptian wall painting is absolutely new information, isn't it? The Bible focuses on the Hebrews, their oppression and escape, and the power of God, not on the near destruction of Egypt. And, finally, there is the puzzle of the eleventh plague."

"Right," said Darby.

"The press release and other archaeologists must have commented on this eleventh plague."

"You'd think so," Darby said, "but no one did. I believe that the exciting news is the verification of the biblical text. There are, after all, ten plagues described that match exactly. I guess that the anomaly is simply ignored, since no one has come up with a good theory." Darby went on. "Before we finish, there's an odd development that occurred three or four months ago. When we announced our newly restored wall painting, there was immediate and widespread interest among the professionals who follow archaeology. One of the parties that contacted us, and then sent a team, was Belagri, the international bioengineering agriculture company. Have you heard of them?"

"A controversial company," observed Tom.

"Belagri made a date with me through the Supreme Council of Antiquities—through the secretary general himself. Of course I saw them. When the secretary general summons, I jump. When we actually met Belagri, they said they wished to study the grains that had been found in one of the canopic jars. That seemed harmless enough, I thought, so I agreed to take them to the Cairo Museum to show them."

"Why would you, or the American University in Cairo where you teach, or the Supreme Council, for that matter, entertain the idea of giving the most controversial bioengineering company in the world access to these precious materials?" asked Tom.

"Money," Darby said. "The answer's that simple. They made their case powerfully, that their laboratories are the best positioned in the world to perform DNA analysis on the grains, even though the samples are three thousand years old. They pledged that if they were selected to do this testing, they would report their findings and would give the American University in Cairo one million dollars for use in the further excavation of Tomb KV5, as well as Imhotep's tomb. Frankly, money talks. We're always having trouble with obtaining enough funding. Having too little money is why it took us seven years instead of two to excavate the first two chambers of Tomb KV5.

"The Supreme Council and the university, each debated the merits and, in relatively short order, agreed to Belagri's terms. But, when the director of the Cairo Museum went to find the canopic jars, they were missing. There was a small supply of what had been stored in the jars of grain and bones from the cows, but nothing was left of the human tissue in the museum's possession. Belagri was given modest-sized samples of the grain and cow bones."

Tom asked, "Do you know what Belagri found when they analyzed the material?"

Darby said, "No. To my knowledge, Belagri has said nothing about what they have or haven't found by analyzing the material from the canopic jars."

"Belagri has a reputation for being highly secretive. Did they ever tell you what they hoped to do with what they found?"

"They told us nothing," Darby said.

Tom said, "Did you get the million dollars?"

"The first installment—the rest is payable over five years."

"Darby, I'm very grateful for your time and explanations. Your information has been extremely helpful. Many thanks."

Darby replied, "I won't ask you any questions about the details of the Roman Forum tragedy, though I'm very curious."

"Thanks. I'm under restrictions not to talk about what happened," said Tom.

"Fill me in when you can. Next time, why not come to Luxor? I'd like to show you around in person. And, if you come up with an explanation for the eleventh plague, let me know."

"I will. Until I can get to Egypt," Tom concluded, "thanks again."

Almost immediately after his conversation with Darby Smith, Tom was interrupted by a telephone call. It was Ambassador Wilson, whose big, hearty voice projected even over the telephone. "I enjoyed meeting you at Caroline's office. Could we get together? I'd like to introduce you to one of my colleagues in the Vatican. It's about the events in the Roman Forum."

"Meet with me? Certainly, I'd welcome a meeting," Tom said, somewhat surprised.

"Would later today be possible?"

"Where and when would you like?"

"Let's meet at St. Peter's Basilica. Come to the Bronze Doors. Knock and you'll be taken to the front desk, and there'll be someone there to escort you. Is 4:30 p.m. okay?"

"Yes," Tom replied, "but I'm not sure where the Bronze Doors are."

"I'm sorry," laughed Ambassador Wilson. "As you face St. Peter's, look to the right at the end of the Bernini columns, and you'll see big ceremonial bronze doors—these are called the Portone di Bronzo. This is where visiting royalty used to enter the Vatican palace to meet with the pope. It's an imposing entrance, but a great shortcut to our meeting. See you then."

Tom remained seated in front of the computer going over what he had learned from Doc Smith. Caroline entered the room with a worried look on her face. "Tom, did you know that Father O'Boyle died two nights ago?"

"Died? Are you sure?" Tom asked, a shiver running down his spine. "What happened?"

"He was found by his landlady early yesterday morning, in his apartment, dead—apparently of a heart attack. No warning—he wasn't sick. He has no immediate family. It's very sad. Doc was very fond of him, as are most of our scholars."

Tom nodded. "I'm sorry—I only barely knew him."

Tom's mind was racing at the news. He had hoped to persuade O'Boyle to give him the missing piece to the puzzle of the Moses Virus. How would he find out the name of the Swiss banker now?

Caroline continued. "Have you heard anything more about the investigation? Pulesi hasn't responded to my efforts to reach him." She sighed. "It's just like the rest of the city government here. Everything gets so wound up in red tape, nothing ever gets done."

Tom changed the subject. "Have the Belagri people contacted you?"

"Yes, I heard from their foundation. They faxed me the additional paperwork. At least they're efficient, although I don't know how I'll be able to help them if the dig stays closed."

"I'd guess that the Academy will be allowed to reopen the excavation once the official investigation is closed. On a different topic, I had a computer meltdown last evening."

"What about the loss of your manuscript? You must be panicking!" Caroline said.

"I'm fine—at least I had my manuscript on a memory stick, which is intact. But I'd like to borrow an Academy computer to download and send some e-mails."

"Of course. The one you just used for your archaeological research—use that for as long as you like." Caroline's cell phone rang. She glanced to see who the caller was. "Excuse me," she said, "but I have to take this. Talk to you later."

Tom logged onto his e-mail. Brad had left a message saying that he had cleared the concept of a relationship with Belagri with NYU's administration and that Tom should proceed. "Thanks, Brad. Why am I not surprised?" Tom said to himself.

Looking through the rest of his messages, he was struck by one e-mail, whose subject was in Latin, *Pestilentia Moseia*. It was also, Tom noticed, untraceable. Tom felt a rising sense of excitement. Could O'Boyle have sent him the information he needed—and how did he do this if he was dead? The date on the e-mail was noon yesterday, delayed for some reason. He opened it immediately. The message was just a few words:

SIGMUND WARBURG
CORDIER, WARBURG, & CIE., GENEVA
May God Protect Us All

"O'Boyle." Tom whistled under his breath. "It has to be O'Boyle's work. He must have changed his mind and sent the note before he had a heart attack." Tom Googled "Sigmund Warburg," but only got articles on Warburg's career in banking. He assumed that Cordier, Warburg was the name of his bank, found the address and telephone number, and called the office in Geneva.

"Sigmund Warburg, please."

The bank telephone operator was exceedingly precise in her conversation with Tom. "Herr Warburg is no longer at this office. He retired several years ago."

"It's important that I speak to him on a business matter. Do you have a number where he can be reached?"

The operator paused. "I am sorry, but we are not permitted to give out the private contact information of our people. I may be able to give him a message, however."

"Thank you. Please have him contact Dr. Thomas Stewart at this number as soon as possible. I am referred by Father Timothy O'Boyle." He gave her his cell number.

"I will pass this message to my manager," she replied courteously, then hung up.

Satisfied that he could do nothing more, Tom called Alex to see about his new place.

"It's all set. I've even had your things sent over to your apartment at the hotel. You can get settled anytime. You are registered under the name John Jones. Clever, eh? No ID will be required." She gave him the address.

"John Jones as an alias . . . not very original," Tom said, amused. "But, good thinking. It'll be harder for anyone to trace me."

"Best I could do at the time."

"Seriously, thanks. I'll head over there after dark."

"I'll meet you there. There's a little restaurant nearby where . . ."

"No. You're been exposed too much already. If they're following me, you'll be a target also."

Alex agreed. "Then when will I see you?"

"I'll need to let you know. I may be going to Switzerland."

"Switzerland?" Alex asked.

"Sorry," Tom replied. "I'm going too fast. Caroline just told me that O'Boyle died last evening. Heart attack."

Alex seemed shocked. "Dead? How will you find the virus?"

"I've received an e-mail—which O'Boyle must have managed to send just before he died."

Alex sighed with relief. "With the banker's name?"

"Both his name and that of his bank in Geneva."

"Tom," Alex seemed troubled. "You said heart attack. That can be faked. Do you think he was killed?"

"Possibly," Tom replied. "I'd guess there'll be an inquiry. I also tried to verify that it was O'Boyle who sent me the e-mail. But it was untraceable, though I'm sure he wrote it."

"Father O'Boyle wasn't sick, was he?"

"Not that I know of. I called the Swiss bank and asked that the banker contact me. If and when this man calls, I want to meet with him as soon as possible."

"How sad—about O'Boyle. Please be careful. Let me know if I can help."

"The first thing you can do is tell me where I can buy a new laptop."

"That's easy." She gave him the name of a large electronics store in the business district. "But I hope that's not the only way I can help."

Tom smiled. "Hardly. I'll call you later. Ciao." He hung up.

Purchasing a new laptop turned out to be easier than he thought. There was a markdown on a Dell computer, which made buying one irresistible. Still, Tom seriously contemplated a MacBook Air, which was the best looking, thinnest computer he had seen, but he stayed away from it thinking that he still wasn't free from another break-in, and he definitely did not want to lose it.

Tom took a cab part of the way to his new place, near a large piazza, and hailed a second taxi. He was determined to shake anyone trying to track him. He got out at the Termini, walked its length, deciding that it was truly the longest train station in Christendom. The hotel, which Alex's friend owned, was located at 401 Via Giovanni Giolitti directly across the street from the Temple of Minerva. Tom saw that this ancient monument was in ruins, a beautiful hunk of bricks and broken arches.

Tom checked in at the front desk and was greeted by the owner's nephew. They took the old elevator to the sixth floor, and the nephew opened the front door of his aunt's apartment, handing the keys to Tom. The nephew was fastidious, and easily spent ten minutes showing Tom each cupboard and closet. The kitchen was fully stocked with basic supplies. Quietly, Tom took in all the details and couldn't help smiling. It was a wonder—modest in size, with one bedroom, living room, kitchen, small office, and bathroom, but had been "done" in an over-the-top style as a Roman ruin. It had painted sky views on the ceiling, and, on the walls, crumbling bricks (all painted), faux marble sculptures of male and female torsos, and dozens of photographs of the owner with friends. The lighting was soft and dramatic. Yet, though all appeared real, it actually was accomplished with paint, pins, glue, and tape.

Despite the stage setting of the interior, when Tom was shown the view out the large plate glass windows, he saw there was a good reason for making the apartment a contemporary ruin. Across the street were the remains of the Temple of Minerva Medica—or, as the nephew said, "Minerva the Doctor." To the left was the great train station with its tracks running south. The temple itself had been a large domed building, constructed with Roman brick. As the dome was gone, only parts of the arches were still standing. Tom was pleased at the apartment Alex had found for him. After the nephew left, Tom set up his new computer in the small office and brewed himself a cup of coffee on the small modern cooktop in the kitchen.

Around one in the afternoon, Tom descended the six flights, passed the reception desk, and walked to the corner of Via le Manzoni and Via Giovanni Giolitti. There was a small restaurant owned by the hotel where Tom had lunch. He studied a map while he ate so he could familiarize himself with the neighborhood. The apartment buildings around him gave evidence of a fairly modern, though nondescript, residential area. He looked around carefully as he exited, and seeing no one suspicious, felt relieved that for once he might be free from the surveillance of the past week.

He turned onto Via le Manzoni, a wide boulevard leading toward the Colosseum. He walked leisurely for about fifteen minutes when he passed the street where the San Clemente Church was located. Remembering that John Connor had called this church O'Boyle's favorite haunt, Tom entered San Clemente. Tourists were wandering around on all levels. At the Mithraic temple, three levels down, he was impressed by the quietness and sanctity of the place. He sat on one of the stone benches and thought about Father O'Boyle. Had he been murdered? And, if so, by whom? But he found no answers here, and so Tom retraced his steps and continued on his walk.

From San Clemente, Tom went to the Colosseum and into the Roman Forum, observing guards standing in front of the iron gates on the Palatine Hill, behind which lay the archaeological excavation where Doc and Eric lost their lives. Tom could not avoid reliving the incidents that had turned his own life upside down.

Again and again, Tom checked to see if he'd been followed. He headed back toward his hotel. Once more on Manzoni, he saw a large supermarket where he picked up some coffee, soft drinks, cheese and crackers, and a couple bottles of white wine. And, on leaving, he saw that a few buildings away there was a gelato shop with an enormous variety of ice creams, two of which he bought to take back. He was at his apartment around 3 p.m. and thought he'd head to the Vatican. Before leaving, he called Alex and asked if she'd like to meet him and they'd walk over to St. Peter's Square for his appointment with Ambassador Wilson.

"I know we've got to be careful about someone following us. But if you're okay with meeting me, at least we'll be in the crowds around Vatican City," Tom cautioned.

Alex replied, "I'd like to get out. It's a beautiful day, and I'll be careful. Besides, I've been doing some homework on plagues and viruses, which I'd like to tell you about. Why don't I meet you on the walking bridge over the Tiber near the Castel Sant'Angelo?"

"Sounds good," said Tom, and he set off, taking a taxi part way, and a second taxi to the bridge.

Tom and Alex met on the Ponte Sant'Angelo. Alex was waiting midway across the bridge. "Do you see the statue on the top of the drum?" she asked after they had greeted each other.

"Yes. I've seen it dozens of times, but never thought much about it."

"It's the angel that answered Pope Gregory's prayer for help when a major plague was devastating Rome in AD 590. Pope Gregory asked God for help. Saint Michael, the patron saint of doctors, appeared on top of the Castel Sant'Angelo, signaling God's response to the pope's prayer. Saint Michael is shown sheaving his sword, which signifies the ending of the plague."

Tom said, "Okay, what can you tell me about plagues and killer viruses?"

Alex laughed, and proceeded. "You're asking for it. The worst plague—until modern times—was the black death, which arrived by ship in Venice in October 1347. It was carried by rat-infected sailors from a Genoese colony called Kaffa on the Black Sea. Entire crews were infected, and some ships were found grounded on Italian shorelines with no one alive. Within eighteen months, one-third of Europe's population was dead, somewhere on the order of 25 million people."

Tom said, "I didn't know it was that powerful."

Alex replied, "It was horrible. I've found a short account written by an Italian named Agnolo di Tura." Alex read from some pages she had Xeroxed and brought with her. "'They died by the hundreds, both day and night, and all were thrown in ditches and covered with earth. And as soon as those ditches were filled, more were dug. And I, Agnolo di Tura, buried my five children with my own hands. And so many died that all believed it was the end of the world.'"

"That's horrifying," said Tom.

"And I'm not sure that the Spanish flu wasn't worse," said Alex. "I've been thinking. Suppose some group gets hold of the Moses Virus and sets it off? It could be far worse than the black plague. If the Moses Virus is as deadly as the Spanish flu, then the fallout is unthinkable." Alex paused, contemplating the impact of a pandemic killer. "We've simply got to stop this from happening."

Tom surprised himself. In the middle of the bridge, with countless numbers of people walking by, he took Alex in his arms. Her directness was compelling to him, and he felt, with her support, anything might be possible. He kissed her, and she welcomed it. "I'm so glad we met. I need you," he said. Alex pulled her head back, smiled and said, "I'm glad, too."

They walked from the bridge and stood beneath the massive monument, Castel Sant'Angelo. It was a beautiful afternoon, and Tom and Alex sat down at a bench along the quay, which permitted a view of the Tiber as well as a magnificent view of the round drum at the top of Castel Sant'Angelo. There was a mime entertaining tourists.

Tom's cell phone rang.

"Dr. Thomas Stewart?" a man said. He had perfect English, but a very slight German accent.

"Yes, I'm Tom Stewart."

"I am Sigmund Warburg. I understand you contacted me."

"Yes, thank you for calling back so quickly. Father O'Boyle suggested I speak with you."

"Father O'Boyle is an old friend, although we have not spoken for many years. How is he?"

"I'm afraid he passed away yesterday."

"I'm very sorry to hear that. He was a good man. Had he been ill?"

"Not to my knowledge. I understand it was a heart attack." Tom was anxious to get to the point of his call. "He mentioned that the Vatican is a client of Cordier, Warburg."

"I am retired and don't know much about the bank's business these days. The Vatican does business with many Swiss banks."

"Father O'Boyle mentioned Cordier, Warburg specifically. Apparently, there was one transaction in particular concerning a valuable possession of the Vatican. It occurred some years ago. He said that he made the arrangement with you personally."

Warburg was silent a long time.

"Herr Warburg?"

"I am forbidden by law to discuss any bank business related to specific clients."

"I am aware of that. I can assure you, however, this is a matter of some urgency."

"Dr. Stewart, I'm an old man, seeking to live the rest of his life in peace. I'm no longer actively involved in bank business of any nature, routine or urgent. I'm afraid I can't help you."

"Even if it could jeopardize the lives of hundreds of thousands of people?"

Again, more silence.

"I cannot help you."

"It is complicated and very serious. My own life has been threatened as a result of my connection to O'Boyle and this matter. It's not something I feel comfortable discussing over the telephone. Could I meet with you to explain it more fully?"

Silence again. "I'm agreeable to a meeting," Warburg said at last. "However, I no longer travel. You will need to come to my home in Blonay, a small town outside of Geneva."

"I would be happy to meet with you. When would be convenient?"

Warburg said, "Tomorrow or the next day?"

Tom said, "If I can get a reservation, I could fly to Geneva tomorrow morning."

Warburg replied, "If you let me know what flight you've been able to get on, I'll have my driver pick you up at the terminal and drive you to my home. Is that acceptable?"

"You are very kind. I appreciate your willingness to meet with me on such short notice."

"My driver's name is Hubert. He'll be waiting."

Warburg gave Tom his e-mail address and his telephone number. Then he concluded, "Until tomorrow, Dr. Stewart." He hung up.

Tom quickly called the airline and made a reservation, then e-mailed his flight information to Sigmund. "This might be another dead end," Tom said to Alex.

"You have no choice but to follow it. By the way, we should get going if you're to be prompt for your 4:30 p.m. meeting with Ambassador Wilson at the Vatican."

"You're right," he said. "It's a walk of about fifteen minutes." Alex accompanied him to St. Peter's Square, whose great expanse of space never failed to impress Tom. Several thousand pilgrims from all over the world were making their way into or out of St. Peter's, and they were momentarily in the square itself, yet it seemed empty. Tom walked to the right side of the massive Bernini colonnade, saying goodbye to Alex who was returning home.

Tom stopped at the huge, closed bronze doors at the end of the colonnade. He banged on the doors with his hand, thinking that this might be a fruitless effort. His fists made no discernible sound. No one came. He banged a second time. Still no response. He was about to walk a football field's length away to the main front doors of St. Peter's, but he guessed finding the place inside the church where Wilson had suggested they meet would not be easy.

Then, slowly, one of the huge, twenty-foot doors opened. A Swiss guard appeared and beckoned Tom to enter and follow him. He was dressed in his red, yellow, and blue Renaissance costume, with its white ruffled collars and black beret. Looking to his right and left, Tom saw only other guards in identical costumes. He knew he would never have been allowed in this area if he had entered by the main front doors. He dutifully followed the guard to a large reception desk where other guards as well as several clerics were standing. He gave his and Ambassador Wilson's names to the attendant, who entered the information in a computer in front of him. The attendant asked Tom to wait for Fra Giuseppe.

Within a minute or so, a monk, dressed as if from central casting, appeared at the desk. He had a brown robe with a rope belt, sandals, short-cropped hair, and a kindly look in his eyes. Fra Giuseppe motioned to Tom to follow him, and together they climbed a monumental flight of stairs.

Fra Giuseppe smiled benignly at Tom and said, pointing to the stairs, "Scala Regia." Tom smiled back, acknowledging his having heard the name of the ceremonial stairway pronounced, but he already knew this was the royal entrance.

At a landing on the Scala Regia, Tom passed the marble equestrian statue of the Roman emperor Constantine, a famous statue by Bernini. They went up another flight of stairs and Fra Giuseppe continued, passing the Sala Regia as well as one of the doorways into the Sistine Chapel.

During the Renaissance the arriving kings, queens, or ambassadors were asked to wait in the Sala Regia after making their climb. Here, the popes would detain them long enough to observe the wall paintings, which showed those visitors, obedient to the wishes of the pope, leaving Rome on ships laden with treasure. For those who failed to pay their dues, their boats were on fire and sinking in the harbor. Tom wondered if he'd be asked to wait and whether his boat would be afloat or burning when he left.

On the opposite side of a wide corridor Fra Giuseppe walked Tom into a modest-sized chapel where he made it clear that Tom was to wait. Tom sat in the back of the chapel. Almost immediately, the tall, physically strong figure of Ambassador Wilson strode in, wearing a business suit. "Tom, good afternoon," Wilson said, shaking Tom's hand. The ambassador motioned Tom to sit in one of the pews, and he joined him.

With gusto, since this is what Ambassador Wilson seemed to be full of, he expounded. "Pauline Chapel," he said with a hint of pride. "It's the pope's private chapel. The pope prays here and reads mass to private audiences."

Wilson continued. "On your right, Michelangelo's Crucifixion of Saint Peter, one of the last two frescoes he painted. And, on your left, Michelangelo's Conversion of Saint Paul. This is my favorite part of St. Peter's. Almost no one gets to see this chapel or these two last frescoes. C'mon, let's go. I'm going to take you to our meeting room." With this, Wilson abruptly stood up and led the way out of the chapel, walking briskly down the wide corridor. Tom had to move quickly to keep up with him.

Halfway down the passage, Wilson pointed to the left. "That's the pope's balcony out over St. Peter's Square where he makes his speeches, especially his Easter address, 'From the City to the World.' Here," he added, "let's take a look."

Tom quickly said, "Sure."

Wilson pulled aside the curtains in front of the balcony, opened the door and stood aside. Tom walked out onto the balcony. As he stood, high over St. Peter's Square, he saw that the Bernini colonnade below curved outward, like two arms extended toward Rome, even the world. Tom could see thousands of people in the square below. He could imagine them all looking up to see him. He thought to himself, What a sense of power to stand here. Then he asked Wilson, "How many people does the square hold?"

Wilson replied, "Bernini designed it to hold 400,000 people."

Tom said, "Amazing. Very impressive."

"I thought you'd enjoy it," said Wilson.

The ambassador to the Holy See continued a bit further down the corridor, then stopped at a door that he opened and waved Tom to enter. "I'd like to introduce you to Reverend Monsignor Henrik Svenson, the pope's personal secretary."

Svenson immediately stood up and extended his hand, giving Tom a very firm handshake. Tom looked at Svenson, a Swede, who had a chiseled face and light brown hair and was wearing a crisp white shirt with a clerical collar and a neat black jacket. He had strong blue eyes, which he fixed on Tom's face. The energy in his glance was so strong that Tom thought he could almost feel it.

Tom didn't know much about Svenson, but he had learned from the newspapers that he had become a media personality. While he was noted for his efficiency and analytical mind, Henrik Svenson had gained notoriety in Rome for having the attributes of a star athlete and playboy. He was known as being an avid skier, tennis and soccer player, as well as an amateur pilot.

The three men sat down. Svenson, who seemed very professional in manner, yet friendly as well, said, "Let me get to the point at once. We're fully aware that your life has been difficult, since that event in the Roman Forum."

"Worse than that," Tom said, "it's been downright dangerous."

"Dangerous?" Svenson asked.

Tom decided to expose some of what he had been through. It seemed that this was Svenson's primary reason for requesting the meeting and that maybe the Vatican was involved. "My room was broken into last night and my computer stolen. Two days ago, I was coming back into Rome, and I was nearly driven off the road by a black Fiat sedan with darkened windows. And I've been pursued by two men who claimed I had a supply of something they wanted. Besides these, I've been hounded by the press."

Svenson was no longer smiling. "I'm sorry to hear what's happened. First, we've had nothing to do with any of this. Second, we are as eager as you are to bring a halt to it." Svenson paused and changed the subject. "We know you met with Father O'Boyle two nights ago. Have you learned that he died last evening?"

Tom, surprised by the reference to O'Boyle, said, "I heard the news earlier today."

Svenson proceeded. "O'Boyle had a top secret assignment, working for a powerful cardinal during the Second World War, an assignment that went disastrously wrong. We're now aware—due to the deaths in the Roman Forum—that a supply of a dangerous virus is 'out there' somewhere. Our assumption is that there is a group that will move heaven and earth to get hold of it.

"Your presence at the Roman Forum puts you in the middle of the hunt. Digging up the past serves no one, which is why I asked Ambassador Wilson to set up a meeting with you. We don't know who has been after you, but what's happened to you tells us that whoever it is is deadly serious. The virus must be found and destroyed before it falls into the wrong hands."

"Why is this virus so important to you?" asked Tom.

"The cardinal I mentioned was acting outside his authority. But, one way or the other, if the virus were used—and people died—the trail would lead back to us."

Tom said, "Second World War. The pope then was Pius XII. His canonization process is under way now, isn't it? And it's in trouble because of those who are against his being declared a saint?"

Svenson's face reddened. He said nothing.

Tom continued, "I understand the virus is ferociously dangerous. Did the Church play a role in creating it?"

Wilson was silent, as if frozen. Svenson continued to say nothing. Tom realized how difficult this was for Svenson. He also realized that he was pressing his point against Svenson, releasing years of his own irritation at the hypocrisy of the Vatican.

Finally, Svenson spoke. "We want this virus destroyed. Obliterated. No repercussions. You are believed to know how to find it. You need help? Get hold of the ambassador." Svenson looked directly at Wilson.

"I understand," Tom said with some annoyance. "I'm supposed to 'clean up' after some rogue cardinal who created a devastating virus. You'll deny my existence and expect me to take all the risk. Is that it?"

Surprised by Tom's bluntness, Svenson's own demeanor turned tough. "It's supremely easy for critics to throw stones at the Church for decisions made in good faith long ago. When the world watched, expecting that Hitler would attack the Vatican, murder innocent people, destroy Saint Peter's, and plunder Christian treasures, who would fault a program to defend the Church? No one, I say. This is what happened. Our mission now is keep this program from public exposure, and we will do whatever it takes. We had nothing to do with the incident at the Roman Forum, and we, unlike you, were not present."

Tom realized arguing with Svenson was getting nowhere. He decided to move on. He stood and held out his hand to Svenson.

Svenson stood up, shook Tom's hand firmly and, with Wilson, walked Tom to the door, where Fra Giuseppe was patiently waiting. Giuseppe smiled pleasantly. Understanding no English, he beckoned to Tom to follow him and started walking toward the Sistine Chapel where Tom joined the exiting visitors and quickly found himself in St. Peter's Square. It was 5:30 p.m., and Tom thought as he left how different his experience had been compared to the thousands of tourists. As he walked among them, he could see them sharing their experiences of St. Peter's Basilica, the center of the worldwide Catholic Church.

He had seen parts of the Vatican others would never see. He concluded that the meeting was to impress him, threaten him, and give him notice that the Church would fight to keep completely separate anything to do with from the Moses Virus. Thinking back to the Sala Regia, he guessed his boat was on fire and sinking in the harbor.

Before he left St. Peter's Square, Tom turned and looked up at the pope's balcony. He couldn't be sure, but he thought he saw a person in a white robe standing on the balcony looking down, perhaps at him. But Tom wasn't sure at all.

Tom hailed a cab near St. Peter's Square, giving as his destination the address to Alex's house. He didn't notice that as the cab moved off toward Campo dè Fiori, a black Fiat sedan followed him a few cars behind. The Fiat ducked in and out of traffic, in rhythm with the movement of Tom's cab. But Tom was preoccupied and not aware that he was being watched. He called Alex, who was on her way back to her house, to tell her of the meeting with Henrik Svenson and Ambassador Wilson as well as his visit to the Pauline Chapel.

Alex was quick to recognize Svenson's name. "I'm interested," she said, "in your having met the poster boy of the Catholic Church. Do you know he's nicknamed by the Italian press as 'Handsome Henrik'? Donatella Versace was so taken by him and his 'elegant austerity' that she made a line of men's clothing featuring clerical collar–style black jackets. He's been with the present pope as his private secretary for a good many years longer than the current pope has been in office."

"Are you admitting you read American trash magazines?" Tom said. "How else would you pick up this stuff about Svenson?"

"You obviously don't read Italian newspapers and magazines. Everyone knows about Svenson." She laughed.

Tom told Alex about the tough lecture and warning Svenson had delivered.

Alex said, "The Church has survived for two thousand years. It is the world's toughest bureaucracy. They won't help you. But they will come after you if they think you're a danger to them. Do you remember the statue of Giordano Bruno in the center of Campo dè Fiori? The Church had Bruno's mouth nailed shut to keep him quiet. I hope they don't do that to you!" she joked.

"I know you're kidding, but my meeting with Svenson confirms my own suspicion," said Tom. "I've added the Catholic Church as one more group to watch out for."

As Alex passed through the Campo dè Fiori, she noticed that the tempo of activity had slowed, but not stopped. She spotted the somber statue of Bruno, and her conversation with Tom repeated itself in her mind. It was early evening, and the temperature had cooled. Those in the Campo dè Fiori seemed happy to be there with no cares in the world. But this was certainly not the case for Tom, who had this horrific event settle on his shoulders. She mulled this over as she turned the corner and entered the courtyard in front of the entrance to her house. No one was in the courtyard, but when she placed her key in the lock, she suddenly realized that it was unlocked.

Alex stopped. Enough had happened in the last few days to make her suspicious. She reassured herself, thinking, "Ana simply forgot to lock up when she left." Half believing this, Alex opened the door. The kitchen was a mess, drawers pulled out, contents spilled. Then she saw something on the floor, across the room, partly obscured by a table.

Alex felt her heart throbbing throughout her body. Terror was rising within her. "What's happened?" she said. She walked toward the table. As she drew closer, she realized that her housekeeper was lying behind the table, unconscious. Alex rushed to her, knelt down, and felt her throat to see if she had a pulse. There was a pulse, but it was weak.

Alex remained in possession of her senses. Stay calm, she counseled herself. Call for help. She telephoned the Rome emergency number. After she explained that her housekeeper was unconscious, she was told that someone would be there in five minutes.

She telephoned Tom, whose line was busy. Alex suddenly felt abandoned and alone. She thought she should search the rest of her house, but decided to stay put so she could be on hand when help arrived.

Almost immediately, her cell phone rang. Tom was cheerful. "Alex, did you just call?"

"Someone's broken in, searched through my belongings, done something terrible to my housekeeper."

"Is she okay? Ana, that's her name, isn't it?" Tom's voice turned from one of good cheer to serious concern.

"Yes, it's Ana. I'm not sure," Alex said, "her breathing is shallow."

Ana stirred, making a faint cry, then went totally silent. Alex said to Tom, "I'll put you on hold. Something's happened." Ana had become deathly still and very pale. "Tom," Alex cried, "she may be dead. Now what do I do?"

"Push down on her chest, then relax, then push and relax, in the same rhythm as breathing. That may help her breathe. I should be there is less than ten minutes."

Very quickly, paramedics appeared at Alex's front door. She let them in, telling them what little she knew. They administered oxygen to Ana and gave her a shot of adrenaline to her heart. Nothing happened. But, in thirty seconds, which seemed like an eternity, Ana's body shuddered, and she began to breathe.

The paramedics lifted Ana onto a stretcher they had brought with them, then stood up and hurriedly told Alex they were taking Ana to the hospital. She—Alex—needed to stay to talk to the carabinieri who had been called by the paramedics.

"Are you comfortable staying here? You're alone?" asked the senior paramedic.

"A friend is on his way over. He should be here momentarily."

"I'll have one of my men remain with you until your friend or the carabinieri arrive."

"Where are you taking Ana?" Alex asked.

"San Giovanni—it's the nearest hospital with a major emergency facility."

Tom arrived, running from the taxi on the street into the courtyard to Alex's house. Alex opened the door for him, and Tom grabbed Alex in an embrace. Alex pulled herself together. "I'm frightened for Ana's life—she hasn't done anything to deserve this. It must have something to do with whoever has been coming after you."

Tom said, "I'm so sorry." Then he repeated himself.

Two officers of the Carabinieri showed up. They were sympathetic with Alex's condition, but they were insistent on learning what had happened. Alex told them what she knew. The carabinieri went upstairs to the upper part of Alex's house. They came down again in a few minutes saying, "There're signs of an intensive search, but no one is now in your house. We may find clues so it's important we investigate for evidence. Could you come up with us?" one of them said to Alex. "We'd like to have you help us find out what's missing."

Alex agreed and went upstairs. Tom remained in the kitchen. While Alex was upstairs, Tom's cell phone rang. Tom looked at it and recognized that Dr. Pulesi was calling.

"Tom," Pulesi began, "I understand that Signora Cellini's house has been broken into."

"How in the world do you know this?" Tom asked with disquiet in his voice. "Oh, yes, I remember. You've been keeping tabs on us. Is there anyone else watching?"

"It's likely. As you know, I'm keeping the U.S. Centers for Disease Control informed."

"I remember."

Pulesi went on. "This situation is getting out of control. Your apartment was broken into, then Signora Cellini's, and now her housekeeper's been attacked. I wanted you to know you can call me at any time. And I decided you'd better know we're still watching what happens to you. The CDC is keenly interested and ready to help if you need it."

Tom said, "Alex is coming downstairs, and I should get off the telephone."

"Understood," replied Pulesi. "Goodbye."

Alex reentered the kitchen. "I can't discover anything that was taken. It's a mystery to me."

Alex and Tom remained in her kitchen while the carabinieri finished up. Tom poured Alex and himself a glass of wine. He offered wine to the carabinieri, but they declined.

Alex gradually began to relax, shuddering from head to toe once or twice. To Tom she said, "I was panicked. I tried to contact you, but I couldn't get through."

Tom replied, "I was on my cell phone. Sorry I wasn't there for you."

"It's not your fault," Alex said. Then she added, "By the way, were you just on your cell phone? I thought I heard you talking when I was coming down the stairs."

"I received a call from Pulesi."

"Really? Isn't that odd?"

"He said that he'd heard about the break-in and wanted to help if he could," replied Tom.

"Wait a minute," said Alex. "Just how did they know about the break-in?"

"It was a surprise to me," Tom replied. "But, now it's obvious that Pulesi's group is watching our every move."

"I don't know whether to be angry or reassured," Alex replied.

"A little of both, I guess," Tom said.

The carabinieri told Alex and Tom that they'd leave an official car with two officers stationed on the street outside Alex's house for the night.

After the carabinieri left, Tom asked, "What's troubling you?"

Alex said, "It's bewildering. I'm a part of the American Academy team on a simple, straightforward summer excavation in the Roman Forum. A totally innocent bystander. Something devastating happens that I have nothing to do with. Nothing. Nor do you. Suddenly, you're pursued, hounded. Then I become pursued. What angers me is that Ana is attacked and hurt. I don't even know if she's going to be okay."

"Why don't I call the hospital to see what her condition is?" Tom asked.

"I'd love it, but I'd better do that. Your Italian is good, but I think I'll have a better chance to get through whatever accent the person on the other end of the line has."

It took half an hour of waiting for one person after another for Alex to find out that Ana's condition was stable. She had been knocked unconscious but was making a quick recovery. She would be able to leave San Giovanni the next day.

Tom responded, "I'm so glad that there's no serious harm to her."

"Tom," Alex said, astonished, "Do you think they would have killed her?"

Tom said, "Somebody wants the Moses Virus and will let nothing get in their way. Father O'Boyle died after I met with him—he knew where the Moses Virus was hidden, but wouldn't tell anyone, not even me. The official cause of his death is heart attack. I'm not sure I buy that. If someone did kill O'Boyle, they still don't have the virus, which may be why they came after us."

Her demeanor began to change. Alex was growing angry. "This has gone too far."

"The Vatican refuses to become involved, but they are. They know about the meeting I had with O'Boyle."

"How could they have known that?" Alex asked.

"I don't know. But O'Boyle's death certainly is suspicious."

Alex was quiet for a moment. "Tom, Pulesi's call—you didn't alert him? How did he find out about the break-in?"

"By tapping our telephones, I believe. Disconcerting, isn't it?"

Alex blurted out, "That means Pulesi—and therefore the Italian authorities—have us under surveillance. They aren't admitting anything, but they know more than I realized." Alex went on. "Tom, the break-in to your apartment and mine. The attack on Ana. I assume they're all connected?"

"I think so."

"Do you know who would do this?" Alex asked. "I know we've talked about Belagri. Others?"

Tom said, "I thought the Vatican might be involved, but I think they're trying to stay as far away from this as they can. I believe Belagri is definitely involved."

"Doesn't surprise me," Alex commented. "Anyone else?"

"I don't know," Tom said. "I don't think so, but I'm not sure."

Alex was silent, thinking things over. Then she said, "Until we find the Moses Virus, we're not safe."

Tom replied, "You're right."

Tom left Alex's house the next morning to pick up some crois-
sants and a copy of the *International Herald Tribune*. As he
walked back to Via del Pellegrino, Tom scanned the paper for stories on the Roman Forum. None, and that's just fine, he thought.
There was, however, a short obituary on Father O'Boyle. Lauda-
tory, Tom said to himself, and uninformed on some important
aspects of his life that are better left unreported. Also, the gaps in
the obituary—that was evidence of the long arm of the Vatican
when it wanted to use its power.

After breakfast, Tom was about to leave Alex's place to return
to his room near the Temple of Minerva to get ready for his trip
to Geneva. But, before he left, his cell phone beeped. Caroline was
texting him. "O'Boyle's memorial service at 11 a.m. today at San
Clemente. He's been cremated and his ashes will be placed in a vault
near the Temple of Mithras."

Tom replied, "Can't go. I'll be out of town. Tell Lucia I'm not
fleeing the country, in case any reporters call."

Caroline texted, "Always the joker, aren't you. Talk to you when
you're back. Ciao." On his way to the airport in a taxi, Tom realized
that he shouldn't go to O'Boyle's service even if he were around.
His appearance would surely draw attention to his connection with
O'Boyle.

Tom arrived in Geneva about 12:30 p.m., a few minutes ahead of schedule. With no baggage, he made it through the airport customs quickly. When he got to the baggage area, he noticed a man holding a sign that spelled out the name of Warburg's driver: HUBERT. Strange, Tom thought. Usually drivers held a sign with the name of the company or party to be picked up. Discretion at all cost, I suppose.

Tom walked up to the man and introduced himself. Hubert was embarrassed that it was Tom who had spotted him and not the other way around. He told Tom he'd go to the parking lot to pick up the car and, rather than wait, Tom tagged along behind Hubert to the limo parking area where a spotless black Mercedes was waiting. The driver opened the back door. Tom climbed in, and, within seconds, they were headed out of the airport.

Almost immediately, the driver's cell phone rang. "Yes, sir, the plane was on time," he said in German. "I have picked Dr. Stewart up. Everything's fine. We should be there in about an hour."

When they reached the eastern end of Lake Geneva, the road they were taking began to climb, and the traffic thinned out. They were headed up the hills, through the terraced vineyards. Homes were discreetly set back into the hills but designed to maximize the views of the lake. Tom had much to think about, and the hour passed swiftly.

Around a bend in the road, quite far above Lake Geneva, the driver turned into a long driveway that curved around tall, perfectly manicured hedges. At the far end, there was a stone mansion surrounded by a large lawn sloping down to vineyards. The Warburg house was a two-story stone building that easily dated back to the mid-1800s. There was a slate roof, and ivy clung to most of the walls. As soon as Hubert brought the car to a stop at the entrance, a large polished wooden door opened and a man neatly dressed in a white jacket emerged and walked down the steps. He opened the car door and introduced himself as Julian. Tom followed him into the front hall, then into the living room and through doors that opened onto a large outdoor veranda overlooking the lake. An older, well-dressed man was sitting, studying Tom's arrival.

Julian announced Tom to Sigmund Warburg, who immediately stood to shake Tom's hand. Sigmund was short, thin, and in his late eighties, or even his nineties. He had most of his hair, a mix of gray and black. His eyes were dark but fixed intently on Tom, who surmised that Sigmund missed nothing. He seemed full of energy.

"Herr Warburg," Tom said, extending his hand.

Warburg shook it firmly. "I trust you had a good flight," he said, smiling. "The weather today is so beautiful." He waved at the mountains in the background: "Please allow me to introduce you to my favorite spot on earth. Such magnificent views of the hills, mountains, and the lake below. Now that I'm retired I enjoy living here full-time in this modest place."

"It is beautiful, Herr Warburg," Tom said.

Warburg touched Tom on the shoulder and said in a friendly manner, "Please call me Sigmund. May I call you Tom?"

"Please do, Sigmund," Tom replied. "The views of the lake and mountains are breathtaking. And you must enjoy looking at them from your swimming pool."

"Oh, the pool," said Warburg, glancing down at a long lap pool below the veranda. "That was my wife Eva's idea. She swam any day the weather permitted. Oddly enough, I haven't been in it since she died. My own passion is literature—books I never had the time to read."

"Have you lived here long?" Tom asked.

"I had the opportunity to purchase this property years ago, but I never enjoyed it until I retired. I was involved with my bank, I didn't realize just how restful this place can be. Eva was so fond of Blonay, and she was always trying to get me to spend more time here. She was right. I'm sad to say that she's been gone for several years, and I'm alone in enjoying it now."

"I'm sorry to hear that."

"You must be hungry," Warburg said. "I've had Julian prepare some lunch; if you don't mind, let's eat outside, here in the sunshine."

Lunch had already been placed on a table covered by a white cloth on the veranda. Warburg invited Tom to sit. Julian immediately stepped forward with a pitcher of iced water, which he poured into Tom's and then Sigmund's glasses. Next he came around with a bottle of chilled white wine. Warburg was a gracious host, inquiring about Tom's work, his role as trustee at the American Academy, and his time in Rome. It was obvious that he had done his homework. Julian served a lunch of cold trout, garden salad, and crisp, warm baguettes. Once the dishes were cleared and the coffee served, Warburg inquired about the purpose of their meeting.

"Now, perhaps you can explain a bit more about this urgent matter you mentioned on the telephone."

Tom started with the events at the Roman Forum, the mystery of the modern lab found during the excavation, and his subsequent contact with O'Boyle. Warburg listened with great interest.

"The Italian authorities have admitted to me there was an extremely dangerous virus that caused the two deaths. According to O'Boyle, there is a supply of the virus that a number of international parties are after. I've been questioned by the authorities, harassed by the press, and pursued by unknown parties who seem to be after the virus."

"Tom, I don't understand how I may be of assistance."

"The item your bank agreed to store for Pope Pius XII after his death—I got this from O'Boyle—is a supply of virus developed by Vatican scientists during the Second World War. It is an immensely powerful, dangerous substance. The supply was kept secret from the pope who had ordered it destroyed. O'Boyle was involved in hiding it, but traces of it, which killed the American Academy archaeologists, frightened O'Boyle, who sought me out. Before his death, he gave me your name, urged me to contact you to obtain the virus and destroy it completely before it falls into unfriendly hands."

Warburg recoiled, visibly shaken, at this disclosure of Tom's. "I am speechless. I had no idea of the gravity of this matter. I did a favor for an old friend. But I know nothing of what you speak nor anything about what was given to me."

"Sigmund," Tom quickly said, "I believe what O'Boyle told me is true, just as I believe what you're saying is true. None of this lessens the dilemma I'm in."

Sigmund calmed himself. "If you will indulge an old man, I'd like to give you some background about my relationship with the bank and with the Vatican. Perhaps it will provide some illumination."

"As they say in America, 'You have my attention,'" Tom said and smiled.

"I come from a long line of German bankers and farmers," Sigmund said. "In each generation, the eldest son would inherit the family farm in a small town outside of Munich, and any other sons would be bankers. My great nephew is in charge of my family's farm today. I was the youngest in my family. My oldest bother took over the farm and so, barely twenty and newly married, I joined a bank in the 1930s in Berlin. It was in the middle of the Great Depression, and Germany—as with most of the world—was in financial and political chaos. Fear was everywhere, from out-of-control inflation to hysteria about communism taking over Europe. In this environment, Hitler became chancellor in January 1933.

"Rumors soon surfaced about actions taken against prominent Jewish businessmen, many of whom were my clients and colleagues. It concerned me, and I asked a family friend, Hitler's secretary of state, who owed me a favor, to look into it. Informally of course. He did investigate and later confided to me that Hitler was in fact disenfranchising the professional Jewish class. They were stripped of their possessions and positions, and were just disappearing. And he also said he and I were unwise to be seen together again. The secretary of state's family had a farm next to ours. I could see fear in his eyes.

"After this conversation, I realized I could be in personal jeopardy from Nazi policies. Right then and there, I decided that my wife and I must leave Germany—as soon as possible, no matter what the consequences. I hurried home and explained the situation to Eva. At first she thought I was exaggerating, but after I explained what was happening to several important people we knew, she agreed. Over the next few days, she had all our belongings packed. I resigned from the bank, citing family problems, withdrew our savings. Switzerland seemed to be the best place to go due to its neutrality and large banking community. We were on the train to Geneva before the end of the month.

"When we arrived in Geneva, we settled in a flat outside the city. Through a friend, I contacted a small private bank called Cordier et Cie and secured a position there. I worked hard, but being German, I was at a disadvantage. The Swiss banking community is very close knit, you see."

"Yet you became a majority partner in the bank," Tom said.

"Yes, eventually, but I had help."

"From the Vatican?"

"Precisely. Before I left Germany, I had made the acquaintance of the cardinal secretary of state, Eugenio Pacelli. He represented the Vatican to the German government. In his dealings for the Vatican with Hitler, there were some very sensitive issues, and he from time to time, discreetly asked my opinion. Naturally, I gave him my judgment.

"We remained in cordial, though less frequent contact after I moved to Switzerland. Then he became pope in 1939."

Tom asked, "I gather that the pope didn't trust Hitler. Is this true?"

"It didn't start out that way," Sigmund replied. "Pacelli had a large ego and thought he could outsmart Hitler, but this expectation was very short lived.

"To consolidate his power, Hitler acted to weaken the Catholic party's influence in Germany. Cardinal Pacelli negotiated a pact with Hitler, called a concordat, in which Hitler agreed to permit the Vatican to regain control of the appointment of German bishops—something the pope and Pacelli desperately wanted—in exchange for the Vatican's promise not to involve itself henceforth in any domestic German political matters."

"A pact with the devil?" Tom asked.

"As it turns out, yes. Hitler reneged on his promise to the Vatican. Then, after Hitler's armies invaded Poland, another stronghold of the Catholic faith, and it looked like Germany might not stop until it controlled Europe, the Vatican realized that it had made a terrible mistake in its dealings with Hitler. My friend Pacelli, now pope, ordered all the Vatican assets in German banks to be transferred to Switzerland. He instructed his envoy to contact me, and we, at Cordier, were most generously favored. Needless to say, our large new account was very helpful in my being made a partner. That envoy whom the pope sent—cut from the same cloth as Pacelli—was Cardinal Visconti, an intensely ambitious man.

"Go forward in time to the pope's death in 1958, and then a further three years—I was visited by Visconti's former assistant, a young Irish priest, whom I'd met several times—your Father O'Boyle. He gave me a letter from Visconti with an unusual request."

"O'Boyle."

"Yes. He told me that Visconti, on his deathbed, had requested him to carry out one of Pius XII's last wishes, which was to safeguard an important Vatican treasure. Since Visconti could no longer perform the pope's directive, Visconti asked O'Boyle to contact me. I found this request by the pope to be strange, as the Vatican has some of the most secure vaults in the world to keep its valuable objects. I asked O'Boyle what the item was, but he said that the nature of the item must be kept secret from all outside parties. Swiss banking law would ensure this, of course. The Vatican still had a substantial account at Cordier, Warburg, so I agreed to accommodate O'Boyle.

"The next day, O'Boyle arrived at my office in Geneva with a small leather suitcase. I arranged for a highly safe and secure place for this package, but—I swear to you—I had no idea or even suspicion of what was in the leather suitcase. This all happened years ago, and I had completely forgotten about it until you contacted me."

"I believe you. Will you help me retrieve it?"

Warburg grimaced. "Only the holder of the lockbox key can gain entrance. It is against the Swiss banking laws for me to give you or anyone else access to the package on any basis. One would have to obtain permission from the source."

"You mean the Vatican?" Tom asked. "That is highly unlikely. The current pope and his staff wish to have nothing to do with this cache. Visconti destroyed all records before his death. He charged O'Boyle with contacting you. Now O'Boyle's dead.

"My problem is this: Other groups know of this powerful biological weapon. And they know I was present when the two American archaeologists were killed. I've been tracked down and threatened. I believe Father O'Boyle may have been tortured and then killed. I'm at risk. Many people's lives are at stake if the weapon falls into the wrong hands. I appeal to you. Please help me."

"Even if I were still active in the bank's activities, I couldn't violate the Swiss secrecy laws."

"Sigmund, surely this situation trumps the existing laws. Please reconsider."

At this point Sigmund seemed to want the afternoon conversation to come to an end. He stood and extended his hand. "I'm afraid I cannot. I'm grateful to you for coming to Blonay, and I hope you'll succeed in your quest. I'll have Hubert drive you back to the airport."

Warburg showed Tom out. Hubert was in the driveway, standing by the Mercedes, the door already open. Tom looked out the back window of the car as they drove away. He saw Warburg wave briefly, then turn and walk slowly back into his house.

13

As Hubert drove, Tom sat in silence, thinking. He was disappointed by the abrupt end to his conversation with Sigmund. Could he somehow have presented his case with a greater sense of urgency? Maybe, he told himself. He understood the ironclad nature of Swiss banking secrecy laws, but was there no exception to this, especially when the stakes were so high that a huge loss of human lives could occur? What could he do now? The Moses Virus was still locked away, somewhere, and Belagri—and perhaps others—were intent on possessing it. And they believed that he, Tom, knew where the supply was.

Maybe he should seek Pulesi's help, as Alex suggested. The first step would be to call Alex, he concluded. Tom was grateful for her very presence as well as her advice, but when he thought about Alex, he also worried that she was being drawn deeper into the danger he was already in. He felt trapped. Nevertheless, Tom called her the moment Hubert dropped him at the Geneva airport. His plane was due in Rome around 9:30 p.m. Tom suggested they meet at his apartment at the hotel, recommending that she change cabs twice to get there.

"But I thought this is not a spy thriller," she said, a bit playfully.

"I'm not taking any chances. Someone may be watching you."

Around 10:30 p.m., when Alex asked for "John Jones," Tom's alias, at the front desk, she was told that Mr. Jones had left a message for her to meet him in the small café restaurant around the corner of the building.

Tom stood as Alex approached. They hugged.

"Thanks for joining me. I've ordered some wine."

She looked around. "I haven't been to this café since Antonia opened it. It's very attractive."

"Yes, and so informal that there's no printed menu. There's a blackboard with what's currently available. The special today is sea bass."

"Fine with me."

The waiter approached, and they ordered.

"How was Switzerland?" Alex asked.

"Interesting but frustrating." Tom related his meeting with Warburg. "The man knows more than he lets on, but says he can't help. He's a retired banker but still bound by the Swiss banking laws."

Alex frowned. "Old men and their rules. What will you do now?"

"I'm not sure. I'll wait a day and contact him again. Maybe he'll change his mind."

"What about Pulesi? If you get him involved, he might use the weight of the Italian government to force the issue with the Swiss."

"I've debated that and wanted to discuss this with you. I trust Pulesi but not the rest of the Italian government. It's risky. There has to be another way to convince Warburg."

The food came, and they ate as they talked.

"How do you like your new place? I know Antonia has a great eye for decoration."

"Over the top—I really do like it."

Alex smiled.

Tom said, "I found a supermarket nearby, and a few doors further there's the best gelato store I've seen in Rome. My fridge now has two large containers of ice cream—double chocolate and butter crunch."

Alex laughed and said, "Bring it on."

He called for the check, and they made their way up to his apartment.

The next morning, Alex had to leave before breakfast for a morning meeting with her dissertation advisor.

"One cup of coffee," Tom teased. He didn't want her to go quite yet.

Alex kissed him. "Sorry, though I love being in this Roman ruin, I have to get back home to change. Besides, Ana will be worried."

"Oh," said Tom, "I've been so preoccupied with my own problems, I forgot to ask you: Is Ana okay?"

"Shaken up, but she seems to have had a complete recovery. Oddly enough, she was so frightened by her attackers that she has no memory of the person or persons who came after her. The hospital released her and told her to resume her normal schedule. Okay, I'm off. I'll call you later then."

He took her hand, "And thanks."

"The pleasure was mine. Ciao, caro."

Tom ate alone, put his breakfast dishes in the dishwasher, and made another pot of strong coffee. Then he sat at the desk in the living room and turned his new computer on. He enjoyed the peace and quiet of the apartment and was thrilled to be doing nothing more than editing one of the chapters of his book. The day vanished. He broke for a quick lunch—a couple of slices of pizza, which he picked up from a local pizzeria across from the café. He returned to editing.

Late that afternoon, Tom stood up and stretched. He'd spent all day working on his book and was making considerable progress. The new laptop made the work much easier. Now that he was sequestered in a safe place, neither the media nor the stalkers would bother him.

He was just about to take a break at the café for a coffee when his phone rang. "Signore Stewart, this is Lucia. A special messenger dropped off a package for you—it has your name on it, but no other markings. The messenger said to tell you his name was Hubert."

Tom couldn't believe that Sigmund had relented. "Thank you, Lucia. I can be at the Academy in twenty minutes. I'll come directly to your office." Tom felt a rising sense of excitement. Perhaps he'd been more persuasive than he realized with Warburg. With luck the package might contain the information he needed to find the Moses Virus.

"Could you arrange to let me in the side entrance of the Academy? I don't want to be too conspicuous."

"Certainly, Signore. Just ring at that entrance. I'll have Fabio looking out for you. He'll buzz you in and have the package with him."

"Thanks." Twenty minutes later, when Tom arrived at the Academy, he instructed the cab driver to turn left before Via Angelo Masina, avoiding the front gate, and following the street around to the side entrance. Tom was buzzed in at the side gate—he presumed by Fabio. He entered the Academy grounds near the Casa Rustica and headed toward a rarely used door in the main building. Before he had a chance to ring, Fabio opened the door and handed him the package. Tom looked around to see if anyone was watching.

In broken English, Fabio invited Tom in. In the safety of the vestibule leading down to the cryptoporticus, Tom undid the outer envelope of the package, revealing a small box about the size of a paperback novel, wrapped in tan paper, unmarked, except for Tom's name. The box was carefully sealed. Inside there was an envelope containing a sheet of note paper with Sigmund Warburg's name printed at the top, and a brief typewritten message: "To Mr. Pierre Villechaise, Managing Director, Cordier, Warburg & Cie., 16, Rue de Hollande, Geneva. Please extend every courtesy to the bearer of this letter. Thank you." It was signed simply, "S. Warburg." There was also a key in the envelope with Sigmund's note.

Tom knew what this meant. Warburg had seen the urgency of the situation and allowed him to pick up the trail to the Moses Virus.

He called Sigmund's telephone number and let the phone ring for a dozen times. No answer. Tom decided he'd call again later.

This package was too important for Tom to carry back to his room. He'd been lucky so far to avoid being followed. He needed a secure place to keep the letter and key until he figured out his next move.

Fabio, who had stood aside while Tom opened the package, now asked, "Do you need anything, Signore?" in Italian. Tom was struck by a thought: The hidden room in the aqueduct would be the perfect place.

"No, thanks, Fabio. But I do need to see Lucia."

It was only a few steps from the side entrance to Lucia's office on the main floor, and, once there, Tom said, "Lucia, I've decided I need to revisit the aqueduct for a few minutes. May I borrow a flashlight? Also, I'm going to walk in the aqueduct down the Janiculum Hill to its end. I assume that's okay?"

"If you want to do this, be our guest. Do you need any help, however? Someone to come with you? I'll be glad to ask Fabio . . ."

"No, thanks," Tom replied. "I'll be fine. If the aqueduct's blocked, I'll just come back."

Lucia gave him a flashlight, and Tom headed back into the main hallway. No one was in the large stairway leading down to the cryptoporticus, nor was anyone around when Tom reached the stone cover over the entrance. When Tom lifted the cover, at first it didn't budge. But he tried a second time, and with a little effort, he found that it lifted enough for him to slide it aside.

Tom descended the ladder far enough to reach up and pull the cover back onto its normal position. Then he turned on the flashlight and continued downward to the floor of the aqueduct.

He found his way to the secret room, entered it, and deposited the package and the key in the small concealed alcove in the far wall. He slid the panel back over the opening, closed the door of the room, and stood for a few seconds in the aqueduct.

He realized he could return to the Academy, but the more he thought about it, the more the idea of leaving at the exit of the aqueduct down the Janiculum Hill appealed to him. If he took this route, he'd know that this was the way he could use to retrieve the key and letter without involving the Academy. It also could be done anonymously, so that no one would know of his coming or going.

Tom started walking in the ancient waterway. The pitch of the entire passage was sharply downward, but not so precipitous that he couldn't handle it. About a hundred yards down the Janiculum, he saw the remnants of the debris that had been moved to the side to keep the water from pooling. He thought to himself that he must be directly under the Norwegian Academy, whose construction project had led to the invasion by the mosquitoes at the American Academy.

Further along, he thought he heard something. Rustling. Scratching. "Rats, again," Tom said to himself. He shined his flashlight down the pathway. The light from the strong beam caught the reflections of dozens of small beady eyes belonging to the inhabitants of the aqueduct. Once again they scurried away, anxious to avoid him. He dropped his flashlight's beam to the path immediately in front of him and continued on his downward trek.

The remainder of the underground passageway proceeded without further incident. He knew from his walk aboveground when he was searching for where the aqueduct led, that the entire trip should only take about fifteen minutes. Sure enough, the aqueduct came to an end as he expected. He was confronted with a door that blocked his way. He pushed on it, knowing already that it wasn't locked. The door opened into the modest room that he had come across only three days ago.

Tom closed the door and emerged into the alley at the back of Piazza Trilussa. The experience had not been unpleasant, he realized, once he'd grown used to the heat, the stale air, and the downward pitch. It was mostly a matter of knowing what to expect that eased the apprehension of being in the aqueduct. Once in the fresh air of Trastevere, however, and hearing the bustle of Romans walking on the street in the midst of their routine tasks, seeing the open-air restaurants situated around the piazza—Tom admitted it was joyous to see Rome alive and well. He wondered at his reaction, and guessed that his elation might be the knowledge that the key and letter in their secure hiding place might mean he was nearing the end of his ghastly experience with the Moses Virus.

Tom hailed a cab. He looked around as the taxi drove away to make sure he wasn't being followed.

Once he was back in his room, he tried again to reach Sigmund but the telephone just kept ringing and ringing. Why didn't Julian pick up as he did before? This was not good, he thought. Tom recalled what had happened to Father O'Boyle after he had met with him. What if something similar had happened to Warburg? Tom called Alex. "There are new developments. Can we meet later?"

"What happened?"

"I'll explain at dinner. Helpful developments, though. Do you have a preference for where we eat?"

Alex said, "I'll meet you wherever's convenient. But, I'd planned to visit the Canova exhibition at the Galleria Borghese. It's ending today. I can't get there much before its closing time."

"When is that?" Tom asked.

"Eight," Alex replied.

"Okay," said Tom, "eight it is. I'll make a reservation at La Terrasse, the restaurant on the seventh floor of the Villa Borghese Hotel. It's very near the Galleria Borghese. If I can make it, I'll join you at the gallery beforehand."

"See you at 8 p.m.," she said and hung up.

Tom returned to working on his manuscript. Totally absorbed in his book, he was feeling good about the changes he had made when he suddenly realized it was 7:30 p.m., and he would surely miss the Canova exhibition, and might even be late for his date with Alex. He left her a text message that he'd probably not be able to get to the museum, but would see her at the restaurant. Tom took the elevator downstairs where he asked the clerk at the front desk to call a cab for him. He waited in the lobby for a longer time than he liked. When the taxi pulled up, he quickly climbed in and gave the Villa Borghese Hotel's address to the driver. Two men in a dark blue Mercedes were waiting a few doors down and watched intently as Tom left his hotel. They followed the cab.

Tom didn't realize this, but his careful efforts to disguise his whereabouts had proven inadequate. The dark blue Mercedes that had followed him from St. Peter's Square to Alex's house two nights earlier had led the two men to Alex's house, and the next morning the car followed Tom to the Rome airport. His trip to Geneva was noted and an agent in Geneva waited for Tom's arrival and followed him to Blonay. The team had both Tom and Alex in their focus, discreetly staying out of sight in the shadows. Waiting. Waiting for further instructions.

A few minutes after 8 p.m., Tom's cab pulled up across the street from the hotel. He paid, then got out of his taxi. He looked around. The street was quiet, only a couple of cars. He didn't see anyone near the hotel entrance.

Suddenly, Tom felt a piece of steel poke into his back and heard a voice, with a German accent, tell him to get into the dark blue Mercedes, which pulled up quickly in front of them. The German with the gun opened the back door of the car and signaled for Tom to get in.

"What's going on?" Tom demanded to know.

"Schnell!" The German with the gun pushed the gun into his ribs. Tom got in, the gunman followed him into the backseat, and the car took off.

"Who the hell are you?" Tom demanded.

Silence.

The man with the gun sitting next to him took white cloth and a small bottle out of his pocket. A sweet smell filled the car. Quickly he put the moist cloth over Tom's mouth and nose. Tom struggled, but it was too late, and he passed out.

Tom eventually regained consciousness, though he felt drugged and his ribs were sore. Where was he? How long had he been out? The world seemed to drift in and out of focus as he struggled to stay awake. He realized that he was on a plane when he felt it touch down and roll to a stop and heard the engines shut down. His captors had bound his hands and now they pulled him up roughly, walking him brusquely down the stairs to the ground and pushed him into a waiting black Mercedes.

As the car took off, Tom saw a large sign for Frankfurt International Airport.

"Where are you taking me?" Tom asked, trying to remain conscious.

"To the country," one of the men said.

What seemed like hours later, the car drove through a large dark forest and pulled up to a tall black iron fence. The massive entry gate opened, and the Mercedes drove through, following a long, winding driveway to what looked like a medieval castle. Its massive stone walls loomed high overhead, lit by ground lights. The Mercedes pulled up and stopped under a porte cochere in front of the castle's solid wood doors.

"Get out," the driver said, opening the door on Tom's side. He had a gun.

His captors walked Tom through the lobby, into the great hall. Tom looked up as they made their way to the main staircase leading to the second floor. The coffered ceiling in the great hall was easily twenty-five feet overhead. At the far end of the room, at least fifty or sixty feet away, there was a giant fireplace, big enough to walk into. Tom's captors pointed him to the stairway and told him to "climb."

At the head of the stairs, there were five doors. The center one was open. They entered and proceeded down a wide hallway at the end of which they stopped.

"This is your room," one of the men said, as he unlocked the door.

"Look," Tom said, "I demand to know what's going on. I . . ."

The man pushed him inside the bedroom. As Tom entered, he did not see the person waiting for him behind the door. This person stepped out, behind Tom, with a cloth in his hand. He placed it over Tom's nose and mouth and held him securely. Tom smelled the sweet acrid odor but barely had time to say, "Not again." Blackness followed.

The next thing Tom knew, he was lying in bed. He was wearing a pair of pajamas, which certainly were not his. There was a light beside the bed that was lit. He had no idea what time it was, but he got up, and walked to the only door. It was locked. He went to a large window and pulled back the curtains. There were bars over the windows. "No getting out of here," Tom said to himself. It was just beginning to be light outside. A mist covered the dense forest that seemed to surround the lawn, one floor below.

"Where the hell am I?" he said aloud.

Tom saw a closet, in which his clothes were neatly hung on hangers. He fished inside the pockets of his jacket. His wallet, passport, cell phone, and money were gone.

Gradually it all came back. He had been abducted by two Germans in Rome outside the hotel where he was meeting Alex. They drugged him and had taken him in a private plane to Frankfurt. He was inside some kind of castle in the country outside Frankfurt. That was all he knew. Suddenly he was struck by a thought: Had they done anything to Alex? He certainly hoped not, but he realized he had absolutely no way to know.

He heard a key in the lock, and the door opened.

"Guten morgen," a tall man dressed in black said. He was carrying a silver tray.

"Where am I?"

The man ignored him and placed the tray on a side table.

"I suggest you eat this," he told Tom in German. "Get dressed. I will be back in one hour." The man turned and walked out, locking the door behind him.

Smelling the full breakfast, Tom realized he was hungry. Poisoned food? He wondered. No, I don't think so. I was brought here from Rome. Certainly not just to poison me. He sat down and ate, then showered and dressed. Precisely one hour later, the door opened again.

"Let's go."

Tom followed the German down a wide corridor that led to a large conference room. A glass chandelier hung from the ceiling, and the parquet floors were buffed to perfection. There were mirrors on either side of the room, so that the chandelier with its lights was caught in the reflections of both mirrors and gave the impression of there being an infinite number of rooms and chandeliers. Tom was asked to sit down at the conference table, whereupon his captor left the room and closed the door.

After a few moments, a man walked briskly into the room from another door. He was of average height, of slightly stocky build, with short salt and pepper hair, a thin mustache, and long ears. His most distinctive features were his light blue eyes. He walked with an air of authority. Tom instinctively rose from his chair.

"Dr. Stewart, my name is Hermann Bailitz," he said in perfect English, though with a slight German accent. He extended his hand. Tom did not take it. Bailitz appeared not to notice Tom's unwillingness.

"I apologize for the rather unorthodox circumstances of our meeting. The urgency of the situation seemed to call for this special approach."

"What situation?" Tom said. "Your thugs drugged me and stole my belongings. I demand to be released immediately."

"All in good time, Dr. Stewart. Please sit down." There was real authority in his tone.

Tom decided to listen rather than respond. Bailitz went on. "As you may know, I am chairman of Belagri, the world's largest biogenetic seed manufacturer. These days, transparency is a virtue, so let me tell you that you are in my private quarters in the quite famous Kronberg Castle, outside Frankfurt. I hope we will be friends.

"I should explain the urgency. You confirmed for my colleagues what happened in the Roman Forum when they met you for lunch at Tivoli."

"What are you talking about?" Tom demanded.

"The existence of an extraordinary virus. Something we had been looking for—academically at first, but recently as a critical part of our strategy. We followed up to learn as much as we could. But we discovered that someone else has been watching every one of your moves."

Tom, surprised, said, "I don't know of any such group."

"Come, come, Dr. Stewart. You surprise me with your naïveté if you mean what you say. They are an undercover unit."

Bailitz continued. "They were coming after you. They are very shrewd. They're like a spider watching its prey, ready to pounce when the moment is right. They would have been successful, but we realized we'd better intervene first. We had already offered you a generous consulting contract, which you seemed intent on taking. But when they showed their hand, we had to take precautions."

"Are you suggesting," Tom said with irony, "I should thank you for capturing me?"

Bailitz replied, "Dr. Stewart, you'll have to be the judge. I will say that it gave me unusual pleasure to 'pluck' you out of Rome right in front of their faces. But, enough of this background. Let me change the subject."

Tom was irritated by Bailitz's high-handed way of treating their conversation. "Wait a minute," Tom said. "You mentioned a minute ago the virus was of academic interest to you, then suddenly it's become a part of your critical strategy. What's this all about?"

"We face competition every day—that's fine, we always win against our competitors. But we're fighting avarice and entrenched power that can take our business away from us, and we have no defense against this. I just returned from Nairobi. Belagri's seeds have been declared genetically altered and illegal for us to sell. This wipes out the Kenyan market. Other African nations may follow their lead. It means millions of dollars of lost revenue to us."

"Bad, but not catastrophic. You have the rest of the world."

"Last week I was in Brazil arguing our case. The government plans to outlaw our products. The irony is that farmers who use Belagri have bigger, better crops. If we're kicked out of their markets, they lose and we do, too."

"Can't the farmers rise up and demand Belagri products?"

"The governments in these countries are corrupt. They collect pay-off money under the table and outlaw us publicly. We have no recourse but to out-think our competitors."

"Can't you plead your case before the authorities?"

Bailitz's voice raised in frustration. "I personally have been named persona non grata in Kenya. We can't even legally enter Kenya. Word of our being ejected is getting around." Bailitz was visibly shaking. This discussion was angering him to the core. He was quiet for a few moments, trying to contain his fury.

Tom thought that he wouldn't like to be confronted by a hostile, angry Bailitz. Then he realized he, too, was confronting him.

Bailitz continued, "Belagri seeds and other products account for roughly half the world's food supply. It's a source of great satisfaction to me personally to feed the world."

"Your powerful company and its . . . methods are well known."

"Ah, yes. Our competitors engineer all kinds of lies and false charges against us. Sour grapes, if you'll forgive me a modest pun." To this statement, Tom made no comment.

Bailitz went on, "But having one government, like Kenya, or two or three others, like Brazil, outlaw us will have a resounding and devastating effect on our reputation and, more to the point, our business."

"What does all this have to do with the virus?"

"We can beat the competition—maybe we can even beat the things Mother Nature throws at us. But we can't beat corrupt governments. I have to take action.

"Despite our monumental contributions to agroscience, we've been encountering growing resistance by political bureaucrats in many countries. Regulations about bioengineering have been written to stop our progress. If we were paranoid, we would believe that there is a well-orchestrated plan to remove us from our critical role in the global food supply. Without Belagri, the world would go back to antiquated methods.

"I won't let that happen. It would be disastrous for Belagri and for the millions upon millions of people around the world who will starve."

"This is all very interesting," Tom said, "but I'm an archaeologist, not a politician."

"It is precisely archaeology which brings you and me together."

"How is that?" Tom inquired.

"Our foundation funds numerous archaeological explorations," Bailitz said. "I believe that the past informs the present and the future. The dig at the Roman Forum was just one of many, but there were some interesting aspects to it."

"Yes, Crystal Close told me of your personal interest in the effort."

"I believe you are aware of Dr. Smith's rediscovery of the mural from the architect Imhotep the Younger's tomb confirming the Biblical account of plagues in ancient Egypt?"

Tom admitted to himself that this last comment by Bailitz surprised him, but he kept that surprise to himself. He said in a measured tone, "Yes, I keep up with significant finds."

"So do our researchers. News several months ago of Smith's substantiation of the famous biblical plagues that wiped out man and beast intrigued us. Our researchers visited Smith. We learned of the unusual contents in the three canopic jars found in the tomb, and we followed the trail of evidence to Rome.

"I did some checking, and it became evident to me that the Vatican had taken the canopic jars from the Imhotep tomb back in the 1920s. I knew from other sources that the Vatican's Propaganda Fidei has always had modern laboratories to test the veracity of religious claims. What precisely was discovered by their labs, however, I could not discover. Our trail grew cold, due to the impenetrable bureaucracy of the Vatican."

"Until Doc Brown's unfortunate accident?"

"Ah, yes, Dr. Brown was a very dedicated archaeologist, but it was through the circumstance of his death that we confirmed our suspicions about the existence of a devastating virus, and we found the trail again which brought us directly to you."

"I assume you've 'persuaded' the authorities?"

"Let's just say that we have many advocates in governments throughout the world as well as detractors. In any event, once we met you, we knew that you would not rest, or, rather, could not rest, until you discovered the truth about what killed your colleagues, so we had you followed. It was you who led us to O'Boyle, who—eventually—told us much of the back story of what he called the Moses Virus. Set loose, this virus could have devastating consequences. We kept any 'competitors' for the virus from getting to O'Boyle."

"You mean you had Father O'Boyle killed," Tom stated with an edge in his voice.

"Father O'Boyle was an elderly man, and physically not very well," declared Bailitz. "That he died of a heart failure should have surprised no one."

"But why would Belagri, 'the world's largest biogenetic seed manufacturer,' as you put it, be interested in a powerful virus?"

"I grant you," Bailitz said smoothly, "it may not seem obvious— that is, a connection between Belagri and a deadly virus."

"I don't follow you," Tom said.

Bailitz continued. "The future for humans on our planet is dire. Food production will have to increase 50 percent over the next twenty years." Bailitz paused, then repeated the number with emphasis. "Fifty percent, just to feed the world's expanding population. How will this be done? It won't. Left in the hands of the greedy bureaucrats, there will be far more than one billion people actually *starving* and dying, not just hungry.

"Politicians from third world countries, through graft and corruption, enrich themselves by stealing billions of dollars each year that were intended for food production." Bailitz raised his voice to enforce his next statement: "Africa's birth rate is much higher than the rest of the world's. We give them Western medicine, which spares their children's lives from infant diseases. They have more children so they can till the pathetic little patches of ground where they live. Then politicians keep them from getting our seeds; their crop yields are anemic. This will end in cataclysmic starvation."

"And I suppose Belagri has a solution?"

"A God-given opportunity! And you've found it for us—a powerful virus. Suppose a devastating virus were to attack the population of Kenya, with the result that thousands would die. Much of the government will perish, but those politicians who survive will panic because they don't have a solution, and they can't 'talk' their way out of their predicament."

"But," replied Tom, "the Moses Virus would not harm the food supply of that country."

"We know that. But if we used the virus, we would also use other means to wipe out that country's agriculture."

"So," said Tom, "you'd destroy agriculture, livestock, and the population, including the politicians?"

"It's a stark way to describe it, but, yes, you're essentially correct," said Bailitz. "After most of the country's politicians are eliminated, Belagri will offer our antidote for the virus, and we will immediately supply the country with the means to reestablish its food production. With our state-of-the-art facilities, I am confident we can find the antidote for the treacherous pestilence of the Moses Virus.

"With the antidote we will have a perfect weapon. Our competitors won't stand a chance to keep up with us. We'll feed the people in that country—forever."

"And there will be enough food for everyone?" Tom asked.

"Exactly," replied Bailitz, with obvious excitement.

"The sacrifice of the few to benefit the many?" Tom said, feeling both sick and sad.

"Just so."

"And put billions of dollars in Belagri's pocket?"

"It's a win-win situation. We are the leader in a growth industry that is essential to man's survival. It dwarfs Apple's or Google's opportunities. Man can live without computers, Dr. Stewart, but *all* men must eat to survive."

"You are mad."

"Dr. Stewart, I'm a practical man. I run a large global company. We have a problem, and I have a solution. The world wins. Belagri wins. We will profitably solve the world hunger problem."

"What makes you think I'd help you, even if I could?"

"You've already been quite helpful to us, thanks to your impressive investigatory skills."

"Well, apparently you know more than I do."

Bailitz smiled. "You are too modest, Dr. Stewart. We persuaded Father O'Boyle to help us understand the Vatican's role in all of this. Sigmund Warburg on the other hand was not quite as cooperative."

"What have you done to Sigmund Warburg?" Tom asked.

Bailitz smirked. "Nothing. He was an old man in frail health. I will simply say that he . . . didn't respond well to our interview techniques."

"What makes you think I was any more successful than you with Sigmund Warburg in learning the whereabouts of the virus?"

"Call it an educated guess. We'll find out soon enough." At this point, Bailitz pressed a button on a signaling device by his place at the table. The door opened and—to Tom's surprise—Crystal Close walked into the room. She looked surprised to see Tom.

"Good morning, Dr. Stewart," she said. "Nice to see you again." Tom didn't respond.

She turned to Bailitiz. "Hermann, I had the impression that Dr. Stewart was under my direction. I was not informed . . ."

"I decided that more aggressive methods were required."

Tom, who was watching Crystal, thought he saw a flicker of anger flash across her face.

Crystal sat down next to Bailitz without saying anything.

Bailitz continued. "We need to know what you know, Dr. Stewart. Your cooperation could make you a very rich man."

"Blood money," Tom said scathingly.

"Spare me your moralizing," Bailitz barked. "You are in a position to save millions of starving people, victims of the shortsightedness of their leaders."

"And you would put hundreds of thousands, maybe millions, at risk to prove this point?" Tom cried out. "This virus may start a pandemic. Without an antidote you would be committing mass murder."

"Semantics," Bailitz answered. "There are hundreds of thousands, if not millions, of people starving and dying every year because of small-mindedness and corruption. Aren't these corrupt leaders really the mass murderers you should care about? Besides, we would only proceed if we have the antidote."

"You'll never get away with it. Once your plan is exposed, every country in the world will hunt you down."

"Exposed? Who will expose us? You?" Bailitz laughed. "I hardly think so."

Tom was silent.

Bailitz became serious and stared directly into Tom's eyes. "Make no mistake, we will get the virus, whatever it takes."

Bailitz stood and Crystal followed suit. "Please follow me," Bailtiz said to Tom. "I will explain further."

They walked down a carpeted hallway and stopped at what looked like a laboratory door, highly secure, with a heavy glass panel permitting a person on the outside to see everything going on inside.

Crystal opened the door and led the way into a large room filled with a huge oval conference table around which were placed leather chairs. It looked like the boardroom of a major multinational corporation.

Quietly sitting at the large oval table was a distinguished older man, with a shock of white hair. "This," said Bailitz proudly, "is Stephen Harrington, the former president of the World Bank, and, before that, one of the most venerated chief executives in the global economy, the former head of the Bank of America."

"What's this room for?" Tom asked.

"It's comforting for Stephen. He sits here every day, never saying anything, waiting for something to happen."

"Will something happen?"

"Not directly—he's 'retired,' you might say. But he remains a potent symbol. We'll paste his picture on a website at the appropriate time, to go along with the speech the world will hear from his lips."

"Even though he doesn't say anything?"

"We have 'organized' a speech for him. It's one he gave years ago, which shocked quite a few people."

"I must have missed it," Tom said, with some interest.

"In short," Bailitz replied, "Harrington had grown exasperatingly frustrated at the plight of third world countries—death by malaria, AIDS, and a dozen other causes, starvation of the masses, scandalous corruption by the rulers. During an interview by Mike Wallace on *60 Minutes*, Harrington said: 'The solution to Africa's problems should be a massive downsizing of its population.'

"'How would this happen?' Wallace had asked.

"'By some act of God, a fearsome virus, perhaps. Wipe the evildoers and sinners out, lock, stock, and barrel.'

"Wallace immediately broke for a commercial, and when the show returned after the commercial, Harrington was gone, and the next guest was sitting in Harrington's seat. That was the last time Harrington appeared in public view."

Bailitz then said, "You know, at that moment, I saw that Harrington was correct. It was exactly the wrong thing to say politically. But it was the equivalent of 'Let the law of the jungle take its course.'"

Tom finally grasped Bailitz's meaning. "You would set the virus loose somewhere killing people indiscriminately, and have Harrington's words blame the tragedy on the righteous wrath of the Almighty?"

"No better place for retribution to come from," Bailitz said. "What's more, the people who must be silenced, who must be removed, are the bureaucrats. Anyone else is collateral damage."

Bailitz looked directly at Harrington, who gave no sign he was even listening.

"How would this work?" Tom asked. "You don't have the virus supply. You don't have an antidote for the virus. And you only have one old man—and barely that, just to look at him."

Bailitz reddened. "We will find the antidote once our labs have the supply of virus for testing. And, we have a specific target."

"Where?" Tom asked caustically.

"Nairobi. Once we strike, killing grain, livestock, and the population, we will devastate Kenya like Moses devastated Egypt," Bailitz said.

Bailitz gestured to Harrington. "Stephen Harrington, our 'Moses,' will pronounce over his website that God has spoken. That corrupt governments must fall. People must be fed. We will let the perilous situation in Kenya fester. The world will wonder, then worry, that the plague will spread wider. Perhaps to their countries. Hysteria will be rampant. And at an auspicious moment, Belagri will announce—with there being no connection with Harrington—that our humane and efficient laboratories have discovered the antidote for the virus. We will offer this to the world agencies for distribution.

"We will also offer newly bioengineered seeds immune from the disease to farmers in the third world whose crops have been destroyed. These seeds will be available from us at rock-bottom prices."

Tom countered, "What if the world finds out Belagri released the virus in the first place?"

"The Vatican certainly won't say anything," Bailitz said. "Their hands are tied with having produced it in the first place. They need to put as much distance between the Church and the virus as possible. Everyone else who knows about it is dead—except you."

Tom said grimly, "I've been thinking about this."

Bailitz stared at Tom but said nothing.

Tom continued. "The real tragedy is that the virus is likely to kill vast numbers of people. That's what happened in 1918 with the Spanish flu virus. There is a chance that the virus will become a pandemic, unable to be stopped. This is much more than a 'local killer.'"

Bailitz said without hesitation, "The real scourge of these countries is their leadership. That's what we'll fix."

Tom looked at Harrington. He had a worldwide reputation for absolute integrity. He was a tall man, six feet five inches tall. His reputation around the world had been made and remained intact. There would be many who would listen to the words of this distinguished world citizen. But Tom grasped the truth. Though he was looking at Harrington, the august man of the past was no longer there. He had declined into dementia. He was solely an instrument for Bailitz to play.

Bailitz said, "I know what you're thinking. But you're wrong. Harrington has been retired and out of the public's eye for eight years. After his wife died, he appeared at her funeral, then he went into seclusion. No one has seen or heard from him since. We kept him out of the press so that the world would not have to see his decline. The beauty of the Internet is that Stephen Harrington can make public statements and even brief appearances over the Internet and no one need know that he has been 'assisted.'"

Tom realized he needed to know more about Bailitz's plans if he were to stop this madman. "Frankly," Tom said, "what you've told me sounds like the view from thirty thousand feet. How will you actually inflict this Moses Virus on the government and people of Nairobi?"

Bailitz grabbed Tom by the arm, enthusiastically leading him to the next room.

Tom could see several long tables against the far wall with many computers and large monitors. Lights on the monitors showed that the computers were active. He spotted two young women keeping an eye on the computers and screens, walking back and forth, occasionally typing on the keyboards.

At this point, Bailitz seemed to be on fire with enthusiasm.

"On the evening prior to our operation, our team will arrive by plane from Paris," Bailitz said. "They'll check into their hotel and spend the next day tracing and retracing the steps of the plan as well as familiarizing themselves with the area. Nairobi has an urban population of four million, three million of whom are concentrated in the central part of the city. This group is the prime target for the virus—and there's the real objective: the central district contains most of the major government officials of the country. To the world, Nairobi is notable: it's Africa's mile-high city, with Mount Kenya to the north and Kilimanjaro to the southeast. Kilimanjaro's famed snow-capped flat top has already been receiving international attention for its ice cover which is melting due to global warming. Kenya's central position in Africa, its prominence, and its history are ideal to demonstrate the message we wish to deliver. In recent years, Nairobi has become world-renowned as a corrosively evil city overrun with crime out of control. It is its government that has failed to keep order. Time for a change, wouldn't you agree?"

"How will you use the virus to infect the population?" Tom asked with—he admitted to himself—morbid curiosity.

"We've selected the Kenyatta International Conference Centre. It's among the highest buildings in the central business district, has iconic status, and is in walking distance of several five-star hotels.

"Around 10 p.m., our three team members will be waiting in the lobby of the Kenyatta Centre. They'll take the elevator to the top floor, the Conference Centre's observation deck on the thirtieth floor. They'll carry a small canister of the virus, a supply of oxygen to breathe via their face masks, but also oxygen to aerosolize the Moses Virus so that it can be dispensed as a vapor. Once on the observation deck, the leader of our team will lean over the edge of the deck, letting the pressurized oxygen force the aerosolized contents in a spray out in the evening air, falling toward the streets of Nairobi.

"Their orders are to remain on the observation deck for only fifteen minutes, time enough for the first effects of the virus to occur, but not enough time to become widespread. The team will then summon the elevator and descend to the lobby.

"It's expected that men and women in and around the building—by that time—will be slumped, dead, or dying. The dying ones are highly dangerous as they immediately become agents for spreading the virus. The beauty of this virus is that death spreads geometrically by contagion.

"Our team, with oxygen masks still in place, will put Red Cross insignias on their arms in case there's anyone to ask them what they're doing. They'll walk to their rental car and drive quickly to the airport. We have studied all aspects of typical wind currents. We did this when we thought we'd be using anthrax. But we're already studying what changes we'll need to make to accommodate the virus. I can tell you, we're excited about using it. After disposing of their equipment, our team will board a private jet at the airport, and yes, we've made provisions to deal with panic and hysteria which may close down the airport altogether. I believe," said Bailitz proudly, "that we've thought of everything."

He paused, then continued. "The circle of those infected by the virus will be spreading out from the Kenyatta International Conference Centre. The livestock similarly infected, but by the anthrax spores, will be a major loss to the farmers of Kenya. The world wire services will cover the incident. There will be no tie to Belagri. Kenya will have been paralyzed—the country will come to a complete halt. Hysteria will spread rapidly from Kenya to the rest of Africa. Europe will experience the fear. So will the United States. News will get out that the virus is the same powerful contagious virus that the Bible spoke of in the Book of Exodus. Some will believe that this is God's wrath."

"And," Tom asked, "as hysteria spreads, what will Belagri do?"

Bailitz said, "We will step forward and offer the antidote. But we'll also offer attractive terms—not steeply priced—seeds, to assist in this rebuilding effort. The cost to Kenya and the farmers will be in the seeds they are obligated to purchase in future years."

Tom said, almost in awe, "I had no idea that this operation has been so carefully orchestrated."

"And, we'll pick a second target if the corrupt bureaucrats miss the point. This time we'll run short of the antidote. We won't stop until we have a monopoly for our business." Then he proceeded. "I was hoping you'd understand what we're going to do and how the world will significantly benefit from our plan. You have made our work easier and more effective with the virus. But, as I told you before, I need your supply supply the Moses Virus."

Definitively, Tom declared, "While I'm impressed with your organization and the completeness of your plan for the world, under no circumstances can I stand by and aid you in the outright murder of thousands if not millions of innocent people. No. My answer is absolutely *no*. I don't have it, and even if I did I would not turn the virus over to you."

Bailitz remained unfazed by Tom's resolve. "I thought you might take this position. You're misguided, and I suspect I can't argue you out of this. I'll leave it to my colleagues to persuade you to be more helpful. Crystal, will you show Dr. Stewart to our interview facility?"

Tom thought he saw surprise and concern in Crystal's face at this suggestion. Crystal asked Bailitz, "Are you sure this is the best plan?"

Bailitz said with grim determination, "I've made up my mind. Go. Goodbye, Dr. Stewart. It is a pity you won't see the bright future of the world unfold." He stood and walked out.

Accompanied by one of Bailitz's fully armed guards, Crystal led the way down a wide corridor to a small conference room. "Please wait inside. Dr. Krebs will be here soon to visit you."

"Who is Krebs?"

"The most persuasive man you'll ever meet, I'm afraid," she said, and left, locking the door behind her.

Tom looked around the room. There was a table off to one side, and a couple of chairs beside the table. In the center was a high-backed chair with leather straps attached to each arm. There was nothing else in the room. The walls and ceiling were covered with soundproof material.

After a few minutes, the armed guard who had walked Tom to the room entered.

"Take off your jacket and sit in the chair," he ordered in German.

"Go to hell!" Tom said.

The man backhanded Tom hard and forced him into the chair. He ripped Tom's jacket off and threw it on the table. Even as Tom struggled, the man was able to secure the straps around his arms and tied Tom's ankles together before leaving the room.

What seemed like hours later, the door opened quietly, and a man entered and closed the door behind him. He was carefully dressed in a lab coat, with gray hair neatly in place and a perfectly trimmed mustache completing his presentation. In the lapel of his lab coat, he wore a small white rose. He carried a black bag. "Good morning," he said pleasantly, as he moved closer, sounding very much as if he was a congenial family doctor. "I am Dr. Krebs."

Tom inwardly clenched his teeth and began to sweat. Dr. Krebs put his black bag on the table, opened it, and withdrew a syringe and a couple of small bottles. "There are so many ways we can do this," he said softly. "Making my work easy will make it easier on you. However, I am a patient man and have all the time in the world to achieve the desired result."

Krebs held his syringe up, then put its tip into one of the small bottles, filling the syringe with a colorless liquid. "Let's start with this. It will keep you awake, but make you highly sensitive to pain. I've found that it's an excellent opener." He moved closer to Tom, and prepared to give him a shot. "Do you care which arm I use?"

Tom remained silent.

"No? Then I will choose the right arm." He began to roll up Tom's sleeve.

Krebs stood with his back to the door, about to administer the drug. Tom heard a small thud, and as Krebs straightened up, a look of surprise swept over his face. Then his knees buckled and he sank to the floor unconscious.

15

"Are you all right?" Crystal asked as she moved into the room and shut the door.

"Yes, I'm fine."

"There's no time to explain. We have to act quickly."

Stepping over Krebs's body, she quickly freed Tom from the chair.

"I don't understand. Why are you helping me like this? Bailitz certainly won't be pleased."

She ignored him. "Here, take these." She handed Tom his personal items. "I'm sorry to say I didn't find your cell phone. That may mean Bailitz's men are trying to extract information from it. Follow me."

Crystal walked quickly from the room into the corridor. Tom followed her without comment. About twenty feet further along, the corridor turned right. Crystal touched a panel on the wall and a door slid silently aside. She ducked into the passageway, and Tom followed. "It was built as an escape route four years ago," she said. Lit by small emergency lights every five feet or so, the corridor was narrow.

"Why are you doing this?" Tom asked again.

"I thought he was all business, engineering a new era of technology with superantidotes to the pestilence. Anything that could knock out a virus as powerful as yours would give us valuable information that would help us deal with other dangerous viruses." She shook her head. "I've admired the man as a leader of a cutting-edge global company and a broad thinker of vital issues facing mankind. There's no one like him. But, somehow in his thinking he's decided that the ends he's striving for justify the means. It horrifies me that he'd be willing to kill innocent people to achieve his goal. He sees the elimination of world hunger and the cash windfall that it brings to Belagri as one and the same thing. But I can't subscribe to his using any means to reach that goal. The only way to stop him is to destroy the virus first. It's our only chance, and you're the only one who can do it."

They stopped at the end of the passage. "This is a back stairway, leading down to a door at the back of the castle," Crystal said. She then tapped a code into her iPhone. "I've disengaged the security cameras and unlocked the door."

Tom looked at her in surprise.

"Only Bailitz and I have this code. My driver is parked just outside. He won't be questioned at the front gates of the castle and will take you to the airport. Get out of Frankfurt as quickly as possible."

"But what about you? When Bailitz finds out, he'll kill you."

"Don't worry about me. I'll just tell him that Krebs let his guard down and you escaped. They'll be too busy trying to follow you to ask any questions. Where will you go?"

"Back to Rome, for now."

"Good luck. Now go. I've got to get back." Crystal was turning to leave, but then paused. "Tom, here's my card. My personal cell number is there in case you need it."

Tom nodded goodbye to Crystal, and moved quickly down the stairs.

At the foot of the stairs, Tom saw a small stainless steel rectangular plaque to the right of the door. He touched it, heard a click, and pushed the door open. Once outside, he saw a similar plaque outside, and found he was in the midst of tall evergreens growing close-up against the castle wall.

Tom pushed through the foliage and saw a car with its motor idling on the drive. The driver jumped out and opened the back door.

Tom got in, and the driver gunned it. They moved quickly around the castle, joining the main road that threaded its way through the eighteen-hole golf course to the massive entrance. The guards at the front gates recognized the car and waved it through.

Forty minutes later, the driver pulled up to Terminal 1 at the Frankfurt airport. Tom got out without a word and melted into the crowd.

What he didn't see was the driver flipping open his cell phone and saying into it, "He's heading toward the Lufthansa terminal," or the two men who followed him at a discreet distance.

At an ATM Tom withdrew €500 and proceeded to the ticket counter where he booked a one-way ticket back to Rome. He only had to wait an hour now before his escape was complete. He settled at a coffee bar full of students and waited. One hour.

But it wasn't long before a commotion broke out among the students.

"Attention," one of the students said aggressively in German, pushing back at two men who were bullying their way through the crowd. The student's shouting was enough to draw the attention of security, and a guard came over to investigate. It was then that Tom got a better look and saw the two men in black.

"Damn," he said under his breath. He recognized them as the two men who had abducted him in Rome. That meant, he began to realize, that his escape from Bailitz was a clever deception to get him to lead them to the virus. He had to think fast—they were closing in on him.

Tom left by another exit from the coffee bar that opened into a large passenger area. He ducked into the nearest men's room and waited. After a few minutes, he looked into the passenger area. No sign of the two men. They probably assumed he'd gone through security to catch his flight. Moving quickly, he exited the terminal and flagged a cab.

"Frankfurt Hauptbahnhof," Tom said, and the cab took off toward the central rail station. Of all the places where he wanted to go, Geneva made the most sense. That was the most logical place to find the stash of Moses Virus—and it might throw Bailitz's men of his trail, if only briefly.

When Tom entered the train station, he was greeted with a cacophony of sounds. People were advancing to the trains and coming from them. Shops were everywhere. He looked up and spotted Geneva on the arrivals and departures board, with a departure time of 4:05 p.m. It was two hours before departure. When he checked further at the ticket window, he learned that the train arrived in Basel at 6:55 p.m.; there was an eight-minute layover before another train departed Basel at 7:03 p.m. and was scheduled to arrive in Geneva at 9:46 p.m. He bought a one-way ticket to Geneva and paid with cash.

Back at his stronghold, Bailitz was in a fury. "What do you mean he wasn't on the flight?" he said sternly into the phone. "Where is he?"

"We're not sure, sir. Perhaps he didn't go to Rome."

Bailitz slammed down the phone. "Idiots! Stewart is smarter than we thought."

"Warburg's bank is in Geneva," Crystal said. "I imagine that's where he'll go."

Bailitz thought a moment. "You're right. Alert our team at the Frankfurt airport. Have them check on flights to Geneva—and on the trains as well. He might try to surprise us by taking the train. Either way, he'll have to show his passport when he arrives in Switzerland. See if we can make contact with Swiss immigration—we need to confirm he's on the way to Geneva. And put that team we sent to Warburg's house on the alert. We'll need someone watching Stewart and someone else watching Warburg's bank just in case we miss him in Geneva."

"I believe we have Warburg's bank entrance under surveillance already." Crystal opened her cell phone and began making calls.

"And check for recent hotel reservations," Bailitz said. "Watch for his arrival at the train station and airport in Geneva and watch the hotels in case he drives there."

He turned to Crystal. "I think you were right to let Stewart lead us to the virus. Our men had better not let him slip through their hands. Is Krebs okay? He won't like having been the fall guy."

Crystal replied, "He should be coming out of it about now," and continued making her calls.

With his train departing Frankfurt at 4:05 p.m., Tom rechecked his watch, which read 2:30 p.m. He had time to kill. He went to a branch of a German department store inside the terminal and bought toiletries, a small suitcase, some clothes and a Bic precharged, prepaid cell phone. He had seen these new gadgets advertised but never guessed he'd find one useful. He changed in the men's room and then, finding the card Alex had given him in his wallet, with her address and telephone number, called her. But the call went straight to her voicemail. "Alex," he said, "this is Tom—I've had to buy a new telephone, so you won't recognize this number. I'm okay now, in Frankfurt, and soon to be on a train to Geneva. I'll explain everything when we connect. Call as soon as you can."

Tom exited the train station and started walking. He had gone two blocks when he spotted a small restaurant that seemed to be doing a brisk business. It was the kind of typical German restaurant that offered reasonably priced food and excellent German beer on tap. He found a table toward the back that gave him a good view of the front door of the restaurant. He was safe for now. Tom relaxed—a bit—and ordered. A few minutes later, the waiter brought Tom some rolls, a stein of beer, and a wurstsalat. He ate quickly, paid the bill, and headed back to the terminal.

As the train left Frankfurt without any further incidents for him, Tom evaluated his situation. Bailitz was insane. Tom admitted he had never met a truly mad person before. Everything Bailitz said made sense from a certain cold, detached perspective, but it was stark, raving madness nonetheless. It was scary precisely because it was so logical. What he had learned about Bailitz's plans was terrifying—Bailitz would set off the Moses Virus, which might become a global pandemic, and Bailitz was prepared to take this risk to accomplish his selfish, crazy agenda. Tom realized he had to get help. Without Crystal's intervention—whatever her motivation—he might still be in that chair being tortured by Dr. Krebs. He could call Pulesi, but could he be trusted? He tried Sigmund's number once again.

After the fourth ring, the receiver was picked up, to Tom's relief. "Sigmund?" Tom asked.

"This is Julian. I work for Herr Warburg."

"Julian, I'm Tom Stewart. I met you two days ago when I visited Sigmund. I've been trying to reach him." From his meeting with Bailitz, Tom suspected that Sigmund was dead, but thought it better that he hear the news from Julian. "Is he available?"

There was silence at the other end of the line. "I'm sorry, Professor Stewart. Herr Warburg has had an accident."

"Is he all right?"

Julian shook his head. "No, sir, he died yesterday."

Though he already knew Warburg was probably dead, the confirmation was still a blow. "Julian, I'm so sorry to hear this. Can you please tell me what happened? I mean, what really happened?"

"He was found, dead of a heart attack, in the swimming pool," Julian replied.

Tom's mind was racing. First O'Boyle, now Warburg. Were these deaths directly traceable to his meeting with these men? Or was it just coincidence?

Then a second thought occurred. Swimming pool. Sigmund had said he never used it—only his wife. There was no heart attack. Bailitz all but admitted that he did it. That was it. That was what Bailitz was referring to—Warburg, a frail, older man. Murder, a calculated murder. Tom thanked Julian, expressed regret about Sigmund one more time, and hung up.

When the train pulled into Basel, Tom glanced at his watch. Tom's train was not only on time, but the train to Geneva was waiting. Within the scheduled eight minutes, Tom was on his way to Geneva. Remarkable, he thought, German and Swiss efficiency. He realized that he had more than two hours before he would arrive in Geneva. Since there was a dining car on the train, he decided to have dinner. He was mildly hungry now, but realized that he might not find many restaurants open when he arrived at nearly 10 p.m.

Tom walked to the diner, which was two cars forward. There were not that many people on this particular train, and certainly no one who looked suspicious. There were several tables free, so he chose a seat at one of them. A waiter came over to ask if he'd like a drink. Tom ordered a glass of wine and chose from the menu.

While Tom waited for the food to arrive, and, again, while eating his dinner, the reality of his position weighed upon him. The information that Sigmund Warburg had been brutally murdered was simply the most recent data, but somehow it drove home just how isolated Tom felt. It bothered him—not being able to reach Alex. Just talking with her would have cheered him up.

Tom concluded that he was alone and safe on this train headed to Geneva. Probably alone—he corrected himself. But when his passport had been checked as the train entered Switzerland, Tom realized his identity had become known to the Swiss authorities and perhaps to Bailitz as well. Once in Geneva, Bailitz undoubtedly would have men watching for his arrival. Within the grip of such somber thoughts, Tom decided not to have another wine after his meal. He needed to be alert. He resolved to be supercareful, because he was certain that he would be followed, and he didn't want to think about the consequences if he made a misstep.

The train pulled into Geneva at 9:46 p.m., precisely on time. Tom asked at the information desk in the station for a recommendation of a hotel near Rue de Hollande. A helpful agent suggested the Hotel d'Allèves, a small, family-run place located on Rue Kleberg, only an eight-minute walk from the Gare de Cornavin, the Geneva train station. Tom bought a map to the city as well. He opened the map and saw that Hotel d'Allèves was not far from the Pont de la Machine, a bridge that crossed the Rhone River and ran into the Rue de Hollande where Warburg's bank offices were located.

Tom left the Gare de Cornavin, heading toward the hotel. Out on Lake Geneva, there was still enough light to see the spray from the huge fountain in the lake. But Tom did not feel like a tourist. He felt more like a hunted animal.

And this was not far from the truth, because two of Bailitz's men had spotted Tom as he left the train. They confirmed this by comparing Tom's face with a picture of him sent to their iPhones. They discreetly followed him as he walked the eight minutes to Hotel d'Allèves. They reported seeing Tom to Bailitz, who ordered them to remain outside the hotel entrance throughout the night.

The Hotel d'Allèves was a modest stone building built in the mideighteenth century, but restored many times over the intervening years. The most recent renovations were carried out, the reception clerk said, in 2008, when a wireless Internet connection was installed throughout the building. Tom booked a room for two days and paid in cash in advance.

Tom's third floor room had two floor-to-ceiling windows. There were wooden beams overhead and a chandelier hanging from the ceiling. A desk was near the windows, and a large television was on the bureau at the end of the bed. The room was not vast, but it was comfortable.

Tom's cell phone rang. He saw that it was Alex's number.

"Hello," Alex said tentatively, and her voice was like a balm.

"Alex, it's me, Tom."

She exhaled in relief. "Thank God it's you! I've been worried sick. Where are you?"

"I'm in a small hotel in Geneva."

"Geneva? Are you safe?"

"For the moment, yes. They think I'm back in Rome."

"Who?"

"The men who kidnapped me last night." And Tom explained the events beginning with the last evening.

"So, Belagri is behind it all," Alex said.

"Yes. They'll stop at nothing to get the virus. They killed O'Boyle and Sigmund Warburg."

"How horrible!" Alex said. "This has gotten out of control."

"I agree. I've been thinking. We'll need to dispose of the virus once we've been able to get hold of it. I've got a plan, and I need you—urgently."

"Tell me what I can do."

"Before Warburg died, he sent me a small package containing a letter of reference to the bank manager at Cordier, Warburg in Geneva, and a key to a safe-deposit box. I suspect that the contents of the safe-deposit box will help us find the cache of the Moses Virus.

Before I was kidnapped, I hid my package from Warburg in the small room just off the Trajan aqueduct, near the American Academy."

"And you want me to get the package and meet you in Geneva?"

"That's the plan."

"But how can I get to the hidden room without arousing suspicion at the Academy?"

"I discovered that there's access to the aqueduct from the Tiber. Here's the way to go." He gave her detailed instructions, with her starting point being the Piazza Trilussa.

"I want to warn you," Tom added, "you'll probably run into rats."

"What? Rats?"

"They're more afraid of you than you are of them."

"I'm not so sure of that."

"They'll scatter when you yell at them."

"You're going to owe me one," Alex said.

Tom continued. "Be sure to take a flashlight. And wear comfortable walking shoes."

"When do you want me to do this?"

"Now. Once you have the package, I need you to fly to Geneva as soon as you can. Make sure you're not followed. Call me at this number when you get in. Rent a car at the airport. We may need it."

"How will I make certain I'm not followed? Don't they already know what I look like from breaking into my house?" Alex asked.

"Take every precaution you can think of. Someone may be watching your house. Change taxis. That may help."

Alex said, "I'll have to make a few calls first, and then I'll be ready. I'll take the first flight out I can get tomorrow morning."

"Alex, you're the only one I can trust. Thanks. I'm so glad to be talking to you."

"You sound exhausted," Alex said. "Get some rest. I'll see you tomorrow."

The sun was up before 6 a.m., and Alex was up with it. She looked out the window at a clear blue sky. It was going to be a hot summer day. Alex thought about her planned activities. Walking in an ancient, abandoned aqueduct: Sensible shoes? Check. A bag to carry Sigmund's package? Check. A flashlight to see in the dark? Check. Disguise for going to the bank to avoid being recognized. Now what could that be?

Then she knew: a blond wig she had used for a costume party last year. It worked then and would be perfect now.

Locking her front door, she walked to Via del Pellegrino. She turned left and then left again into the shortcut she had shown Tom. No car could follow her. Once on Via dei Cappellari, just out front of the Taverna Lucifero, she safely hailed a taxi. She changed taxis once and got out on the east bank of the Tiber, then crossed the Ponte Sisto Bridge to the Piazza Trilussa in Trastevere. Alex looked around her—the street was empty of cars. No one had followed her.

"All's going extremely well," she said and smiled to herself. But this was before she got lost finding the entry to the aqueduct. Be careful, she thought. I can't mess this up. Then, on the second try, she found the alley Tom had painstakingly described, and realized she was well on her way to finding the aqueduct entrance.

Once Alex was in the aqueduct, she found that walking was not easy, as the floor of the tunnel was uneven. "Damn," she said aloud this time as she tripped on a small indentation in the brick surface under her feet. "It's hot, unpleasant, steep, and hard to walk on. I should have worn running shoes instead of these. How was I to know that sandals wouldn't work so well?"

After what seemed like miles, Alex stopped. She heard a scratching sound and saw a dozen pairs of eyes staring at her. "Rats," she said, gritting her teeth. "I was warned. I don't mind them," she tried to convince herself. "They're as afraid of me as I am of them. They'll go away."

She gave a kick in the direction of the staring eyes and cried, "Get away!" The rats immediately scattered. Alex continued on, checking the walls with her flashlight for the wood-paneled door Tom had told her about. She finally found it. She shone her flashlight at the door, gave it a push, and it opened. She stepped inside. There was the table and, behind it, the opening in the wall covered with a sliding panel. She approached it, slid the panel door open, and saw the small box that Tom had described. Alex opened the box and confirmed for herself that the key and the letter were inside.

She placed the package in her leather bag and retraced her steps as quickly as she could back to the entrance. Alex spotted a taxi when she got out, hailed it, and went directly to the airport. She arrived in Geneva around 11:30 a.m., pleased with her efficiency and that of Alitalia Airlines.

Once in the terminal, she went to the ladies' room, where she pulled out her secret weapon: the blond wig. Pinning up her dark hair, she put on the wig in the mirror. Not bad, she thought. I wonder if Tom will recognize me?

She called Tom from the car rental office. He gave her the address to the hotel, his room number, and the address of the bank. He told her to park the car near the bank and walk the short distance to his hotel to meet him. It would make it easier to leave the city if they needed to.

She rented the car for two days, and within minutes was sitting behind the wheel of a gray, four-door Saab sedan. The agent gave her directions to the bank, and it took Alex fifteen minutes to locate 16 Rue de Hollande, where Sigmund Warburg's bank was. She parked the car a block away from the bank's front entrance, checked the directions on her iPhone, and walked to Tom's hotel in no time. She passed Bailitz's men who were still stationed across the street from the hotel's front door, but what they saw was a striking blond woman walk into the hotel. And though they thought her beautiful, this blond woman did not match the photograph of Alex Cellini that they had with them.

Alex asked the desk clerk to ring Tom's room. He did, announcing to Tom that a woman was on her way up. The clerk looked at Alex, his eyebrow lifted in disapproval, nodding toward the elevator. "Third floor, first room on the right."

She knocked on Tom's door.

"Who is it?" Tom asked.

"Alex."

The door opened swiftly, and Tom grabbed her by the arm and pulled her into the room. "I'm so glad to see you," he said, embracing her. They remained in an embrace, then kissed.

"I like you as a blonde," he said.

She smiled. "So you do recognize me?" She laughed.

"You must be exhausted," Tom said.

"I slept on the plane. But I'm starving."

"I thought you might be." On the small table there were some sandwiches, fruit, and white wine.

As Alex ate, Tom laid out his plan. Alex would go to the bank, just in case it was under surveillance by Bailitz's men. Now that Bailitz knew Sigmund Warburg's connection with the virus, it was logical to assume that the bank would be monitored. But few knew of Tom's connection with Alex, and certainly none knew a blond Alex. Tom felt that Alex, rather than he, had a better chance to escape detection.

Alex rehearsed her part of their agreed-upon plan. "After leaving the hotel, I retrace my steps, and go to Sigmund's bank, Cordier, Warburg & Cie. I'll ask for the managing director, Pierre Villechaise, to assist me. I'll call you when I'm finished and have the contents of the safe-deposit box. You'll meet me at the Saab. Here are the car keys."

"Exactly right. If we're lucky, the canisters holding the virus will be in the box. If not, well, this has been a wild goose chase."

Alex said, "I know you're reluctant to call anyone in to help us, because you don't know who would be on our side. Still, wouldn't it be prudent?"

"I know you're right, but everyone I've talked to has wound up dead. Let's see what happens at the bank. I'd call Pulesi if I called anyone. Are you ready?"

Alex showed no hesitation.

"Okay," Tom said, looking at his watch. "Showtime."

She took her purse as she prepared to leave and kissed Tom as he followed her to the door.

"Good luck," Tom said. "I couldn't do this without you."

Alex walked by the reception desk. A new person was behind it and smiled at her. Alex smiled back and pushed through the front door.

Alex took about ten minutes to arrive at the Rue de Hollande. Cordier, Warburg & Cie took up the entire block and was more imposing than she had remembered from her first view of it. She walked down the crowded street to the massive marble entrance, but didn't notice the two men across the street watching the doorway.

Alex went in the entrance of the bank. In front of her was a flight of steps up to the main lobby, which she took, arriving at a brightly lit large area, which had highly polished wood floors. A receptionist sat behind a glossy black granite desk, with a rank of telephone buttons in front of her to contact the officers of the bank. She looked up as Alex approached, politely, but not in an overly friendly manner. Alex identified herself and asked to see Pierre Villechaise.

If the receptionist was surprised, she was too professional to show it. She asked Alex if she could help by telling Monsieur Villechaise what the purpose of her visit was. Alex replied that it was of a confidential nature, adding, "Please tell Monsieur Villechaise that Sigmund Warburg sent me." The receptionist looked a little taken aback, but then called over a uniformed guard and asked him to escort Alex to one of the guest waiting rooms. Alex was quickly and efficiently placed in a small waiting room. The room had deep red linen on the walls, a chandelier hanging from the ceiling, an attractive wood table with inlaid top in the center of the room, a clock, and several innocuous oil paintings on the walls. There were three chairs placed around the table. The room exuded a quiet elegance. A few minutes later, Pierre Villechaise entered the room. He reminded Alex at once of Cary Grant. He was handsome, tall, and broad shouldered. He had black hair with some gray around the temples, and a dimple in his chin. He was tanned and had a warm smile.

"Bonjour, Madame Cellini," he said in French. "I am Pierre Villechaise."

Alex smiled and greeted him in French.

"I was expecting an American professor," he said smoothly.

"He and I are working together," Alex said, continuing in French.

"Did you speak to Herr Warburg?" asked Alex.

"Herr Warburg called—a day before he died—to alert me to expect someone who would want to see his safe-deposit box."

"Oh," said Alex, masking her surprise with a smile.

Villechaise then said, "Would you prefer I speak in Italian?"

"Am I that obvious?" Alex asked.

"No, of course not," Villechaise replied, "I just thought I'd ask."

Villechaise turned extremely businesslike and asked, "You have the key and his letter, I presume?"

Alex nodded and handed him the letter.

Villechaise read it quickly. "I worked with Sigmund for a number of years before his retirement. He was a friend and a mentor."

Alex thanked him. "Along with the letter, he gave me this key."

"Yes, this is the key to one of our security boxes. Would you accompany me, please?" Villechaise said, leading the way down a different flight of steps to a large vault, one level below the street. The vault's thick, oversized steel door was wide open, and there were two guards standing at attention in the room.

Alex followed Villechaise up a very small step over the raised edge of the vault's opening. Once inside the vault itself, Alex saw rank after rank of steel boxes set in the shining steel wall, each one with openings for two keys. Villechaise stopped before one group of boxes, took out a key from a lanyard he wore around his neck, and placed the key in its proper keyhole.

"This safe-deposit box belonged to Sigmund for many years, though I never saw him open it. Please use your key on this lock."

Alex turned her key in its lock, and Villechaise turned his key. There was a click, and the door to the safe-deposit box swung open. Villechaise retrieved a long steel safe-deposit box. He carried it to one of the small rooms adjacent to the vault and placed it on the table inside.

"I'll wait for you outside. Just press the button on the table to let me know when you are finished." He left, closing the door behind him.

She opened its metal cover. Inside was a small black lacquered box. Too small for canisters of virus, she thought. There also was a small brass plate engraved with a twelve-digit number and what appeared to be a royal crest—probably the bank's insignia, Alex thought. There was nothing more in the lacquered box. Alex put the box into her bag and the brass plate into her pocket. She pressed the button. Villechaise appeared almost immediately.

"May I replace the safe-deposit box, Madame?"

"Yes. Thank you."

He did so and turned to lead them out of the vault and into his office.

"Is there any other way I can be of assistance?"

"Actually, yes." She produced the small metal plate and handed it to Villechaise. "Can you tell me what this might mean?"

Villechaise looked concerned. "That's a combination to a locked container in our most secure offsite facility."

"Offsite facility?" Alex asked.

"Twenty years ago, we realized that some of our clients needed a facility that could hold larger objects of value. To accommodate them, we converted the vast dungeon area of the Chateau de Chillon into an underground vault. My colleague, Henri Brocard, is the general manager of our Chillon facility."

"I don't know anything about Chillon."

"Chillon is a famous fortress, built a thousand years ago by the bishop of Geneva."

"Where is it?"

"Forty miles from here, on the shore of Lake Geneva, at the eastern end of the lake, about two miles from Montreux. It's big—more than a hundred buildings joined into one complex. And, popular, with over 300,000 visitors a year. But, with all the tourists, it provides the kind of anonymity that our clients require when they visit. We have an arrangement with the Swiss government where we act as conservator of the facility through a foundation set up for the purpose. In exchange, we have exclusive access to the underground dungeon through a private entrance behind the main building. It was used to transport prisoners secretly."

"How do I gain access to the facility?"

"Normally, it's highly restricted. An appointment needs to be made months in advance and the identity of the applicant checked thoroughly before access is allowed."

"I'm afraid I can't wait that long. I'm in Geneva for a very short time."

"I see," Villechaise said. "It's against bank policy to let anyone who is not the principal owner gain access. I'm not sure I can—"

"Monsieur Villechaise, I'm here on a matter of some urgency. Herr Warburg knew of my mission, and he surely was aware of your rules. I'm certain he gave me your name since he knew you'd help me. Unfortunately, it has turned out to be his last request."

Alex knew she was stretching the truth, but she had come this far and did not intend to fail. She looked straight at this bank manager and said, firmly, "Please," and smiled again.

Villechaise looked torn. Then he seemed to decide. "Sigmund was one of the most respected members of the Swiss banking community. I will make an exception. I will ask you to fill out a few forms first, however. Please give me your passport. And, I'll need to keep his letter of introduction for the file."

"I'll be more than happy to follow your procedure."

"My assistant will draw up the forms immediately. I'll contact the director of the facility and let him know to expect you. I'll explain the background of your unusual request. Brocard, like me, was also very fond of Sigmund Warburg."

"I'd appreciate it if you told Mr. Brocard that I'll be accompanied by a colleague, Dr. Thomas Stewart. He met with Herr Warburg shortly before his death."

"That's not a problem. Please wait here while I collect the papers. If you'll excuse me."

Alex called Tom while she was waiting.

"How did it go?" he asked.

"Smoothly, although we need to take a trip to another facility, the Chateau de Chillon."

"Warburg was more discreet than anyone imagined. How long before you'll be finished with the formalities?"

"Not more than fifteen to twenty minutes, I think," replied Alex.

"Good, I'll meet you at the car."

"I'll see you there."

Tom left the hotel by a back entrance, evading Bailitz's men who were stationed across the street from the front of the hotel. Seven or eight minutes later, he arrived at the Saab, unlocked the car, and climbed in to wait for Alex, who joined him a few minutes later. Neither noticed that they had once again drawn the attention of Bailitz's men. But this time, the men recognized Tom, and, by association, finally, Alex.

Alex and Tom took off in the Saab, not realizing yet that they were being followed. As Tom negotiated the busy traffic, he asked Alex, "Do you know where we're going?"

"I looked it up on my phone. Once we get on the autobahn, we follow it along the shore of Lake Geneva. The entry to the autobahn will be on the right."

But abruptly, the traffic ahead came to a standstill.

Tom honked the horn at the snarl of cars in front of him.

"What's the problem?" he said.

"Looks like some kind of accident," Alex said. "There's a police car with flashing lights ahead."

Tom looked in the rearview mirror. There were a dozen cars lined up behind him. He couldn't back up.

"What time is the manager expecting us?"

Alex replied, "Sometime today before closing. We've got time."

"What do we know about Chillon?" Tom asked.

"Only what Villechaise said. Apparently, it's one of the most popular tourist sites in Switzerland. It's about a thousand years old. It used to be a fort, then served as prison. Cordier manages the facility through its foundation and has exclusive access to the underground dungeon. That's where they keep the vault."

"Chillon seems like a brilliant move on Warburg's part," Tom said. "Top security masked by crowds of tourists. Let's just hope it's where he put the virus."

While they waited, Tom noticed a white BMW that was following them. When the traffic began to move again, he floored the accelerator. The BMW similarly kept pace. He knew he couldn't lose his pursuers, but he could hold them at bay. It was a cat and mouse game, where Tom would pull ahead of the white BMW by passing cars in front of him, increasing the gap between the two cars. As soon as Tom had done this, the BMW would accelerate, gradually reducing the gap again.

After about forty minutes of attempting to pull ahead of the Belagri car, there was a sign indicating that the Montreux turn-off was just ahead.

Tom pulled off the autobahn onto the Montreux exit ramp. He followed the signs, which led to the large parking area at Chillon Castle. There were a dozen tourist buses in the parking area. There were also many passenger cars. Nearby, there loomed a gigantic castle, and beyond that the serene blue of Lake Geneva seeming to stretch out forever. In the distance, Tom saw a wooden passenger ship bearing additional tourists heading toward the castle.

"Villechaise said there was a private entrance to the bank's offices," Alex said as Tom pulled into the main Chillon parking lot. "He said it was behind the main building."

Tom glanced to the left of the entrance and spotted a small road that looked like a service driveway leading behind the main building. "That must be it," he said and turned onto the road. At the end was a very small parking area, hidden behind a stand of pine trees. He stopped and they got out of the car.

Tom and Alex looked for the BMW.

"Where do you think it went?" asked Alex. "Could we have lost them?"

"I doubt it. The stakes are too high. We may have fooled them by coming to this remote parking area. They'll cruise the main parking area and eventually find our car here. Let's go in the bank."

Directly across from the lot was a small building made of the same granite as the castle. A door opened and a uniformed guard met them.

"May I assist you?" he said.

"Yes," Alex said. "We have a meeting with Monsieur Brocard."

"Please follow me." The guard closed the door, which immediately locked behind them.

Once inside the building, the guard ushered them to a private elevator. He inserted a key and the elevator door opened.

"The reception desk is on the bottom floor."

Tom and Alex entered the elevator. The doors shut automatically. Within seconds, the elevator stopped, its doors opening onto a spacious wood-paneled room. The floor was polished wood, made of wide boards of rich cherry. There was a modern granite reception desk that reminded Alex of the reception area in the main office of Cordier, Warburg in Geneva. An attractive young woman was sitting behind the reception desk and smiled as she asked how she might be of service.

Alex introduced herself, saying that the managing director of the Geneva office, Pierre Villechaise, had arranged a meeting with Monsieur Henri Brocard. The receptionist seemed to be expecting them. She pushed a buzzer by her desk and almost immediately, a well-dressed man entered the reception area. He was in a gray suit but wore a thin maroon sweater under the jacket, despite this being a warm summer day.

"Bonjour, Madame Cellini. I am Henri Brocard, manager of the Chillon Castle branch of Cordier, Warburg." He spoke with a heavy French accent. "This must be your colleague, Dr. Stewart. It is a pleasure to meet you both. May I see your passports, please?" He checked them and handed them back.

"Monsieur Brocard," Alex said, "Monsieur Villechaise said that you would be able to assist us in retrieving an item stored here."

"I'm at your service. May I offer you some tea or coffee first?" Brocard asked politely.

"Thanks," Tom replied quickly, "but we're rather in a hurry. Also, Monsieur Brocard, we're being followed by two men. They may try to gain entrance to the bank. We would greatly appreciate it if they not be allowed in."

Brocard smiled benignly. "No one is permitted to enter for any purpose without prior clearance from the Geneva headquarters. I will, however, alert our guards."

Brocard called the guard, then said, "As you are pressed for time, may I see your combination plate?"

Alex took the small brass plate out of her purse and handed it to Brocard.

"Ah, yes. This is in one of the older sections. Please follow me."

They followed Brocard as he led them toward a door opening into a corridor that took them into the interior of the vast dungeon. The walls were made of large blocks of granite.

"As you can see, the bank took over this portion of the castle twenty years ago, refitting the area with suitable places to store larger valuables for our clients. It may look primitive, but let me assure you that it is equipped with the most modern security equipment available."

Brocard, enjoying the company, could not stop himself from telling his guests more about the Chillon facility. "Over there," he said, pointing to a stone column, "Lord Byron, the great English poet, carved his name. He wrote a poem about a prisoner in the dungeon here."

Brocard seems to be a talker, Tom thought. Aloud, he said, "Monsieur Brocard. Please, we are in a bit of a hurry. It's most important."

The Frenchman, who had slowed down to point out the historic stone column, apologized and fell silent—if only briefly.

Along the corridor there were stainless-steel doors recessed directly into the stone. "It is really quite ingenious," Brocard said. "The former prison cells have been turned into individual vaults, each with its own combination. Ah, here we are."

They stopped in front of a door inscribed with the first four digits of the combination. Brocard punched his own code into the electronic lock pad. Brocard asked for the brass plate again, which Alex produced. Brocard held the plate with the royal crest close to the electronic lock pad. There was a discernible click, and the door opened.

"You will find the vault inside. Simply tap the full combination into the keypad. You will be asked to enter the same combination a second time. I will be waiting outside until you summon me."

"Thank you for your help," Tom said.

Tom and Alex entered the small chamber. The vault was directly across from them. A small table was to the left. Tom took the brass plate and entered the numbers. He then entered the numbers a second time. There was a slight whirring sound. The door opened and a light went on inside the vault automatically.

On a shelf inside, they found a small black leather suitcase. Tom retrieved it and carried it to the table. There were no markings on the leather suitcase at all. It was not locked and the latches opened easily. Inside, there were three quart-sized stainless steel canisters recessed into a molded black felt casing and secured with leather straps. Their tops were sealed with thick red wax and stamped with the letters "PM."

"Pestilentia Moseia," Tom said, with a mixture of fear and relief, while Alex looked on.

"Are they safe to handle?"

"The seals have not been broken, so I assume so," Tom answered, closing the case. "I think we're finished here. Let's go." He closed the vault door.

Tom and Alex exited the security room, rejoining Brocard, who was waiting for them. Brocard said, "One of you may wish to return to your car, and drive it to our lower level. This private exit is to the right, behind the house."

"Good idea," Tom said. "Alex, will you pick up the car? Here, take the keys. I'll keep the suitcase with me. Monsieur Brocard, I wonder if you can accommodate us. The two men I mentioned could conceivably be waiting for Madame Cellini at our car. Could you please have one of your guards accompany her?"

"Certainly," Brocard said. He spoke quietly to one of his security personnel who came over to Tom and Alex. Brocard introduced him, "This is Philippe. He is pleased to accompany Madame Cellini."

Brocard left with Alex and Philippe, guiding them to the elevator to the upstairs entrance. Alex and Philippe then walked to the small parking lot so she could retrieve the Saab and drive it to the lower loading area. Brocard returned to Tom. "Come, I'll take you to the exit for our lower-level pickup."

Brocard and Tom arrived at the glass enclosure leading to the lower loading area at exactly the same moment as Alex's Saab pulled up. Philippe was walking alongside the car. Tom opened the glass security door and walked toward the car, holding the suitcase.

Suddenly, out of nowhere, the white BMW pulled up and blocked the Saab. Two men jumped out and ran toward Alex. Philippe stepped forward with his revolver in his hand to protect Alex. One of the Germans fired his own gun, equipped with a silencer. There was a spitting noise, and Philippe collapsed to the ground. The other German yanked Alex's front door open and pulled her out. He held a knife to her throat.

"She dies unless you give us the suitcase," he yelled at Tom. The other man moved toward Tom, holding his gun pointed at Tom.

"Let her go!" yelled Tom.

"The case," the German in front of him barked.

Tom hesitated, looking for a way out. He took a step forward, seemingly offering the case to the intruder, then quickly swung it, knocking the gun out of his hand.

"No tricks, or the girl dies," the other man, holding Alex, yelled and ran the knife across her left arm. She cried out in pain as the cut started to bleed. Alex fell to her knees.

"You bastard!" Tom cried.

The German who had come after Tom had recovered the gun and hit Tom hard in the head. He collapsed onto the ground.

"I've got the case," the German said to his partner. "Take the girl."

The two Germans, one with the black leather case, and the other literally dragging a bleeding Alex, dashed to their BMW. Alex was thrust into the BMW's backseat.

Brocard had remained inside the glass enclosure when Tom had left through the secure door to join Alex. The moment he saw the BMW pull up, he locked the door electronically to protect Cordier, Warburg from any forced entry that the two armed men might try. Simultaneously, he pushed a concealed emergency button to the right side of the door, which signaled the police in Montreux, the receptionist, and the bank's security people, as well as Villechaise in Geneva. Then Brocard watched and waited. He thought to himself that he was doing the right thing to stay inside. His job, he reminded himself, was to protect the bank.

When he saw Alex, bleeding, fall to her knees, Brocard called the receptionist and told her to have the bank's medical officer join him immediately. Two bank guards who had been summoned by the emergency button were already standing beside Brocard, waiting for orders. The medical officer came running up, out of breath. The BMW had now left the area with the two Germans, Alex, and the black leather case.

Brocard released the electronic locks on the glass security door. The two guards, the medical officer, and Brocard walked quickly toward Philippe. It turned out that the bullet had grazed Philippe's head, entering his left cheek and exiting without doing permanent damage. Philippe was regaining consciousness, but was bleeding profusely. The medical officer told Philippe that the ambulance was on its way to take him to the hospital. The medical officer gave Philippe a sedative and applied a bandage to the wound to cut down on the bleeding.

The medical officer next examined Tom and realized that Tom had been knocked out, but had not sustained any serious injury. He waved a vial of smelling salts under his nose and Tom began to come to. He coughed at the acrid scent of the smelling salts that burned his nostrils. Seeing that Tom was going to be all right, the medical officer returned to Philippe to stay with him until the ambulance arrived.

Tom stood gingerly, his mind cloudy as he pulled himself together. Suddenly, everything came back to him. He saw that Alex had been taken, and the suitcase with the virus was gone as well. Tom suddenly felt helpless—everything had gone wrong. He had been working desperately to find the Moses Virus; moments ago, it had been in his hands. Abruptly, it was gone, taken by Belagri, which would use it for destruction of human lives. Bad as this was, Alex now also was gone, taken from him, and hurt. Then a wave of anger and urgency swept over him. He cried aloud to no one in particular, and to everyone, "We've got to go after them—they've got the suitcase and Alex."

"Monsieur," Brocard said as he hurried from Philippe to Tom's side, "they headed toward the autobahn. I've alerted the Montreux police. They'll be here any minute."

"There's no time to waste! Tell them to follow my car. I'm going after the white BMW." Tom got into the Saab. Alex had left the keys in the car. Tom started it and sped off, just before the police arrived.

17

The two Germans raced through Montreux on their way to the autobahn. The driver had been watching through his rearview mirror. He noticed a car that he thought was following them—but it turned off the road after a time. Then he spotted a second car. A gray Saab catching up fast.

"We've got company," the driver said.

The driver veered off onto a side road that led through a wooded area. "This should take us to the next entrance to the autobahn to Geneva."

"We should have killed him and the girl when we had the chance," the second German said.

"Damn," the driver said, looking in the rearview mirror. The Saab turned, following behind. "It'll take about an hour to get to the Geneva airport and turn in the car, so we'll get our flight to Frankfurt without any trouble. But we can't have that Saab on our tail the whole time."

The second German looked in the backseat at Alex, whose arm had stopped bleeding and was now caked with dried blood. "She's not seriously hurt," he said. "The knife wound was superficial."

The driver said, "We've got to throw the Saab off our trail. I think what we need to do is leave some bait for Stewart."

"Bait?"

"Bait. The girl. I'm going to increase speed and pull ahead of the Saab. Then we'll dump her in the middle of the road, and Stewart will have to stop and pick her up. We'll escape."

The BMW surged ahead. Neither of the two Germans particularly noticed that the road was becoming bumpier, and the forest through which they were driving was growing denser and denser. The BMW began to pull away from the Saab.

Suddenly, the driver slammed on his brakes, bringing the BMW to a skidding stop. "Get her out of here," he shouted.

The second German jumped out of the car, opened the back door, and pulled Alex out, dragging her onto the road. She didn't resist in the slightest. The second German quickly tied her arms and then her legs together. He left her in the center of the road. "You'll be lucky not to be run over," he said, giving a little laugh. He climbed back into the BMW, which spun its wheels, leaving Alex behind.

The BMW was going as fast on this back road as possible. The driver said, "We need to get back on the autobahn. Take a look at the map—where can we turn?"

"I've been thinking," said the second German.

"About what?" the driver asked.

"We're too obvious if we stay in this car."

"What do you mean?"

"Back at Chillon. Any Swiss bank is sure to be overrun with security cameras. Someone must have spotted our car as we left. Hell, Stewart may have called our license plate numbers in to the police. We'd be better off ditching this car and finding another."

"You've got to be crazy! We're in a dense forest. We haven't seen any cars in either direction."

"I know, I know. But, if we do see one, we should swap, destroy the BMW, and keep traveling in the new car, incognito."

"You've got a good point," the driver said as he swerved on a sharp curve in the road.

"And," said the second German. "I've got another thought."

"What now?"

"Our plans were to fly back to Geneva. With the black leather case."

"Right," said the driver.

"Well, we certainly aren't going to check that leather case, and, if we try and carry it through security at the airport, we'll have a lot of explaining to do. The briefcase might be held or confiscated. I'd hate to have to explain to Bailitz that we had the suitcase, and it was taken away at the German border."

The driver said, "So, we should drive straight to Kronberg Castle?"

"That's what I'm thinking. It'll take three hours. Not that much longer than checking in, going through security, flying, and going through security again at the other end."

The driver kept the speed of the car up, despite the worsening of the surface of the road. Though they hadn't noticed it, the road they were traveling was heading upward into the mountains. Abruptly, a large truck loaded with logs appeared, bearing down on them in the opposite direction.

"Watch out!" shouted the German who wasn't driving.

"I see it, I see it," the driver said testily. He swerved the car off the road onto the shoulder to avoid a head-on collision. "I'm not sure why the road is so rough and narrow. Or why a monster truck is coming the other way." As the truck whooshed by, their BMW was buffeted by the force of the air moving along with the truck. The driver of the lumber truck looked down at them, and honked his horn both in irritation and warning.

"Idiot!" said the second German. "We should be on the major route to Geneva—not on a feeder road for someone taking trees out of this forest. Is there any way we can get off this?"

"No, we can only get off by turning around." The driver then pointed. "Look, there's a car stopped on the other side of the road!"

"Pull over. This may be exactly what we're looking for."

The stopped car was a maroon four-door Opel. There was no driver in the car. The German driver of the BMW crossed over and parked behind the Opel. The driver of the Opel, seeing the BMW, emerged from the woods. He had a pair of binoculars hanging around his neck, probably returning from some bird watching. The German approached the Swiss birder and said, in English, "We've got a sick woman. She's unconscious and needs help."

The Swiss birder, a middle-aged man, walked quickly toward the BMW to see what the problem was. The German struck him across his neck with the sharp edge of the back of his hand. The driver fell forward, knocked out. The German searched for identification and carried the unconscious man around to the passenger side of the BMW.

Then, the German driver said, "Switch the suitcase to the Opel's trunk, and I'll drive it. You drive the BMW. We'll find a place in the forest to dump the BMW and the driver."

Tom was madly driving the Saab trying to catch up to Alex. He was panic stricken that the Germans would do something to her. Yes, of course the Moses Virus was critically important, but he was focused on trying to save her. He was suddenly aware how attached to her he had become.

Abruptly, about two hundred yards in front of him, Tom spotted something in the road. At first he thought he could maneuver around it and scarcely cut his speed. But as he drew closer he began to make out a human form in the middle of the road. He applied the brakes with force, bringing the car to a stop. It was a human. Suddenly Tom realized—it was far more than a human lying in the middle of the road—it was Alex. Tom burst out of his car and ran to her. She saw him running toward her and began crying, and it seemed more in relief and joy than from discomfort or pain.

Tom immediately removed the ropes binding her, pulled her up to her feet, facing him. "How is your arm?" he asked.

"Superficial wound," she replied. "It's stopped bleeding."

"I'm so glad to see you," Tom said and gave her a strong embrace.

"Do you still like me without my blond wig?" said Alex.

"I sure do," replied Tom. "I like you better the way you are now."

Then, Tom asked, "Why did they let you go?"

"To throw you off their trail," Alex said. "They're no dummies."

"Do you know where they're headed?" Tom asked.

"To Geneva, the airport, and Frankfurt. But, I wonder . . ."

"What do you mean?" Tom asked.

"I'm thinking that they'll have to go through security twice, in Geneva and again in Frankfurt. That means Swiss and German security, both known for their thoroughness. That might be a problem for them since they're carrying a leather suitcase with metal tubes inside. Those metal tubes will show up on any metal detector. They'll have some questions to answer that they won't want even to be asked. It might be easier for them to drive straight through to Frankfurt," Alex said.

"On the other hand, the police have their license plate numbers," Tom added, "since I gave this information to them over the phone."

"That bothers me," said Alex. "If I were they, I'd change cars to protect my anonymity."

"Let's hope you're wrong, for the sake of the driver whose car they might have taken."

He helped Alex into the Saab, and they took off in the direction the BMW had been heading.

The two Germans were now proceeding in tandem, the Opel followed by the BMW.

The road rose even more vertically and wound furiously to the right and to the left. Another gigantic truck laden with huge logs was bearing down on them.

The German driver, seeing the truck coming toward them, froze momentarily. Then he swerved. Focused solely on the danger in front of him, he made a calculated gamble. He veered to the right, swerving off the road onto the shoulder to avoid the momentum of the truck, which was coming at them at a speed and a downward pitch that made it impossible to stop even if the driver had tried, which he didn't.

The Opel roared onto the shoulder, barely missing the massive log truck careening by them. The German driver slammed on the Opel's brakes, and the BMW followed. Without warning, the forest ended on the edge of a large pit, which was being mined for the recovery of gravel. The road swept around to the left, following the contours of the pit, but the right shoulder abruptly stopped with only a wooden barrier to warn of the shoulder's termination.

The two Germans looked at the precipice and agreed: "This cliff is perfect for destroying the BMW."

They walked to the edge and looked down the one hundred fifty feet to the bottom. They moved the unconscious driver to the driver's side of the BMW. They opened the trunk, pulled out two red gasoline containers and emptied gasoline throughout the interior of the BMW, including onto the unconscious Opel owner. They pulled the wooden barrier aside. The two Germans got in the Opel. The driver maneuvered the Opel to the back of the BMW. Then he used his vehicle to push the BMW over the edge of the cliff.

The BMW began to fall in a long graceful arc, one hundred and fifty feet. Seconds later, the car, with its unconscious occupant, smashed into the huge rocks and unattended machinery below, at the bottom of the pit.

The BMW made a crunching noise as it collapsed like an accordion. The gas tank exploded in an orange fireball, and the explosion set off the gasoline in the car's interior. The flames turned black with oil and gas as the smoke plume rose as high as the top of the pit. The heat of the consuming fire in the heap of twisted metal melted the interior of the car and incinerated the dead passenger. Soon there was nothing but the acrid smell of smoke and twisted shapes. The Germans turned the Opel around and soon found a road that would take them to the autobahn.

From inside the Saab, Tom and Alex could see billowing black smoke rising high into the sky. They headed toward the source.

Tom said, "I'll bet something has happened to the BMW. It may have crashed. We can't be far from whatever is causing the smoke. We should be there in five minutes."

Alex nodded but said nothing.

Tom continued. "If that is the BMW, and if the Moses Virus was in the car it may have been destroyed in the crash and fire."

"Just what I was thinking," Alex replied. "A virus would be destroyed by the high temperatures of a gasoline fire. It may be for the best."

Tom increased the speed of the Saab.

As the road's turns became more torturous, Tom found that he had to keep his speed down. When the road reached the large pit, he stopped the car. He and Alex jumped out of the Saab and went to the edge of the pit where they peered down at the twisted metal and remains of a car. They were engulfed with black, acrid smoke. Tom stated, "That's the BMW all right, whatever's left of it." Tom called the Montreux police and asked them to send firefighting equipment.

Alex asked, "Could the virus be a part of what we're breathing?"

Tom said, "I'm fairly certain that if the virus was in the car, it's been consumed, and the smoke doesn't contain any of it. But, standing around here is just asking for trouble. Breathing acrid smoke can't be good."

"Tom," said Alex, "we don't have the virus. Maybe it's been destroyed in the fire. Or maybe it hasn't. If the virus is still in the Germans' hands, we've got to find it. Don't you think we should get help?"

"Do you mean Pulesi?" Tom asked.

"He's the one—the only one—you seem to trust," Alex said.

Tom didn't need any more persuading. "He gave me his cell phone number just in case I needed to reach him." He dialed Pulesi's number, who picked up right away. Tom brought Pulesi up to date.

Pulesi was quick to say, "I'm glad you called. With the virus supply in dangerous hands, we need to take action quickly. I can't do much for you from Rome. But I can contact David Baskin, head of the CDC in Atlanta. He knows the situation since I've kept him informed."

"I hate to ask," Tom commented, "but is the CDC to be trusted?"

Pulesi replied, "You can definitely trust them. They desperately want to keep the virus from falling into hostile hands. This is of the highest priority."

Then Pulesi continued, "I've got Baskin's number, and I'll call you back the moment I've reached him. I'm glad you've reconnected with me. Good luck."

With that, Tom turned to Alex, who had overheard the conversation and seemed relieved. He said, "Let's get down to the bottom of this pit. I'm anxious to see if the virus was destroyed."

About a quarter of a mile farther along the road Tom discovered a service road, which wound precipitously downward to the bottom of the pit. Within ten minutes he and Alex were standing near the burning hulk, where little remained of the BMW.

Tom surveyed the scene: "I've an uneasy feeling about this."

Alex replied, "If the virus has been eradicated—that's good news."

"But," said Tom, "we need to look inside the car. What if the Germans aren't there? What if they escaped with the virus?"

Tom's cell phone rang. It was Pulesi, who said, "I'll be brief. I've spoken with Baskin. He's dispatched one of his best men from E.I.S. to assist you. His name is Gerard Pinet. He happens to be on temporary assignment in Geneva, which is a piece of great luck."

"What is the E.I.S.?" asked Tom.

"Sorry," replied Pulesi. "Epidemic Intelligence Service. One hundred and sixty elite U.S. medical operatives—think the equivalent of Navy SEALs, but dedicated to epidemiologic work. They're extremely good. But Baskin will call off Pinet if you don't want him."

Tom decided quickly. "We need help. The sooner the better. Please give Pinet my cell phone number and have him call me. The sooner he can be here the better."

As if to show just how much urgency the CDC was putting on the situation, Tom received a call from Pinet two minutes later. Tom explained his and Alex's position, telling Pinet of the crashed BMW in front of them. He also explained that he did not know yet whether the virus had been consumed by fire or was now in the hands of hostile parties.

"Where precisely are you?" asked Pinet.

Tom replied, "We're at the east end of Lake Geneva, not far from Montreux. The car's still red hot, but little more than a burned-out hulk. Our suspicion is that Belagri's men may have escaped in another car with the virus. If so, they're likely heading to Frankfurt to Bailitz's castle where I was held captive."

"Why would you guess they're driving instead of flying?"

"To avoid airport security and customs with the virus in their possession."

"Good point," said Pinet.

Tom continued, "We've called the Montreux police, and they said they've already spotted the smoke. They're on their way."

Pinet said, "I've got a car. I'll check with the police, and I'll get to you as soon as I can. Probably half an hour. Do you need anything?"

"Your brains. We must get that virus," Tom said.

"I'll see you soon," Pinet said.

Two police cars and firefighting equipment arrived within fifteen minutes. An EMS vehicle from Hôpital Riviera in Montreux arrived in another ten minutes. It took forty minutes and considerable firefighting foam to tamp down the smoldering fire so that the contents of the car could be inspected. Only one body was found in the car, a man, burned beyond recognition.

Gerard Pinet pulled up at that moment in a car driven by a police officer from Geneva. Pinet rode in the front seat beside the driver. He jumped out of the car and came right over to Tom and Alex.

Gerard Pinet was five feet ten inches tall and looked like he weighed 180 pounds. Probably not an ounce of fat on him, thought Tom. Pinet thrust his hand toward Tom, looked Tom straight in the eyes, and introduced himself. Pinet had gray eyes looking out intelligently behind brown horn-rim glasses. He had a full head of brown hair and maybe was—Tom estimated—thirty-five.

Tom introduced Pinet to Alex.

"I'm pleased to meet you," Pinet said, smiling and extending his hand to Alex, seemingly warming to this highly attractive woman with black hair, a firm handshake, and a welcoming smile. His eyes dropped to the blood stains on Alex's blouse. "Are you okay?"

"An old wound," Alex answered, then laughed.

Tom then said to Pinet, "There should have been at least two bodies—the Germans—and some evidence of the three canisters."

Alex replied, "One unidentifiable man and no canisters? That confirms the virus and the Germans are gone in a car we can't trace."

Tom replied, "My guess—the Germans seized a car which was driving by. They put its driver into the BMW sending it over the cliff. They took off with the virus in the stolen car."

Pinet commented, "Are you certain they'd go to Frankfurt?"

Tom replied immediately. "Bailitz wants the virus as soon as possible, and he's at Kronberg Castle, which is near Frankfurt."

Alex asked, "What do we do now, Tom?"

"Get this dead man to an examining room at the closest hospital, where they'll have the proper equipment to examine the body, and perhaps obtain an identification."

Pinet immediately agreed.

"We'll go to whatever hospital the EMS is going to take the victim," said Tom. "If we can identify him, we might get the man's license plate number and then the make of his car. The Germans will probably be on their way to Frankfurt, or wherever they're headed, but we'd have something to go on if we know the car they're driving."

"Spoken like a true forensic archaeologist," Pinet said. "I'll find out what I can from the police."

The EMS team put yellow tape around the burned-out hulk of the BMW. The charred human body was carefully removed from the BMW and readied for transport to the Riviera Hospital, which was a well-equipped emergency facility located within half a mile of Chillon Castle.

Tom drove Alex and Pinet, while Pinet's car and driver went separately. Both vehicles followed the EMS team into Montreux. Once at the hospital, the body was taken to an examining room. The doctor in charge at invited Pinet to work alongside him. And, as he worked, the doctor and Pinet conversed in French.

"Can you perform autopsies?" Alex asked Pinet.

"I'm standing beside the expert. This is not my training, but I do have a bona fide medical degree. I can interpret what we find."

"What are you looking for?" she asked.

"No clothes, no papers—we've only got DNA or dental work. I'm afraid that DNA analysis will take more time than we have. His teeth may provide us what we need."

Alex asked, "Will the dental analysis be reliable enough?"

"As reliable as DNA testing, and, quicker, provided Montreux has electronic dental records."

The doctor looked up from his work on the man on the operating table and said, "Two years ago, Montreux introduced a voluntary program of collecting dental records digitally. The Montreux police keep the updated electronic files. I'm ready now to take digital photographs and transmit them to the police department."

Once photographed, the images were sent.

Tom asked Pinet, "How long will this take?"

"Twenty minutes, if there's a match," the doctor said, answering Tom's question.

With some time to kill, Tom called for information on the next flight to Frankfurt from Geneva. There was a flight at 8:30 p.m., three hours away.

The Montreux police were able to identify that the dead man was a fifty-five-year-old, widowed, retired schoolteacher living in Montreux. The police records department established where he lived and the fact that he owned a ten-year-old, four-door maroon Opel. The police shared with Pinet the man's car license plate numbers.

Pinet commented to Tom and Alex, "We've got what we need. If we find the Opel we'll get the Germans and the virus. In the meantime, we need to get to the Geneva airport at fast as possible." Then Pinet added, "I'll have my driver accompany us in his car. You'll need to turn your Saab in, and we'll have the time."

Tom drove the Saab, while Pinet purchased tickets over the Internet for the evening flight to Frankfurt for himself as well as for Tom and Alex. Pinet checked with Interpol on the BMW. He told Tom and Alex, "The destroyed BMW's license plates have been traced to a car rental agency at Geneva airport. Dead end, by the way—they paid cash. The BMW was registered in the name of John Jones."

Tom smiled. "Not very original."

Alex looked up, grinning. "John Jones? Why, I know a 'John Jones,' in Rome."

"What does she mean?" Pinet asked.

"That's an inside joke. Alex registered me at a hotel in Rome under that alias."

"Oh," said Pinet, smiling. "And, please, call me Gerard." Then he added, "I've given the Opel's license plate numbers to Interpol, and the police between here and Frankfurt will be on the lookout for them."

Tom added, "We might even get there first."

Gerard said, "Can you describe anything about Belagri's set-up in Frankfurt? I suspect we'll get a warm reception. We'll need help."

Tom described Kronberg Castle as he remembered it. Then he described Bailitz and his plans to use the virus. He covered the rooms he had seen or been in, the back entrance. When he finished, Gerard said, "We've still got some time before the flight to Frankfurt. I'll get busy rounding up some support in Frankfurt for us."

While driving to the Geneva airport, Gerard contacted the head of his E.I.S. unit in Geneva, who gave Gerard the name of the E.I.S. counterpart in Berlin. Gerard immediately called him. The German E.I.S. officer's name was Carlo Schmidt.

Pinet explained to Schmidt the circumstances surrounding the Moses Virus. He made clear to Schmidt that "having the Moses Virus released could lead to uncontrollable hysteria—worldwide— perhaps the worst pandemic we've ever seen."

Schmidt, sobered by what he heard, said, "What do you need?"

Gerard replied, "I've two requests, one straightforward, the other more complicated."

"Tell me."

"A car and driver at the Frankfurt airport to pick up the three of us and to stay with us," Gerard said.

"Done," said Schmidt. "I'll have that car waiting for you. What's the second request?"

"We have to assume that Bailitz—the man behind Belagri—will stop at nothing to defend his position, especially once he has the Moses Virus in his possession."

Schmidt asked, "You mean they've got weapons?"

"In the hands of mercenaries," Gerard replied. "So I think we need a team—maybe no more than four or five men, in plainclothes, but armed. We'll need them immediately—by the time we land in Frankfurt."

Schmidt paused. "From what you've told me, the best group for this job is the Grenzschutzgruppe 9. We've worked with them in the past, and they're outstanding."

Gerard, pausing in his conversation with Schmidt, asked, "Grenzschutzgruppe 9?"

"They go by a nickname—GSG-9. You might have heard of this," Schmidt said.

Tom, who had been listening to Gerard's side of the conversation, said, "Still haven't heard of them."

Gerard said, "Not surprising. GSG-9 is Germany's elite counterterrorism unit. Formed after the Munich Olympics massacre in 1972, it performs mostly behind the scenes. And it gets the job done—if possible—without firing weapons."

Gerard resumed speaking with Schmidt. "The GSG-9 is exactly what I was hoping for. Belagri presents a terrorist threat."

Schmidt said, "I'll take care of this. Where do you want the men?"

Gerard said, "We need them at Kronberg Castle outside Frankfurt. And we arrive at the Frankfurt airport about 9:45 p.m. tonight. We'll meet them at a point near the castle grounds, a specific rendezvous we'll have to figure out. That reminds me, we'll need a briefing about Kronberg—its grounds, and, inside, the layout. Also, make sure that GSG-9 has an expert present who is fully familiar with biological and chemical weapons."

"Will do," Schmidt said, "and we'll see that we get the information on Kronberg's grounds and blueprints of the interior. I'll get to work now. We don't have much time."

After his conversation with Schmidt ended, Gerard turned to Alex and Tom. Tom looked relieved, and he was actually smiling.

"Perfect," said Tom. "The GSG-9 unit sounds efficient and discreet. If they've got someone familiar with biological and chemical weapons along with them, that'll be great. We don't know what we'll run into."

Gerard added, "You may not have heard him speaking, but Schmidt has the slow, easy drawl of a southern Bavarian gentleman, yet I know the E.I.S. They immediately get the situation—they're highly efficient and make things happen. And, I'm sure, if Schmidt says so, the GSG-9 will be fully familiar with biological and chemical weapons."

Around 8 p.m., Gerard, Tom, and Alex pulled into the Geneva airport. They parked their Saab outside the rental agency, checking it in with attendants. Gerard turned to Tom: "We've got a lot to talk about, but let's get to the boarding area since they should be announcing our flight momentarily. We'll need to pick up boarding passes."

Gerard added, "The flight's not crowded, and I talked my way into having us sit next to each other, as well as separate from anyone else."

Once on the plane and bound for Frankfurt, Tom and Alex were seated together, with Tom on the aisle. Gerard was in the other aisle seat. The plane was half-empty, as Gerard had predicted, and there was no one close enough to hear their conversation.

"Your name is French," Alex said.

"You mean, I don't act French or even have a noticeable French accent?" Gerard said, anticipating what Alex seemed to be thinking.

"Well, yes," Alex said, "that's what I had in mind."

"I'm highly flattered by that," Gerard said, smiling. "I give credit to Harvard Business School, Harvard Medical School, Mount Sinai for residency and further study of communicable diseases, and training with E.I.S.—all of these activities have drummed my French accent out of me."

Alex apologized, "I know I have a definite Italian accent in my English."

"Not true," said Tom and Gerard in unison.

"Anyway," Gerard added, "I take your comment as a compliment."

Tom said, "Gerard, I have no idea how well Bailitz protects himself, but I have to assume he'll be heavily defended."

Gerard replied, "The GSG-9 can handle just about anything."

"What role do we play?" Tom asked.

"You've been at Kronberg Castle recently and know more than anyone else where the virus might be. I won't kid you—there is considerable danger," said Gerard, looking closely at his two traveling companions.

Tom was silent. Alex looked at Tom, concern spreading across her face.

Then Tom said, "How do you do this, Gerard? You're in as much danger as Alex and I are. Yet you don't seem to show concern."

"It's my job, so I don't think much about it. I weigh what happens to the world if I don't intervene. Here, it's an open-and-shut case. From what I know, the virus would probably be the most dangerous virus ever to be set loose on mankind."

"You believe that, really?" Tom asked.

"Baskin told me our labs at CDC examined minute particles recovered from the green moss in the Roman Forum. It's the real Mc-Coy. More virulent even than the Spanish flu." Gerard continued. "You tell me that Bailitz will set the Moses Virus off in Nairobi?"

"That's the first stage of his plan," Tom stated.

"We're concerned by what may happen in Kenya, but extremely worried that he won't stop there. Suppose he sets off the Moses Virus in another major metropolitan center, like Paris, Hong Kong, or New York?"

"You mean substantially more people could be exposed?" Tom asked.

"Exactly. Sixty million people visit New York City every year. That means 166,000 visitors are in New York on any given day. Think where these travelers come from—virtually every state of the United States, and every country of the world. Infect any or all of these 166,000 visitors, and they will carry the virus to their homes. We stopped the outbreak of SARS a few years ago because we tracked and isolated those carrying the virus. Virtually every person was tracked down. But there isn't enough manpower to prevent a worldwide pandemic like the one that this virus could cause."

Tom concluded, "So, the danger is less to the world from Belagri starting an epidemic in Kenya than from starting one in New York or Paris?"

Gerard said, "The power Bailitz possesses with this virus is awesome. From what I understand, a man like Bailitz, so strongly driven, may use the power to extort all he wants. He will convince himself that the end justifies the means. When I see the risks to the world from substances like a virus as potent as this one, I willingly take personal risk to keep the unthinkable from happening."

Tom said, "Bailitz is charismatic, driven, brilliant. I'd hope he would wait to use the virus until he has the antidote and can control it. Am I wrong?"

"Tom," Gerard replied, "Bailitz certainly knows you are still alive. That was not his original plan. He'll assume you're going after help. That's us. He knows we will do everything in our power to stop him. Hand over the virus to us? He'll never do that."

"Why wouldn't he wait until he's got the antidote?" Alex persisted.

"Antidotes are tricky—they may take too long to develop, and he'd have to deal with us. No, if I were Bailitz and believed in my mission, I'd set off the virus as he's planned to do in a place like Nairobi, then I'd follow up with a strike in New York. There's a fine line between brilliance and madness," Gerard concluded.

Tom looked at Alex, then at Gerard. "I'm not a professional in these matters, as you are. But I couldn't live with myself if I shrank from offering my help."

Alex said, "I'm on board, as well."

Tom then said, "Let's go over again what we're trying to get done. With the Moses Virus in dangerous hands, and time working against us, we can't afford to make a mistake of any kind."

When their flight touched down at the Frankfurt airport, passport control had been prearranged by the U.S. Embassy so that Tom, Alex, and Gerard descended from the plane and got into a black Mercedes station wagon waiting next to the plane on the tarmac. The station wagon was driven by a uniformed officer who spoke flawless English. "I'm an officer of Bundespolizei, our federal police force. We were asked by the E.I.S. in Berlin to assist you. We're coordinating with a unit of the GSG-9 which will meet us near Kronberg Castle."

Tom said, "If we could stop the Germans in the Opel before they reach the castle with the virus, we would make life much easier for ourselves."

"Agreed," said Gerard. "Maybe we can get the local police to set up a roadblock." Speaking to the Bundespolizei officer, Gerard asked, "Can you help to arrange a roadblock?"

The Bundespolizei officer radioed his home base in Frankfurt. After a few minutes of conversation he switched off the radio: "Headquarters says they're not hopeful the local police chief will set up the roadblock."

"Why not?" Gerard asked.

"Jurisdiction," he answered. "We're part of the federal police force. The roadblock would have to be set up by the local police force, which reports to the State of Hesse."

"Why is this a problem?" asked Tom.

"Belagri has a lot of power in this region, which means they've given plenty of money to local politicians. The police won't cross the local politicians, and we can't make them. This means no roadblock. Sorry."

"So," said Gerard, "we'll just have to proceed with entering the castle grounds."

The driver continued, "I've got plans of the castle, and I also am familiar with its grounds, the forest, and towns nearby."

Gerard asked, "Please give me a general picture."

"Kronberg is in the middle of a large forest. Its entrance gates are closely guarded, and this is the only way in. There's an eighteen-hole golf course between the entrance gates and the castle itself, built when the castle was a hotel before being purchased by Belagri."

Tom asked to see the building diagrams for the second floor. After he looked at them, he admitted his surprise. "These plans don't match my recollection of the second floor, which is a series of labs, conference rooms, and some bedroom suites, organized on either side of a wide corridor. There's also a hidden internal passageway, which I've been told very few people know about."

Gerard said, "Looks like that floor was changed by Bailitz, which means we'll have to rely on your memory of what's there. Tell us what you learned in your encounter with Bailitz. You know more about him than any of us. He's always kept a low profile."

Tom said, "Bailitz uses his suite of rooms on the second floor of the castle as his personal headquarters. He has a private bedroom, and, from what I learned when I was held captive, there are a series of rooms, loaded with computers, in which teams of Belagri personnel prepare for Bailitz's secret operations.

"Bailitz's first objective is an attack on Nairobi. He was planning this anyway, but once he has the virus—and Gerard has pretty much convinced me that Bailitz won't stop there—he'll create a global incident of terror and panic rather than a local one that plays into his plan of making Belagri an unstoppable force. One of the rooms in Bailitz's suite is the central planning area for the Nairobi operation.

I'm sure there are other planning rooms for other cities on his list, as well as laboratories where viruses are experimented with.

"We're dealing with a man who's blinded himself to the real dangers of what he's doing and will stop at nothing to accomplish his objectives. I believe he's out to create hysteria on a massive scale. He won't stop until he has an absolute monopoly."

Gerard asked, "Did you see any of the laboratories?"

"I only heard them talked about. But I know that once he has the Moses Virus he will be moving as fast as he can to find the antidote for it. Bailitz is anxious to protect himself and Belagri. But he also plans to offer the antidote to countries that 'play ball' with him. By all rights, he should wait to set off the Moses Virus until he can control it with his antidote. But I'm not sure Bailitz will wait—that's not his frame of mind."

Tom added, "There's a secret corridor with a stairway down to the back of the castle, which I've been in."

"How should we enter the castle? The front will surely be guarded," Gerard said. "I would guess that the secret back entrance will be locked and protected by security cameras everywhere."

Tom thought for a few moments. "I have an idea for getting in the castle."

"What is it?" Gerard asked.

"Crystal Close, one of Bailitz's top executives, helped me escape and gave me her cell phone number. She could disarm the security system and unlock the door."

"Why would she? And if she does what's to keep her from telling Bailitz?"

"She's complicated. Yes, she helped me escape, but I also realized that this was a set-up to let Belagri follow me to get their hands on the virus supply. I think she's conflicted about Bailitz's plan to use the virus."

Gerard interjected. "If we seek her help, we'd have to assume she's still on Bailitz's side and that she'll tell him."

"Understood," replied Tom, "but we'll at least get in the castle from the back while GSG-9 fights its way in the front."

"We'll tell the GSG-9 commander when he arrives," Gerard said.

The Bundespolizei officer said to Gerard, "He'll be waiting for us at the checkpoint. We should be there in two minutes."

Alex asked, "Can Belagri stop us at the front gates?"

"Plainly marked federal police cars like ours on an official police mission will not be stopped," the Bundespolizei officer answered. "And the GSG-9 will be using federally marked cars. The guards won't stop us but they'll report us to the castle. Our plan is for two squad cars with the men from GSG-9 to enter the front of the castle. Our car will go around to the back."

The Bundespolizei officer pulled the car over to the side of the road.

"Why did you stop?" asked Gerard.

"We're at the checkpoint—a mile away from the front gate of the castle. The two GSG-9 squad cars will rendezvous here. They should be arriving momentarily."

At that moment, two black squad cars pulled up, then turned their engines and lights off.

Tom said to Alex, "I'm thinking about what could happen: I'd feel a lot better if you stayed behind."

Startled, Alex said, "Why? I want to be with you."

Gerard agreed with Tom, saying to Alex, "Better you stay. We three will go up the back stairs. Alex, we need you in the car near the back entrance. You'll pick us up when we're done, but the car won't be so obviously waiting by the secret entrance."

Alex was silent, and not happy.

Tom was relieved that Gerard had spoken up. He didn't want Alex exposed to additional danger. But—he thought—she is so damned independent, she'll want to be with us.

By her silence, Alex stoically accepted that she would be staying with the car.

The commander of the GSG-9 force got out of one of the black federal cars. As he approached, Tom saw a tall man with an imposing physique. He was dressed in camouflage fatigues, his face darkened with black paint. He had shiny black boots and a trooper's beret.

The officer from the Bundespolizei got out of the Mercedes and walked briskly to meet the GSG-9 commander. They shook hands and walked back to the car. Tom, Alex, and Gerard got out, and they were introduced to the GSG-9 commander. He had a strong, even menacing face, with a nose that had a flattened look as if it had barely survived some serious battles. He introduced himself as Otto Kramer.

Kramer said to Gerard, "My men and I are ready. I have a plan, but I'd like to hear your thoughts." Looking at Tom he added, "Weren't you here recently, Dr. Stewart?"

Tom replied, "There's a secret back door to the castle and a stairway up to Bailitz's quarters. That's where his security force will be concentrated and the virus will be."

"Your plan?" the GSG-9 commander asked.

Gerard replied, "We could go up the back way while you go in the front."

Kramer listened, but replied impatiently, "What makes you think that the back stairway isn't fully guarded? It could be a suicide trap."

Tom then mentioned his idea to call Crystal Close and ask her to turn off any alarms.

Kramer said, "There's significant risk in your plan since you don't know if this woman will turn you in."

Tom added, "I can't argue with you. We certainly have to be along with your team to destroy the virus, one way or another. If we go up together via the front stairway, we're all exposed. I'm only suggesting the back route gives both your team and the three of us a second access that may be useful."

"I admit it's a reasonable idea, but there is considerable risk. For you. If you accept this risk, I'm willing to go ahead with it."

Tom said, "Should I call the Belagri officer—Crystal Close?"

"Proceed," Kramer said.

Tom reached Crystal and told her he needed her help. He added that there would an effort to retrieve the virus.

Crystal didn't deny that the virus was in Bailitz's possession. "I'm concerned," she said. "Bailitz has changed his plan. Now he wants to use the virus even before there's an antidote to control it. You know the danger." She paused and said, "I'll let you in. I'll disarm the security cameras on the back drive and at the entrance to the castle. You'll have to move fast, since even if I disarm them, the system is programmed to reset itself."

"How long do we have?" Tom asked.

"Ten minutes," Crystal said.

"As we enter the castle grounds, I'll call you. Then you should immediately disarm the system."

"I'll do that. Be careful. Bailitz is on edge tonight. He has his scientists already working on the virus with orders to test it and begin looking for the antidote."

Tom related the substance of his conversation. Kramer outlined his plan to enter the castle from the front demanding to see Bailitz. "He'll know why we're there." The commander paused. "This virus. Tell me what we're dealing with."

Gerard summarized the reasons behind the mission to destroy the virus, and at the words "mankind's most deadly virus," Kramer said nothing, but pursed his lips in determination.

Gerard continued, "I'm sure Bailitz will deny any knowledge of the virus and will certainly deny having it. He'll order you to leave."

Kramer smiled and said, "We're a tough enough looking group, and he'll know we mean business. He'll demand a search warrant."

"But," said Gerard, "we don't have one—unless you have already taken care of that."

Kramer said, "I've ordered a warrant—but we don't have it yet. Frankly, with what's at stake, we're going in now with or without a warrant."

Tom asked, "I heard you prefer not to use weapons."

"We definitely carry guns and are ready to use them. In most cases we prefer to intimidate—we'll try that first. I'll tell Bailitz to avoid unnecessary bloodshed—but I doubt that'll work," Kramer said. "We carry Heckler & Koch MP5s, which are 9-millimeter submachine guns, and 0.38 caliber revolvers. No one in his right mind should want to tangle with us. Now, let's go over what you'll be doing while we go in the front."

Tom replied, "The entrance to the back stairway is heavily disguised, but I know the way in. It goes up into a passageway that

Bailitz uses to spy on what's happening in any of the rooms on the second floor—the entire second floor is Bailitz's secret headquarters. I think there are only two exit points from the passageway into the second-floor rooms."

Tom continued, "I've been told that the passageway terminates in Bailitz's bedroom suite—that's one exit point. The other exit is near what they call the Nairobi room. I was taken through this door when I escaped."

Kramer said, "So you can enter the rooms on the second floor through this back passageway?"

Tom nodded affirmatively. "The first thing Bailitz will do—or already has done—is hand over some of the virus to his scientists to test it and begin making an antidote. He'll move fast. I'm sure we'll find the virus in the lab—likely under refrigeration since it's less dangerous that way."

"What about the scientists working in those labs, or security guards or Bailitz himself?" Kramer asked.

"There are one-way mirrors in the passageway that open into every room. We'll have a great vantage point as long as we stay in the passageway, but we'll have to be very careful."

"I'm still uneasy about your plan. We're excellent at defense but we're downstairs making a ruckus. You'll be at the center of the action, and we'll be downstairs. You're not used to shooting guns, are you?"

Gerard said, "Yes," but Tom said, "No."

"Do you even have weapons with you now?"

Both Gerard and Tom said, "No."

"I can fix that," Kramer said. "I've extra pistols. But I want one of my men to accompany you."

The Bundespolizei officer spoke up. "I'm planning to join Dr. Stewart and Mr. Pinet."

Kramer said, "What about the woman?" The commander looked at Alex as he asked his question. "Where's she going to be?"

Alex stiffened when she heard herself referred to as "the woman," but said nothing.

The officer from the Bundespolizei replied, "She would stay with the car."

"No, I'm having one of my men, fully armed, go with Dr. Stewart and Mr. Pinet. You," Kramer said, looking at the Bundespolizei officer, "will stay and protect her."

Kramer withdrew three small pins from a box in his jacket. "Here," he said to Tom, Alex, and Gerard, "put these somewhere on your clothing, out of sight."

"What are they?" Tom asked.

"Microtransmitters. In case you get separated, we can find you by keeping track of their signals." Tom, Gerard, and Alex did as instructed. Then the commander gave them tiny earplugs. "Insert these in your ears. You'll hear me through them. They're virtually invisible. Talk at a normal sound level as you start down the passageway. We can hear everything that's going on. If things escalate, we'll know where to find you." Kramer concluded, "If we're agreed, let's go."

"One additional thing," Gerard said to the commander. "As you approach the castle, keep your eyes open for a maroon Opel. That's the stolen vehicle that Bailitz's men used to transport the virus from Switzerland. We'll be able to confirm that the German couriers with the virus actually arrived."

"Let's get going," Kramer stated.

Tom nodded and said, "I'll call Crystal Close."

Kramer said. "Yes, call her. But you should know I'm not depending on her. I've had our men combing over the castle's building plans. We know where the incoming master power lines are. We'll cut the electrical power about the moment we arrive at the castle. We believe that there's emergency backup power, which will start immediately, but not be sufficient to power the major surveillance systems. We're also certain that there are emergency generators which will fire up, but there will be a ten- to twelve-minute window during which you can move through the secret corridor unseen."

Tom said nothing but smiled to himself. He suspected Crystal Close capable of changing allegiances at will. A failsafe option where they would not be relying solely on Crystal's promises appealed to him.

Everyone returned to their cars. Almost immediately one of the GSG-9 commander's men came over to Gerard's car. He stood at attention and introduced himself as Diethelm Hoener. Then Hoener burst into a smile and got in the car.

The three cars moved out toward Kronberg Castle's front gates. Getting by the guards—who recognized that these were federal cars—was easy. Bailitz's guards called their contact at the castle and said that the federal police demanded to speak with Bailitz. The three cars proceeded, winding around the golf course surrounding the castle. Tom's car turned onto the back drive that swept around to the rear of the castle.

The two federal squad cars approached the formal entrance, which was a gigantic, imposing structure made of stone, lit by exterior spotlights. The cars drove through the entrance and went directly into the general parking area beyond. Otto Kramer left his car. The rest of his squad, four men, all in camouflage fatigues, with black paint on their faces, followed. On the way to the large oak front doors, Kramer spotted a maroon Opel parked near the entrance. The hood was still warm to the touch. He spoke into his microtransmitter. "Gerard, didn't you say that a maroon Opel was the car that carried the virus? Well, it's here."

Gerard gave Kramer the numbers on the license plate for the stolen car. The GSG-9 commander confirmed these matched the numbers on the Opel's plates in front of the castle. Then he moved into the reception area.

It was about 10:15 p.m., but there were still Belagri employees in the reception area, as if the company were expecting visitors.

There was an imperious-looking Belagri security official behind the large reception desk. "What can I do for you?" he inquired of Kramer, who presented himself at the desk. The tone of this question was unfriendly, signaling that he viewed the commander as an unwanted intruder. The GSG-9 commander, who was a good foot taller than the haughty Belagri employee, displayed no reaction.

"I'm here to see Dr. Bailitz."

"Really?" came the reply. "On what subject? And at this hour?"

"I'm a commander of the GSG-9, here on orders of the federal police. My business is with Dr. Bailitz exclusively. Relay my message to him, now." Kramer and his four men looked deadly serious. Still, the receptionist persisted.

"Let me see your identification," he said.

The GSG-9 commander produced it.

The receptionist sighed, guessing that he was not going to get them to leave. He dialed a number on his telephone, then said, "Sir, there is a commander of the GSG-9 demanding to speak with you. He's here with four troopers."

After a moment's delay, the receptionist said, "I've passed on your message. You'll be responded to directly. Take a seat if you like."

He nodded in the direction of a grouping of furniture in the reception area. Kramer moved to this area, but remained standing.

Precisely at this moment, lights in the castle flickered, then went off. The receptionist picked up the telephone, which continued to work, and called security. The commander could hear what the receptionist was saying.

The haughty receptionist complained loudly, "How am I supposed to do my job if you can't keep the power on? Oh, the power's out everywhere?"

Electrical lights for emergencies came on. The receptionist duly told security of this development. Then the receptionist whined, "You mean that the full emergency backup won't be working for another ten minutes? You've got to be joking. This is outrageous."

Kramer was pleased. He said quietly in his microtransmitter, "Power's out here, with emergency backup in ten minutes."

Gerard replied, "Power's out here. Small, dim footlights in the corridor, but we can see. The cameras, however, are likely to be out. Thanks."

From where he was, Kramer could see into the large, but now shadowy, ceremonial hall adjoining the reception area, and in the center of it he could also see the grand stairway.

Several minutes passed. The emergency power surged through the castle, and the lights came back on. Then, abruptly, at the top of the stairs, a most striking blond woman in a close-fitting red dress appeared. Otto Kramer was taken completely by surprise. The woman paused briefly, lit by a huge glass chandelier above her, then descended the grand stairway. She took each step effortlessly, looking down at those in the room, her eyes seeking the man in charge. She zeroed in on the GSG-9 commander, and as she reached the main floor she started walking toward him, holding out her hand to shake his, and presenting him with a warm, gracious smile.

Otto Kramer felt the radiant smile and the seductiveness of this beautiful woman as she approached him. He thought, this must be the woman Stewart referred to—Crystal Close. He returned a tight-lipped smile that displayed courtesy. A siren, he thought to himself.

"My name is Crystal Close," she said as their hands touched. "I'm senior vice president of Belagri." She continued smoothly. "Chairman Bailitz apologizes but is tied up with some important business matters and asked me to meet with you. What is the purpose of your visit?"

The GSG-9 commander said, "I'm here to secure a shipment of dangerous material contained in steel canisters. They were transported from Switzerland in a maroon Opel. I did notice that vehicle just before we entered the building."

Crystal replied, "We have no canisters of any dangerous substance, and that Opel belongs to Dr. Bailitz's secretary. It has been hers for ten years, and she has been here all day—she arrived early this morning as she always does and has yet to leave. Aren't Opels one of the most common cars in Germany?"

"The Opel in front of the castle, with its hood still warm from a long drive, has a Swiss license plate with numbers matching those of a stolen car in Montreux," Kramer said.

If Crystal was taken aback, she showed nothing, but stood her ground. The commander remarked to himself—this woman is tough, no pushover at all. Crystal continued, "Dr. Bailitz asked me to convey to you that unless you have a valid search warrant signed by the Frankfurt superintendent of police, you are out of order being here, and you and your men should leave at once. Do you have such a warrant?"

"We're not leaving," Kramer said. "Tell your Dr. Bailitz to have his security force stand down. My team will be coming up."

The man at the reception desk looked at the GSG-9 commander with sudden respect. The commander had stood his ground.

Crystal remained in her place, watching Kramer who had refused to leave. The smile on her face changed from warm and engaging to polite but absolutely firm. She turned and walked up the steps of the grand stairway to the second floor.

Gerard commented to Kramer over his microtransmitter, "We're continuing to move through the secret passageway on the second floor. The lights have been on for the last few minutes, even though the lighting is dim. We assume the surveillance systems are working, and we've been noticed if anyone is monitoring the equipment."

The three men, Tom, Gerard, and Hoener, the GSG-9 soldier, had entered the secret corridor and climbed the back stairway. They stopped at each window along the passageway, looking into the rooms.

Tom said, "We need to figure out where the virus is."

Gerard added, "Keep a lookout for refrigeration equipment. They'll be storing any unsealed virus under heavy refrigeration."

The first two rooms they observed from inside the passageway had tables with computers and technicians working on papers at their desks. The view of what was in the third room, however, caused all three to gasp.

In the center was a platform, about four feet high, holding a giant model of a city with miniature skyscrapers, roads, hotels, and houses. They could make out that there were small cars and larger trucks on the roads, but also cars parked along the edges of the streets. Trees, public fountains, even scores of people walking were also shown. The detail was impressive: there were railroad tracks, a couple of factories, and even several oil derricks, which looked substantial, probably made out of cast iron. On the periphery, there were papier-mâché mountains ringing the city. There were tall fans on four sides of the city.

"Amazing," said Tom. "This must be a model of Nairobi. It's a room I didn't see when I was here yesterday."

"You told me about Bailitz's first target," said Gerard. "But this model is so complete. Hearing you talk about it is one thing. Seeing it makes Bailitz's plan more sinister and real. Every one of my colleagues at E.I.S. has the same nightmare: being unable to stop a virus pandemic that rages out of control."

"Like SARS?" asked Tom.

"Exactly. In three to four weeks, it spread from one province in China to thirty-seven countries. We stopped it, but only barely."

Gerard was silent for a few moments, staring into the Nairobi room.

"What do you see?" Tom asked,

"I've spotted at least two cameras. Bailitz can watch everything going on in this room without being in the secret passageway."

Otto Kramer interrupted, speaking to them over their earphones. "We have to assume that the woman Bailitz sent down to meet me has told Bailitz about your going up the back passageway. In any case, with the power back on, the surveillance systems will be working again. Check to see if the passageway's been booby-trapped."

The soldier accompanying Tom and Gerard shone his flashlight in the passageway. "There are some simple black boxes on the floor every twenty feet or so."

In Tom's and Gerard's ears, from the microtransmitter, came the voice of the GSG-9 commander to his soldier, Hoener. "Check them out, now," said Kramer.

Hoener knelt down while Gerard held his flashlight on the black box. The soldier studied the box, then said, "It's wired into the wall. There are eight wires leading from a hole in the box into the wall."

In their ears, again, from the microtransmitter, came Kramer's voice. "Don't fool with any of those wires. Some are real, others are fake. If you cut the wrong wire, the system will short out and—I would guess—an explosion of some sort will occur. Even worse, I'll bet that all the other boxes would go off simultaneously. Bailitz has planned for the possibility that a hostile might enter the secret passageway."

Tom said to Gerard, "Bailitz knows about the GSG-9 down-stairs and undoubtedly suspects we're in this passageway. We must hurry."

Gerard nodded and moved further down the corridor, with Tom and the soldier close behind. The next one-way mirror in the hidden passageway showed the interior of a gleaming laboratory. There was a metal door with a thick glass panel on an adjoining wall. From where Tom and Gerard stood, there was no entrance from the secret passageway into the laboratory.

Inside, half a dozen scientists were dressed in cotton scrubs and disposable gowns. They were wearing latex gloves and had headgear on, clear plastic shields enclosing their faces. Tubes ran out of the back of the shields to sets of filters strapped to their waists. At the entrance, there was a retina scanner and at the other end of the room there was a large freezer against the wall.

Tom said, with some excitement, "We're here. These must be Bailitz's scientists working on the virus—under orders to find an antidote."

Hoener quietly said, "I see two guards at the front door to the lab."

Tom spotted them. "They've got Hazmat suits on."

Gerard added, "That's dress code for anyone in a room with a communicable virus in it. What are they doing?"

"They're each carrying Eliseo R5 6-mm BR repeaters," said Hoener.

"What are they?" asked Tom.

"High power, highly accurate, rapid firing rifles. Deadly. These people mean business."

Abruptly, Tom realized he was outclassed. This was the big time, he acknowledged. No game, at all. How could he, or he and Alex, for that matter, have brought these professional warriors down? He felt fear.

Gerard was staring at the freezer. "I'd guess the virus is there."

The three men were studying the laboratory so intently that they completely failed to notice that someone had come up behind them in the secret passageway. "The canisters are, in fact, in the freezer," a voice said.

Tom was so startled that he whirled around to confront this voice. Standing before him was Crystal, looking as beautiful as ever. But there was also, he thought, something urgent in her eyes. "You're in serious danger here," she said. "Bailitz is in his office. He doesn't appear to know you're in here yet, but the camera surveillance will have picked you up. The arrival of the GSG-9 squad has put him on edge. He'll be on the lookout for trouble."

Tom thought, Bailitz must know about us from your telling him, Crystal. But he said aloud, "Why would I trust anything you say?"

"If you did trust me, I'd say you're a fool," Crystal answered. "But you don't have much choice, do you? I'll give you a reason, though. I never thought Bailitz was mad enough to turn a catastrophic menace like this virus loose on the world. And he's willing to do this without having found the antidote. I think he may destroy the company—a risk he now seems willing to take. I find this unacceptable. He's a wholly different person now that he physically has the virus."

"Why?" asked Tom. "Doesn't he have other toxins?"

"He does," Crystal said, "but with your virus he's like a kid with a new toy. He's as furious with the corrupt officials running the third world as he is deadly serious about cornering the world market in food production. A toxin like anthrax might create the chaos he's striving for, but the virus is a thousand times more powerful and gives him an extremely potent psychological weapon—it kills humans, rapidly, efficiently, ruthlessly. He believes it'll be seen as the vengeance of an angry God."

Crystal went on. "I'm prepared to help you stop him, since no one from the company is willing to stand up to him. Trust me or not, you'll have to agree that standing in middle of the secret passageway that leads directly into his bedroom suite is not a smart idea, right?"

"What do you recommend?" Tom asked.

"Follow me," Crystal said and started walking down the passageway. Tom, Gerard, and Hoener followed. Ten yards further down the corridor, Crystal stopped in front of a door. She turned the knob, opened the door, and walked in. "This is my room when I stay overnight," she said.

Tom was incredulous, "You once told me there were only two doors to this passageway—the one you took me out by and the other leading to Bailitz's suite. So, there's a third?"

Crystal said nothing.

They entered a windowless room, with drapes covering the spaces where windows might otherwise be. Crystal had a double bed, a sofa with three chairs, a table, and a bureau. These added up to a comfortable room, fully appointed. Crystal sat and told that the three men to sit also.

"First," Crystal said to Tom, "tell me who your colleagues are."

Tom replied, "This is Gerard Pinet, a trained doctor and a member of E.I.S., the virus investigative unit of the Centers for Disease Control in Atlanta. This soldier is a member of the GSG-9 team here to help us."

"Your mission being to recapture the virus and destroy it. Is this correct?"

"We are tasked with recovering the virus, and, yes, our mission is to destroy it before it does irreparable damage," said Gerard, with Tom nodding yes to this statement.

"We're on the same wavelength," Crystal said. "Our job, then, is to secure the virus canisters as quickly as possible, and you must escape with them."

Tom was concerned. "What will happen to you? Would you leave with us? If you help us, and Bailitz finds out, he'll come after you with a horrifying vengeance."

"I'm going to have to live with the mess I've created for myself. I've got documents proving Bailitz's insane plans are real, and I've got evidence that will destroy Belagri if anything happens to me. Even with this, I know I'm vulnerable," Crystal admitted with some regret and resignation. "Let's talk about what we need to do right now," she said.

Crystal added, "The canisters with the virus are in the freezer in the lab. Bailitz ordered them to be opened the moment he had them in his possession—he wanted to make sure the virus was there in the quantity he hoped for."

"Was it?" asked Tom.

"Just as he hoped," replied Crystal. "But, once opened, he extracted a few samples for testing for potency as well as for samples to be used for creating an antidote. He also has one vial, which he has with him."

"What for?" Gerard asked.

"He didn't say," Crystal replied. "The canisters are especially dangerous once they're open and need to be kept at extremely cold temperatures. Bailitz is so keen on launching his plan as soon as possible now that he has the virus, that he'll keep visiting the lab to see how the scientists are coming with testing for an antidote. Your best bet is to create a diversion to force an evacuation of the laboratories."

Gerard said immediately, "Make them think there's been a leak of the virus?"

"Exactly," Crystal said. "Everyone in the company knows that we had a similar accident at our major plant in Chemical Valley in West Virginia. One of our best lab technicians was careless, just once, by failing to observe Belagri's strict protocols. A very small mistake but a deadly one. This technician had previously handled the Spanish flu multiple times without consequence. But some of the virus escaped, immediately infecting her. Within hours, she died a horrible and painful death, but she had also become a carrier for the virus and infected virtually our entire team.

"We had a wide-scale minipandemic on our hands. We couldn't report this to anyone, particularly the CDC, and so had to handle it internally. Bailitz decided he had no choice but to isolate everyone who had been contaminated, which meant most of our team of scientists and technicians, as well as certain members of their families. The infected people were rounded up and placed in total isolation, until they all died. There were rumors—never proved—that some of those who were locked up and left to die never had the virus. The process took only a few days. Once it was over, everything was burned—there were no traces left."

Tom interjected, "How would we create panic among the scientists?"

"Set off the warning systems that alert everyone if a virus has escaped. The protocol is for everyone to evacuate as soon as possible."

Tom asked, "How are polluted and nonpolluted areas identified?"

"Wall dividers come down, sealing off the tainted areas."

"Where are the warning systems controlled?" Tom asked.

"There is a monitoring room within Bailitz's private suite, which I know about and can access. I can set off the alarm. We don't have much time. We need to move," Crystal warned. "I'll set off the alarm in one of the unoccupied labs. Once the alarm sounds there will be a mass exodus. Pandemonium will result. That's your chance to seize the Moses Virus canisters from the freezer and escape."

Gerard asked, "What about the retina scanner at the entrance?"

"Don't worry, the evacuation alarms will drown out any other sounds. The lab technicians will already have fled from the lab. There's risk, but I don't think you'll be noticed at all."

Diethelm Hoener said to Tom, "Can we speak in private?"

"Certainly. Crystal, can you let us have a moment alone?"

"Don't take too long," she said and slipped out of the room.

"What did you want to say?" Tom asked after Crystal had left.

"I thought we should check with my GSG-9 leader."

"Right," replied Gerard.

The soldier spoke into his microtransmitter. Otto Kramer immediately responded. "I've heard everything. Trust her or not, what she says makes sense."

Tom added, "If the GSG-9 attacks from the lobby and moves up the stairs, that would draw Bailitz's mercenaries away from us. Once the evacuation alarms go off, and people rush out, there should be enough chaos to give us some time."

Gerard and Kramer agreed. He added, "We've just received our search warrant from the Frankfurt police superintendent. The superintendent is mad as hell at being told to do this, but was leaned on by some higher-ups. We're good to go. We'll begin an assault immediately, starting from the lobby and working our way upstairs. I anticipate that Bailitz will have his mercenaries try to stop us. This diversion should buy you some time. I suggest everyone coordinate their watches."

Gerard told Kramer exactly where the three of them were. Tom asked Crystal to return.

Tom said, "Crystal, we're ready. The GSG-9 force has the search warrant and will engage Bailitz and his men immediately."

Crystal looked surprised, but said, "It'll take me a few minutes to set the alarm off. I'll leave, and you wait here. After five minutes, head toward the lab the moment you hear the alarms." She left them to get to the control room.

After Crystal was out of the room, Gerard said to Tom, "I was surprised you told her about the GSG-9's plans."

Tom replied, "If we're going to throw Bailitz off balance, forcing him to deal with us on one side and GSG-9 on the other may give him more to cope with than he's comfortable with. And, no, I don't trust her."

Gerard said, "She's strikingly beautiful and obviously intelligent. I've never come across anyone like her before. She's like a chameleon. One moment on our side and the next, she's back with Bailitz. If she's being honest with us, she's in a very dangerous position if Bailitz finds out she's the one who betrayed him."

"You're right," Tom replied.

Tom called Alex, who was anxiously waiting in her car. Tom said, "We're hoping that we're about to gain control of the virus canisters in which case we'll be downstairs right away. If alarms sound—they're part of our plan. I've got to go. Love you."

"What did you say?" Alex asked, startled.

"You heard me." Tom laughed. "Wish us luck."

Alex replied, "Good luck and . . . ditto."

This time it was Tom's turn to ask, "What did you say?"

Alex laughed and said, "Over and out."

An excruciatingly loud alarm went off. It repeated itself, again and again. Doors started banging. The halls were filled with people, some in lab coats, others not.

With the alarm sounding, Kramer strode briskly through the lobby into the ceremonial hall. He pointed to the officious Belagri employee behind the reception desk, and one of the GSG-9 team members walked toward the receptionist. He took aim at the Belagri employee. There was a hissing sound as a tranquillizer dart struck his shoulder. The receptionist had raised his arms, crying out he was innocent: "Please spare me," he said. The drug in the dart took effect, and he slumped behind the reception desk. The GSG-9 soldier now stood guard to make certain no one entered the castle.

Kramer headed toward the grand stairway. Far across the room, near the fireplace that glowed with a fire to take the edge of the chill out of the room, there was a small group of men dressed in ordinary business suits sitting at a table, talking. Their briefcases were open on the surface of the table. No one else was in the main hall.

As Kramer and his team reached the grand stairway, the men at the table stood up, taking out their weapons from under papers in their briefcases. Bailitz's security guards began to yell to the GSG-9 to halt. The noise made by the evacuation alarms was deafening. Bailitz's security guards waved their guns menacingly at the GSG-9 team, which had their own weapons out and were already at the stairs and moving up.

Bailitz's guards rushed toward the grand stairway. There were four guards in plainclothes. "Clever," said Kramer to his team. "Posting guards in the ceremonial hall dressed as Belagri employees is a shrewd precaution. Let's go."

Bailitz's security force was no match for the swiftness of the GSG-9 team, who fired tranquillizer darts with deadly accuracy, hitting their targets. Within seconds, Bailitz's security team was sprawled on the floor, breathing, but totally out of commission.

Seeing that the way was now clear, Kramer moved quickly up the rest of the stairs and was only a couple of steps from the top. As he neared the top of the stairs, he noticed that the huge glass chandelier, hanging in the large stairwell, had a hidden video camera, which was in position to photograph anyone on the steps.

Kramer took careful aim at the camera and fired. There was a shattering of glass as the bullets hit the camera and knocked it out of commission. But the bullets also severed the chain tethering the chandelier to the ceiling. There was a crack as the chain snapped. Abruptly the chandelier began to fall—seemingly in slow motion, then it gathered more and more speed. The chandelier hit the stone floor and shattered, sending shards of crystal to all parts of the ceremonial hall.

In the main corridor, between Crystal's bedroom and the lab containing the virus that they were heading toward, Tom, Gerard, and Hoener walked quickly, hugging the wall. It was like moving against a torrent of fish swimming downstream.

Tom arrived first, finding the lab door swinging open and closed as one technician after another raced to get out. Tom, still flattened against the wall, kept an eye on those leaving and tried to get a look at those who remained inside. When he was certain that the last scientist had left, he grabbed the door before it closed and signaled to Gerard and Hoener to follow him. They were inside.

The retina scanning machine alarms, as Crystal had suggested, were ineffective due to the overwhelming noise from the evacuation alarms.

Gerard moved quickly to the freezer. He thought to himself that in the CDC lab in Atlanta, such a freezer would be securely locked. But in this Belagri lab, the retina scanner at the door of the lab provided the security, and the freezer itself was not locked. He opened the lid. "Three metal containers, right?"

"There should be waxed seals, and the canisters should have inscribed on them the words *Pestilentia Moseia*," said Tom.

"Only if they haven't been unsealed," said a steely voice behind the three men. A tremor rumbled through Tom as he recognized the voice. Tom turned to face Bailitz. "I think you'll find all three canisters are missing their seals. Perhaps because they've been opened. Perhaps because a minute amount has been removed." With this, he waved a small glass vial in the air at them.

Tom, Gerard, and Hoener faced Bailitz, who had with him one of the Germans who had kidnapped Tom in Rome, and who had then knocked him out at Chillon. The German held a gun pointed at Tom. Tom felt instant panic. He tried to focus on the vial in Bailitz's right hand. Then he looked at the German. Time seemed to slow. He had—it seemed—all the time in the world to study this German who was holding a gun pointed at him. The German had a prominent scar on his left cheek, which Tom figured was from an old dueling wound. A university skirmish? The scar made his face tough looking. He obviously meant business. Tom chastised himself for this bizarre mood he was in.

Bailitz spoke. "Let's do some housekeeping. Put your firearms on the table in front of you. Empty your pockets. I don't want any half measures. My colleague here is ready to deal with any of you who has a clever idea."

Tom and Gerard had the guns Kramer had given them. Diethelm Hoener had an MP5. They put their guns on the table.

"Go ahead, now. Empty your pockets of everything. Including cell phones." This time quite a few items were placed on the table.

"Looks like an arsenal of guns and electronic equipment, doesn't it?" Bailitz said. "This modern world of ours is really something." At that moment, the blaring of the alarms suddenly stopped. Bailitz smiled. "There, that's over. Now we can hear each other talk."

"Dr. Stewart," Bailitz continued, "did you think that the hidden passageway and the back stairway had no surveillance equipment? Cutting the castle's power was a clever idea, but we have full back-up. I will admit there was some confusion while we switched to emergency power. Your every step was monitored, however, down to the fact that your car occupied by your friend Cellini and a police officer is parked in the darkness a hundred yards from the hidden back doorway. We have a man whose gun—a recoilless rifle, actually—is trained on that car—no one in it will get out alive."

Tom shuddered inwardly at the thought.

Bailitz said to Gerard, "Please step over to the freezer and lift the three canisters out. There are gloves on the shelf above the freezer. Place the canisters in the leather case, which is on the floor beside the freezer.

Gerard went to the freezer, put the gloves on his hands, then lifted the freezer's top, removed the three canisters and placed them in the leather case, and carried it over to Bailitz. "Give the case to me," Bailitz said, extending his hand. He locked the case, then handcuffed himself to it with a handcuff he extracted from his right pocket. Tom observed that Bailitz had now put the small vial in his left pocket and had the case attached by a chain to his right wrist. "No one is going to take the virus from me," he said with strident conviction.

Bailitz continued, "I expect that we have about ten to fifteen minutes before squadrons of police and fire engines from nearby towns arrive." He looked at Tom and Gerard. "I know that I owe you for finding the virus, but I also have you to thank for setting off the alarms bringing a massive invasion of police and security people. The GSG-9 unit is undoubtedly making their way up here. We have little time. I'll be leaving here with the virus in five minutes."

He turned to his German henchman and nodded.

The German pointed his gun at Hoener. It was outfitted with a silencer. There was a muted, spit-like sound, and a scarlet mark blossomed on Hoener's forehead as he sank quietly to the floor.

"Why was that necessary?" Tom cried out, staring at Hoener's lifeless body.

"Evens the odds, that's all," Bailitz said. "There are two of you and two of us."

With the evacuation alarms turned off, there was silence in the room, but outside there was the sound of gunfire. Bailitz said, "I hear the GSG-9. Despite my efforts to assemble the best possible security force, I expect that the GSG-9 will get through. I have at least five minutes and a score to settle: You've given me the opportunity to test the potency of your virus. Let us adjourn to the Nairobi room."

The German waved his gun toward the exit door of the lab, indicating that Tom and Gerard should precede him. Tom and Gerard walked side by side, with the German following and Bailitz last, carrying the suitcase in his right hand. Under his breath, Gerard said to Tom, "Stay alert."

In another part of the castle a few minutes earlier, Kramer and his team had arrived at the top of the grand stairway and found, on the landing, five doors arranged in an arc, all of them closed. They didn't know which door led to Bailitz's suite. The leader called out to one of his men, "Try the door on the far right first. We'll cover you."

Placing himself against the wall next to the closed door, the appointed soldier gingerly turned the elaborate door handle until the lock clicked, then gave the door a firm push causing it to swing open. Nothing happened. "There's a long hallway, and I see no one," he whispered.

Kramer said, "Okay. Try the second."

The soldier moved to the second door, opened it, in the same manner. Again nothing.

The middle door was next. Tension was building. The leader said, "We've got to be lucky on one of these."

The soldier moved into position to open the third door. With the quiet turning of the handle, it opened. He gave the door a push, and it swung all the way open. As it did, there was a hail of bullets traveling down the interior corridor, which burst out through the open door, striking the stone wall on the far side of the grand stairway.

Kramer signaled his team to cover for each other and begin firing back. Their objective was to enter Bailitz's fortified quarters.

The Nairobi room, where Tom and Gerard were being taken at gunpoint, was a short distance down the corridor from the lab. No one was in the hallway, all the lab technicians and other employees having rushed out of the building. The German said to Gerard, "Open the door and go in."

Gerard and Tom entered the large room with its fans and models of the city of Nairobi and the surrounding mountains. Bailitz was last in. He looked at the model city. "Interesting plan, don't you think? Strike a city down with a plague-like virus, kill its animals, and wipe out its agriculture, just like the wrath of an angry God destroying the Egyptians. What do you think the fundamentalists around the world will think? Will the crazy groups that are always predicting the imminent end of the world seize on this virus as evidence of Armageddon? How much will each country pay to make certain this doesn't happen to them?"

Tom was horrified. Bailitz's plans were far more aggressive than he had realized—he now actually planned to extort world governments.

Almost as if he were reading Tom's mind, Bailitz said, "New York is next, after Nairobi. A lot more money is at stake there."

Bailitz said to the German, "We'll be leaving shortly. We need to be ahead of the German police." He withdrew his cell phone from his pocket. Holding it up, he carefully logged in a preprogrammed self-destruct code. At first, nothing seemed to happen. But suddenly, the room they were standing in was rocked by a distant explosion, followed by another and another.

"What's that?" asked Tom.

"The interior spaces on this floor, the labs, the demonstration rooms, are being ignited, one by one. They are set to burn at a fast pace and at an extremely high temperature. Nothing inside can survive. Nothing will be left to be found—no evidence, nothing. I don't like destroying my own property, but I've got what matters most," Bailitz said, holding up his right arm with the leather case containing the virus dangling below, "and I've got other secret locations I'll use after this."

Tom, though his situation was perilous, ignored his own predicament and pressed Bailitz. "Where can you take the virus? You'll be hounded by the police and the CDC."

Bailitz replied, "I've got a second lab—totally private, not known, even to top management of Belagri. There we can work on the virus in complete secrecy. But, no more delay tactics." Bailitz looked up. "It is time to start the fans. We have precisely five minutes until this room is ignited." He took out the vial from his left pocket and a cold smile spread across his face. "I want to see how our two friends do with a taste of the virus."

On Bailitz's cue, the German walked over to a switch on the wall that controlled the fans.

"The virus acts more swiftly with circulating currents of air," Bailitz said as he edged toward the door. "At heart," Bailitz added, "I'm a scientist. And as a scientist, I need to test the potency of your virus. So I'm delighted you've volunteered to be my guinea pigs." There was a look of supreme satisfaction in his eyes. He seemed to be deliriously pleased with the fate he was about to administer to Tom and Gerard.

The German henchman's hand reached out to switch the fans on. In the split second that his back was turned to Bailitz, overly confident that his gun gave him superior power, the German was vulnerable. Gerard grabbed the small-scale model of an oil derrick from the display and hurled it at the German's forehead. As the derrick flew through the air, Tom saw his opening and threw his arms around Bailitz, who didn't see Tom coming. With the vial in his left hand and the suitcase attached to his right wrist, Bailitz was fairly easy to corral. He struggled but couldn't escape, and Tom tightened his grip, immobilizing Bailitz.

Just before he was struck by the flying derrick, the German pushed the switch for the fans and wheeled around, but he didn't have the split second he needed to duck. The flying cast-iron oil derrick struck him on the forehead with a solid thud. His blue eyes widened, then he sank to his knees, dazed. Gerard rushed to grab his gun before the German recovered. It was over in a second. The fans kicked up a strong breeze.

Tom glanced down and in horror saw that Bailitz had intentionally or unintentionally broken the vial. "Quick, the vial's broken!" Tom screamed at Gerard. "Get out the door!" Gerard dove for the door. Tom gave Bailitz a shove, sending Bailitz to his knees. Tom made it to the door a split second after Gerard.

They burst out of the Nairobi room and pushed the door into its closed position. There was the secure sound of an airtight seal forming. Both Tom and Gerard could look through the thick glass panel into the room. Bailitz was struggling to get up. He was encumbered by the leather case strapped to his right wrist. He had a cut on his left hand from the broken vial. Its contents had spilled into his cut and into the air. The fans moving air in the room swiftly picked up the droplets of the virus, spreading it everywhere.

Over near the wall where he had fallen, the German was awake and starting to stand up. The German began to cough. Bailitz was racked with coughing. In a blinding flash, Bailitz must have realized that he had set in motion his own horrendous undoing and death. His grabbed his head in pain; his breathing was labored. His face was a mask of terror as he collapsed. Bailitz, the chief executive officer of Belagri, was trapped inside a ravaged body. Dimly, he must have realized that his dreams were over. He was in pain and having trouble breathing.

Tom turned to Gerard, and said, "Fast—super fast."

"Apparently," Gerard said. "The Spanish flu took effect in a few hours, with death in a day or two. This virus acts immediately. I think you're seeing what happened to your colleagues in the Roman Forum."

Tom shuddered at his memory of Doc's and Eric's deaths.

Bailitz's body contorted in pain. He cried out for help. Then, with almost superhuman strength, he pulled himself together and inched slowly toward the door behind which Tom and Gerard were watching. The leather case with the virus inside was being dragged by Bailitz, who was mouthing a cry for help, to be let out.

"Don't even think about it," Gerard said to Tom. "Without an antidote, which we don't have, the damage to Bailitz and his henchman has been done. They can't survive. Going back in there would only spread the virus to you and, if you left the room, to others. With what Bailitz planned for us, for Nairobi, for the world, this is a suitable fate for him."

Tom said to Gerard, "We should contact Otto Kramer."

"You're right," Gerard said.

"We've been able to hear you since the alarms stopped," said Kramer over the earpieces that Tom and Gerard were wearing. "What are those explosions?"

Tom replied, "Bailitz has detonated each of the labs. He's trapped in one, which is about to be blown up."

"He's dead?"

The lab suddenly exploded. There was a bright fireball of light, coupled with a loud noise that sounded like thunder. Tom felt the shock rock through his body, and he stumbled. But both he and Gerard were unhurt otherwise. The thick glass and steel of the door protected them.

"He is now," Tom said, staring at the carnage.

"What was that?" Kramer asked.

"That was the last lab," Gerard said, "the Nairobi room—blown up. We're standing just outside it."

"And Bailitz?" asked.

Tom said, "Bailitz is inside—burned, or burning, to a cinder. The virus has been incinerated. It's over."

The commander said, "Thank God. We have a couple of snipers between us and you, but we should be there momentarily."

The steel lab had contained the explosion, but Tom and Gerard could see through the thick glass in the steel door that the inside had become a fiery furnace. The room was burning furiously. Heat from the fire made the glass panel in the steel door extremely hot. "Don't touch it," Gerard warned after he came close to burning his own hand.

Bailitz had collapsed, and the fire had engulfed him. The leather case was on fire as well. Tom couldn't see the canisters that were in the case. The German's body was also in flames. The two bodies were twisting into shapes that Tom recognized, from the Roman Forum with Doc and Eric, but also from the videos of the bodies in Imhotep's tomb.

Tom suddenly looked shocked. Gerard spotted this change that had come over Tom and said, "What's the matter? Something wrong?"

Tom muttered, "Imhotep's mural."

"What are you talking about?"

"The Bible names ten plagues, but the Egyptian mural in Imhotep's tomb has eleven panels, one of them depicting Egyptians being devoured by flames. Seeing Bailitz and the German engulfed, I was reminded of the mural."

"So, go on, tell me what you're thinking," Gerard said.

"I think that the Egyptians who survived the final plague—a devastating virus that attacked humans—figured out that the virus could be snuffed out with fire. In the picture showing the flames, three canopic jars are depicted—not the usual four. The actual jars were found in the tomb, and none of them were filled with Imhotep's organs. Their contents had samples of victims, including human samples. What occurs to me is that those highly shrewd Egyptians had figured the virus out—three thousand years ago, and sent a warning about it, how to fight it, and samples for their successors."

"Why do you think that the fire panel was not the last one?"

"I'm guessing," said Tom. "For the Egyptians, the afterlife was so important that everything in their culture was directed to preserving the human body for its next existence. Destroying a body by fire to kill a virus would be seen as treasonous. It was imperative to comment on the plague but not to present it in so obvious a place as either the first or last panel. If I'm right, I'm amazed at how sophisticated this ancient culture was. Some priests have reached to us across a gap of three thousand years. But I may be wrong—it's just a guess on my part."

"Impressive deductions," said Gerard.

Tom and Gerard were mesmerized by Bailitz's fate. They knew, of course, that the other labs would be burned into charred remains with nothing identifiable remaining. That meant that Diethelm Hoener, the GSG-9 soldier shot by Bailitz's henchman, would be lost, as would all papers, documents, and substances within the rooms. Tom guessed that the contained nature of the burning labs might save the castle from destruction, but he wasn't sure of this.

Otto Kramer and his team reached Tom and Gerard. The Nairobi room was still white hot. The commander immediately asked, "Are you okay?"

Tom and Gerard both replied, "We're fine."

"Where's my soldier?"

Tom shook his head. "Shot by one of Bailitz's men and left in another lab. We could do nothing. The lab is one of those that Bailitz blew up."

Kramer sent a detail of his men to see if his soldier could in any way be retrieved. Then he asked, "The virus?"

Gerard replied, "It was in a leather case strapped to Bailitz's wrist. We saw it burning. I assume the virus was vaporized. But we won't know for sure until the room cools down and we can check it out."

Kramer added, "We picked up the blond woman. She was in the secret passage, heading for the back stairs. My men are holding her. We're going to question her. She's protesting that she's not involved."

Tom said, "That's a joke. She's totally involved. You'll want to question her, because she has valuable information. But there's probably no point in detaining her, since she's actually been very helpful to us."

Borrowing the commander's cell phone, Tom called Alex, who was frantic with fear that something might have happened to him. She told him that she had heard the alarms, gunfire, and the intermittent explosions. She and the Bundespolizei officer had driven to the back entrance of the castle where she had been waiting impatiently for Tom.

Gerard said to Tom, "I'll need to stay here until the lab has cooled. I want to make certain the virus is completely destroyed."

"How long will that take?" Tom asked.

Kramer replied, "All the local fire departments are here, battling the fires."

Tom said, "I'd like to go find Alex."

"Understood," replied Gerard. "Once you've done that, come on back up here. It'll still be awhile until we can make a secure examination."

Kramer said, "I want one of my men to accompany you. We've got Bailitz's men rounded up, but if there's a stray, hiding somewhere . . ."

"I understand," Tom said. "Thanks."

Tom, accompanied by a soldier Kramer assigned to him, proceeded down the hidden staircase without any incident and left the castle out of the secret entrance. Alex was standing beside the car, anxiously waiting. When she saw Tom, she ran toward him and he toward her, the two embracing with great warmth. Tom soothed her, telling her, "The Moses Virus was destroyed in the fire. Bailitz planned to use the virus on Gerard and me, but we escaped. Bailitz did not escape."

"You mean it's over? The Moses Virus is destroyed? We're free to go?" Alex asked.

"Gerard needs to make certain that there's absolutely no Moses Virus remaining, but I think the answer to that is yes, once he's verified the conditions in the lab."

Tom and Alex, accompanied by Kramer's soldiers, retraced Tom's route to the second floor, finding Gerard standing at the door to the Nairobi lab. The heat within the Nairobi room had died down enough to enter.

A Hazmat team from a local hospital had accompanied the firefighting teams and was stationed at the entrance to the Nairobi room. Gerard put on a spare Hazmat suit, and the Hazmat team, along with Gerard, entered the Nairobi room. Tom and Alex could watch through the glass panel in the laboratory door. Gerard went first to Bailitz's charred body, or what was left of it. Strapped to the bones of his wrist was a chain. There was a metal handle at the end of the chain, but it had half melted. The leather suitcase had vaporized, but the three canisters lay on the floor. The tops of the canisters had blown off as the virus inside had become superheated. Gerard talked to Tom through his microtransmitter.

Tom asked, "The tops were blown off? What about the virus?"

Gerard replied, "With the temperature of the fire so searingly hot, the virus was vaporized and destroyed. I'm standing beside Bailitz's skeleton, and it is severely contorted."

Tom replied, "Just like Doc and Eric. The virus certainly leaves its telltale mark."

To make absolutely certain, Gerard made another pass through the Nairobi room, turning over all objects in the area. Gerard also went to the lab where the virus had been stored in the freezer. Again, nothing. He returned to Tom and Alex. "You know," Gerard said, "it's closure, but an odd feeling just the same, don't you think?"

Tom replied, "I think I know what you mean. A substance that endured for three thousand years is gone—there's no evidence of any amount, minute or otherwise, of the virus. I should be greatly relieved, and I am. But there's a gap in what we'll ever know about this amazing piece of history."

Gerard said, "Remember, Tom, we destroyed a menace, saved the world."

"Okay," laughed Tom, "I'm over my nostalgia. Just remembering the hell that Alex and I have been living through is enough to cure me. I'm glad it's gone, and we're safe."

"Agreed," seconded Alex.

Otto Kramer had walked through Bailitz's rooms and now returned. "We've rounded up all Bailitz's mercenaries and are taking them in for questioning. That's standard procedure. But they're hired hands, and I doubt we'll learn anything useful."

"What'll happen to them?" Tom asked.

"That's not my call," Kramer said, "but if asked I would try to recruit them. They're good. The other Belagri employees who worked in the labs—we'll let them go. We've got no case against them. The same goes for the woman—Crystal Close."

"You've nothing on her either?" Alex asked, somewhat ironically.

"She was on the scene, but was in possession of nothing illegal. This is, after all, a property owned by Belagri. I checked with my headquarters and was told that if there is no supply of the virus remaining, we have no grounds for holding any of the employees unless we have evidence that some of the people were involved in stealing it or transporting it from Switzerland. But since she's the senior-most officer of Belagri present, I've been ordered to take her in for questioning."

Gerard commented, "Without any of the virus left, we at the CDC have no jurisdiction or reason to detain her. What do you think, Tom?"

"I'm a private U.S. citizen. I've got no view on her at all."

Alex said, "I don't trust her."

Kramer asked, "Would you jail her?"

"No, I suppose not," said Alex, somewhat unhappily.

"Fine, then. I'll be taking her and leaving with my men. Our work is done. The rest of the cleaning up will be handled by the local fire departments. After that, I suppose Belagri will take over the reconstruction of the facility."

"Thanks, Otto. We're very grateful for your help and especially sorry about the loss of Diethelm Hoener," Tom said.

"Diethelm was a very able soldier, and I already miss him. He had a wife and two small children, and I'll have to break the sad news to her this morning. Loss of any of my men is tragic, and nothing excuses this loss. But if the virus had been let loose on mankind, and if we could have prevented it but didn't, then I'd never have forgiven myself." With that, Otto Kramer and his team withdrew, leaving Tom, Alex, and Gerard.

Gerard said, "I've still got my government car and driver. Would you like a lift to the airport? Will you be returning to Rome?"

Tom looked at Alex, who nodded affirmatively. "We'd like a ride. Thanks."

The three walked down the back stairs to the car that Alex had left. Gerard was on the telephone calling David Baskin in Atlanta. Gerard apologized for calling at such an ungodly hour.

Baskin said to Gerard, "Don't concern yourself about the time. Please put me on your cellphone's speaker. I'd like your colleagues to hear." Baskin then continued, with Gerard, Tom, and Alex listening. "What's important is the destruction of the virus. Absolutely the best news we've heard in years. Congratulations. I can tell you that everyone at the Centers for Disease Control will be tremendously relieved when they learn that the threat of a Moses Virus pandemic is over."

Then Baskin added, "The scientist in me—to be frank—will always wonder what we'd have found when we analyzed the virus. True, we did have a few grains of it when we examined the moss that had housed and protected it. But this examination just whetted my appetite to study a larger sample of it. Was there something unusual about it? Did its origin being closer to the beginning of man's recorded history make its properties unique? I'm sorry in a way the mystery of the virus will remain forever that—a mystery."

While Baskin was speaking, Tom chanced to see Crystal being escorted to a police car parked a dozen yards away. She was carrying in her left hand a suitcase filled with—Tom guessed—whatever clothes she had that hadn't been ruined by either fire, smoke, or water. But, in her right hand, she had a much smaller leather suitcase. Crystal looked up, saw Tom, smiled, and while she handed the suitcase in her left hand to the driver, she continued to hold the smaller leather suitcase in her right hand as she got into the car. Her door closed, and the driver, police escort, and Crystal drove off.

Gerard wound up his call with Baskin. Gerard's car pulled onto the drive at the back of the castle and swept around the castle grounds and in a couple of minutes was headed on the major road to the Frankfurt airport.

21

One week later, Gerard called Tom, reaching him at Alex's place at Campo dè Fiori. "You're in Washington?" Tom asked. "I thought you were on assignment in Geneva."

"That's over. I'm about to take off on a new assignment. How are you doing?" Gerard asked.

"It's the most amazing change. From the moment I visited the Roman Forum before the accident until the fire at Kronberg Castle, I felt like I had this gigantic weight on my shoulders. No matter what I did, people wanted me for one thing or another, or threatened me, or kidnapped me. True, Alex came into my life—that's a great thing. But I was seriously concerned for her safety. Now, both she and I are back to where we were, except we're together."

"What about all the attention you'd been receiving?" Gerard asked with a laugh.

"You mean, do I miss articles about me in the newspapers, or reporters calling, or strange, unidentified people tailing me or kidnapping me? No, the silence is deafening and golden." Tom continued, "I'm working on my book, editing, getting ready for courses at NYU this fall, even answering a few questions from the New York Police Department about some criminal issues they've encountered. Alex has returned to her coursework, eager to complete her dissertation on the history of pandemic diseases. It's our plan to live in New York after Labor Day, and see how things go."

"I imagine," said Gerard, "that they'll go well."

Tom said, "Hope so, thanks. You know, Gerard, I wonder about Belagri. What will happen to them?"

Gerard replied, "You may have missed this. Two days ago, the board of directors of Belagri announced their choice for Bailitz's successor as president and chief executive officer."

"Who is it? I didn't hear anything about this."

"Are you ready for a surprise? Belagri's new chief is Crystal Close." Tom was shocked into silence.

Gerard said, "Tom, are you there?"

"I can't believe it," Tom replied.

"The stock market didn't like it at all. A woman CEO of a company as predatory as Belagri? The stock price plunged 15 percent. I don't believe the market has any conception about the kind of person Crystal is."

Tom responded, "If investors knew Crystal they'd have run the stock up, not down. She's incredibly tough. How do you think she got the board to name her CEO?"

"My guess," Gerard said, "is Crystal made clear to the board that she's got 'the goods' on the company. Undoubtedly she also told them in no uncertain terms just what Bailitz almost pulled off. By the way, the company elevated two other officers, putting them into the president's office—a scientist named Winch and a marketing guy named Parker. Do you know them?"

Tom replied, "I've met them—I would consider they're already a team."

Gerard added, "You asked about Belagri's future. My experience is that global companies are almost indestructible institutions. Belagri will plow ahead. Unless Crystal makes the company change directions, it will continue to be the most powerful company in the agricultural field."

"With one difference," said Tom, "there won't be any Moses Virus to intimidate third world countries or start a human pandemic."

Gerard said, "Speaking of third world countries—the Department of Justice—with a little nudge from the CDC—landed hard on Belagri. The DOJ extracted an agreement from Belagri to make its products available for a ten-year period to farmers in developing nations at 'reasonable'—a defined term—prices."

"How did the DOJ do this?"

"They agreed not to investigate Belagri's historical pricing—over the past ten years—to farmers from a group of ten countries. They agreed to let Belagri off the hook in exchange for an agreed-upon formula pricing in the same countries for the next ten years."

"Is that harsh?" asked Tom.

"Better than an investigation with penalties. You'll love this, however. Belagri has decided to call its new program the Hermann Bailitz Initiative to Ease World Hunger."

"Do you mean," said Tom, "that Bailitz actually might emerge as a kind of folk hero?"

"That's the irony. The biggest villain becomes a world philanthropist."

"I can see all sorts of problems with the DOJ, Belagri, and the Hermann Bailitz Initiative," Tom stated, "but I'm finishing my book and heading back to NYU." Tom was quiet for a moment, then added, "What are you up to?"

"I'm off tonight to Africa. There's been an outbreak of SARS, which could get out of control. I'm heading a team, and we're anxious to make certain a minipandemic does not happen."

"Where in Africa are you going?" Tom inquired.

"Nairobi. Strange, isn't it?"

Tom said, "At least you know now what Nairobi looks like, don't you?"

Gerard laughed. "Thanks to Bailitz, yes. More important, SARS has a history of being able to be contained. Quite a different story if I were going there because of the Moses Virus."

Later that day, Tom and Alex were invited to lunch at the American Academy by Caroline. It was a fiercely hot summer day toward the end of August. Rome was like a sauna. Heat shimmered upward from sidewalks, but despite it, the streets were crowded

244   THE MOSES VIRUS

with buses and cars filled with tourists seemingly oblivious to the sweltering temperatures.

As Tom and Alex walked from the taxi through the wrought-iron gates, Norm greeted them from his guardhouse. In front of them was the larger circular stone fountain whose sound of falling water immediately seemed to shut out any street noise and cool the air.

They walked up the two flights of wide steps into the large vestibule of the Main Building. Both fountains in the vestibule were resonating with the sound of falling water. Then there was one short flight of steps, which brought Tom and Alex to the garden level. In the center of the courtyard surrounded by four cypresses was the Paul Manship fountain, which added its cascade to the sounds of water from the vestibule.

Alex said to Tom, "This place is so full of falling water that the sound really does shut out Rome. It's also cooler and a strong buffer against—"

"The sultry summer?" Tom finished her sentence.

"Sultry is the right word, but one I can't imagine an Italian using."

Tom said, "It's fifteen minutes before 1 p.m., and Caroline asked us to stop at her office first."

Lucia rose from her desk and walked toward them. "Tom, Alex, it's good to see you. Rumors have gotten around—everyone's talking about what happened at Kronberg Castle. Congratulations. Let me tell Caroline you're here."

Caroline had a big smile on her face. "Dr. Pulesi called yesterday with—he said—good news. He wanted to know if you, Tom, were around. I told him you'd be here for lunch today. He asked if I would call him when you arrived—he'd save the good news."

Tom said, "Let's make the call."

After some pleasantries, Pulesi said, "The whole Italian government is indebted to you, Tom, for ridding the world of Bailitz and stopping his threat of a pandemic hell."

Tom laughed, saying, "Stefano—the whole Italian government?"

"Let's just say, those of us who know how important your contribution has been. In any case, and this has been cleared with the

Ministry of Italian Cultural Properties and Activities. The American Academy in Rome is authorized to reopen its excavation in the Roman Forum beginning next spring."

Caroline said, "That's wonderful news. We're thrilled."

Tom added, "I wonder if Belagri will continue to fund the dig?"

Pulesi replied, "I have no idea what they'll do—I've not been in touch with them at all. But I have one other thing I want to tell you, Tom."

"What's that?"

"We've hushed up all publicity about the virus to make certain there's no continuing public awareness or possible hysteria. But I worried that some other group that might be seeking to gain possession of it might think you were still involved. So we quietly circulated throughout our departments a highly confidential memo that states that the virus was completely eradicated in a fire in Germany."

"I don't quite follow," said Tom.

"Simple," replied Pulesi. "A top-secret memo issued to the highest officials within the Italian ministries would immediately be disseminated to all interested foreign parties. I know for a fact that the Mossad and a couple of other groups received it. They will investigate the Kronberg Castle fire, I'm sure. So I've done what I can to bury this matter for you."

Tom replied, "I can't tell you how grateful I am. Anything to put distance between me and the virus is great. Many thanks."

As he hung up, Pulesi joked with Tom, saying, "Good luck, and I hope never to run across you again."

To which Tom added, "I suppose I would make the same wish."

Caroline said, "Let's go out to the courtyard—lunch will be served as soon as we get there. I think you'll be surprised. You're both guests of honor with a group of extremely curious fellows. Tom, if you're willing, maybe you'll say a few words."

As the three arrived at the two long tables set for lunch, the fellows remained standing, clapping. Tom, used to speaking before students, remained standing while everyone else sat down. He began with a brief summary of the events, though as he spoke an idea began forming in his mind. As he covered the storming of Kronberg

Castle and the intense fire in the labs, which destroyed the virus, the idea in his mind crystallized.

The waiters had put the food on the tables and everyone began to eat. Tom closed his short summary by highlighting his idea. "You may not realize the tremendous role the Academy played in this adventure. There lies below us and below the cryptoporticus a two-thousand-year-old aqueduct built by Emperor Trajan. With help from research in our library, and from the Swiss Institute, I learned a secret about this aqueduct, which became a key part of the story.

"In fact," Tom continued, "not only have I walked to the Tiber from here in the aqueduct, but so has Alex. Right, Alex?"

Tom smiled and looked at Alex. She laughed and said, in a loud stage whisper, "There are rats down there." This was greeted by nervous laughter.

Tom volunteered, "I'll lead a walk in the Trajan aqueduct anytime any of you want to go."

Tom concluded by telling the Fellows, "I've decided to write about this amazing adventure. At times, I wasn't sure there would be a happy ending. Certainly, we are all devastated by the deaths of Doc Brown and Eric Bowen. But a serious world tragedy was averted, and I sincerely call this a most happy ending. Since things ended well, I'm going to start working on the book, and I hope I can get all of you to help—or at least ask you all to buy a copy."

The lunch continued, and Tom found himself busy answering questions—throughout the meal and afterward in the bar where a larger than normal crowd gathered for coffee and cappuccinos.

As Tom and Alex headed back to her house in the Campo dè Fiori, Alex asked, "Did the idea of writing a book really just come to you as you addressed the fellows?"

"I think that's when the idea jelled."

"Going public with your intention does make the project more real, more of a commitment. Are you sure?"

"I realize that," said Tom, "which is why I decided to go public with it."

"I wonder," added Alex, "how you will handle sensitive issues."

"Which ones?"

"The role of the Catholic Church, for example."

"Good question," said Tom slowly. "If I'm totally honest, I'll tell the back story of Cardinal Visconti."

"That really drags them into it," said Alex.

"Alex—you mentioned to me—and not too long ago, either—that the Church is a two-thousand-year-old bureaucracy that has been tough enough to survive. Well, this certainly can't hurt them—much."

Alex replied with a shrug. "Well, I'm glad you said 'much.' That may cover you."

Tom added with a smile, "If you don't mind, I think I'll get started on the first chapter of the Moses Virus story this afternoon."

"That's your title? Not bad."

Tom and Alex went to New York at the beginning of September. Tom's classes at NYU began; Alex enrolled in NYU to continue working on her PhD. NYU agreed to accept her work at the University of Rome.

On a late afternoon in mid-September, Tom's office telephone rang. He answered. It was Crystal. Immediately a flood of memories came back to him, not all of them pleasant.

Tom said immediately, "Congratulations are in order. I understand you're the CEO of Belagri."

"Thank you—that's a long story. But I'm finding this new job more demanding than I imagined it to be."

"I'm certain that you can handle it brilliantly. Good luck, by the way."

"Tom, I'd like to close the loop on the grant we spoke to you about in Rome."

"Crystal," Tom replied, "I regard that as a commitment that vanished with Bailitz."

"If you would like," she said, "we'll stand behind that consulting arrangement."

"No, thanks. If there is some valid research I can perform, I'd be more than willing to earn some money for NYU. But don't worry. I've told my dean that that grant would not happen."

Tom could imagine her engaging smile as Crystal said, "We'll figure out a way to have you help Belagri."

There was a pause. The conversation was ostensibly over. But Tom was curious enough to pursue one question. "Crystal, you mentioned how demanding your job is. What did you mean?"

"Bailitz was truly brilliant," she said. "He effectively ran the company as a dictatorship. So long as he made rational decisions he earned everyone's respect."

"But," said Tom, "but, what?"

"Off the record," Crystal said, "Bailitz took medication to even out his mood swings."

"Do you mean lithium? Was he bipolar? I certainly have known friends who've had some personal experience with this."

"With lithium, he was rational. If he omitted taking it, which he was in danger of doing when he was on one of his self-confident highs, he became a totally different personality. He saw himself—and Belagri, which was his alter ego—as having every right to be absolutely number one in every respect. Anyone standing in his way could, in his mind, be legitimately put down. By any means available to him."

"He seemed willful but rational," said Tom.

"Appearances," Crystal said. "Just before the end Bailitz became obsessed. He could mask his feelings entirely. But I knew him well. He would not take his medication and would tell me he had taken it. In a more rational state, he would have been able to balance the risk of the virus to mankind with the advantage the possession of it gave to Belagri." Crystal continued, "I hope you'll believe me when I say that I was horrified once I learned that Bailitz planned to use the virus in Nairobi and in New York. It was then that I knew he had become unhinged."

Tom protested, "But Bailitz had that situation room designed for Nairobi long before he ever knew he might be able to get the supply of the virus."

"True," replied Crystal, "but his original mission was to destroy crops, which he had planned to do so that Belagri could step in and control the market in Nairobi, making substantial profits along the way. He intended to use this as a showcase to warn other countries of what might happen to them. Bailitz never intended that anyone would know how the crops had failed. He wanted farmers and their governments to protect themselves by buying Belagri products. I did my best to convince him that one way or another Belagri would be found out as the culprit and that might finish the company."

"But," said Tom, "he couldn't be stopped?"

"No," Crystal said, "he was absolutely sure he could pull it off. I talked about his plan with Winch and Parker. They agreed with me, but we were powerless to stop him. We either had to resign from the company or play along with him, hoping we'd have some luck in persuading him not to destroy Nairobi. That's where things stood when your colleagues Doc Brown and Eric Bowen were killed in the Roman Forum. Naturally, as funders of Doc's excavation, we read about the deaths with sadness and special interest. All we knew, at first, was that there had been the tragic collapse of an underground passageway."

"In other words, what was reported in the press."

"Exactly, but, within a day, Belagri, which has 'friends' in many high places, including in Italy, got wind that something much more serious had happened. Something so important that the Italian government had blocked all mention of the details of the accident and created a cover story to keep the real details private."

"Of course," said Tom, "the Italian government and all its ministries leak like a sieve."

Crystal continued. "We began to understand that other groups, even foreign governments, were figuring out something was going on. That's when Bailitz really began to follow every development.

"Bailitz was brilliant—a trait that made him the leader he was. It was he who understood that when Pulesi's group was called to the scene of the accident, and when the bodies were cremated—these pointed to a dangerous virus as the culprit. That was a clever deduction, but the brilliant part was his spotting the Vatican connection. He knew that Propaganda Fidei had stumbled years earlier into the possession of Imhotep's canopic jars. And Bailitz remembered

Darby Smith's recent publicity of the wall painting in Imhotep's tomb. It was like an incredible game of chess, where Bailitz saw all the pieces on the board and knew what to do."

Tom replied, "I'm impressed."

"So," said Crystal, "were his management team. Bailitz immediately revised his game plan, from wiping out the agriculture to killing the politicians and a good number of the populace, as well as much of the livestock. It was then I realized that Bailitz was on an unstoppable high—and he had ceased taking his medicines."

"But why use the virus in Nairobi?"

"Bailitz's choice. He wanted to demonstrate the power of the virus, and then to deliver an antidote. He chose Nairobi, known for its corruption and crime as well as its agricultural base. Using the virus that had come down from Moses, with the echoes of a Hebrew god taking vengeance—Bailitz believed that this virus would have devastating results in its power as well as its presence psychologically."

"And he might have succeeded," Tom said.

"Beyond his wildest dreams, since the virus, once started, might become the world's worst pandemic ever."

Tom then asked, "Is that why you helped me?"

"I couldn't be part of his mad plan, and I couldn't resign and then be effective in stopping him," Crystal said.

"Well, you gave me—and us—a critical assist. The world owes you thanks—but this is only known to a handful of people."

"It's better that way, wouldn't you agree?" she said breezily.

Tom whistled under his breath. "That, Crystal, is one amazing story."

"An amazing and true story," she corrected Tom. "I must be going. I hope we'll keep in touch," she added.

Later that evening, Tom reported to Alex on his conversation with Crystal. Alex wanted to know every detail, and asked Tom more than once to repeat himself. "Do you believe what she told you? About Bailitz and his being bipolar? About herself trying to stop Bailitz from acting? And how, exactly, did she maneuver to be CEO of Belagri?"

Tom laughed. "I can't answer any of the questions you've just asked. Crystal is the most incomprehensible person I've ever met."

"More than me?" Alex asked.

"Thank God, more than you. I believe you when you make a statement. You are honest, direct—a perfect partner."

"Well, that's better," Alex said, and she moved closer to Tom until they were sitting next to each other on the sofa. Tom put his arm around Alex and hugged her. Then he said, "Okay, ask your next and final question."

Alex pulled away slightly from Tom and said, "Mr. Forensic Archaeologist, tell me exactly what was in Crystal's small leather case when she drove away from Kronberg Castle."

Tom said, "I have no bloody idea. And, perhaps it's better that neither of us know. Furthermore, it will be some time before I join in an excavation in the Roman Forum again."

"Fine by me," Alex said.

And that is the way things stood for quite a while. But in exactly one year and three months, Tom would have the exact answer to Alex's question.